Power Plays
Book 2
in the Mallory and Derek Attend Secret
Parties Series
Ruan Willow

Table of Contents

This book is certified Human Authored number 2918433.

Dedication

This book is dedicated to lovers who play in and out of the bedroom, those who never stop playing, and those who desire to please their partners and get off on getting their partner off, plus celebrate who they truly are because that's how it should be. Mutual pleasure is mutual bliss. Aftercare matters. Before care matters.
During care matters.
Communication is key.
This book is an open door spicy romance, specifically a polyamory romance featuring a throuple living an alternative lifestyle who explore sharing of intimate experiences with others, please read and enjoy it knowing this is the subgenre of romance it is in.
Marinate in your sexuality daily.
Enjoy and never stop seeking pleasure.
Pleasure is your birthright.

Chapter 1

Pain doesn't always come as an avalanche, but more as slivers of ice falling in a mosaic pattern that slowly reveals the full picture. Mallory squints as her brain works hard to fathom what's happening. She watches Derek's face transform from fervent ardor filled with urgency to simple anger. His jaw drops in panic as Wesley and Jasper enter through the sliding door in loud raucous laughter, Jasper spewing the tail end of the story.

She reaches for Derek, her heart wrenching as defeat fills his eyes. Then the anger returns in him with such intensity that it sears her heart like a dagger. He jerks back, then hops to his feet as if it were one movement. He backs away from her, then turns. His swiftness is shocking; he moves too fast for her as she scrambles to touch him. She needs to catch him. He mustn't leave.

"Derek, no!" Mallory exclaims with her arms raised, helplessness filling her heart.

He runs away from her and doesn't stop as he flees right through the front door, not even stopping long enough to shut it.

"Whoa! What's up with my man?" Wesley says in dismay. "He okay?"

Jasper grabs Wesley by the arm and drags him back outside.

Max remains frozen as he makes and holds eye contact with her. The hurt she sees in his eyes devastates her. This wasn't supposed to happen. Not this way.

"Mallory," Max says, his voice laden with disappointment. He looks crushed.

In her desperation to get Derek, she gives Max an apologetic look as she runs past on her way to the front door, her heart burning with pain. "Derek!" she yells out into the front yard, but his car is speeding away.

Her shoulders droop; it's too hard to stand up straight. She gasps, her heart breaking further as she realizes she can't do a damn thing to stop this bomb that has blown up her life. A sob escapes her. Had he not left, she would have said yes, but his leaving at such a moment is hitting her more like crazed abandonment. What happened to their team mentality? He's deserting it, discarding it as if it were a granola bar wrapper. Is she not worth him staying and fighting for? There's no passion in leaving. It hurts that he just ran as if her plea was nothing.

Max joins Mallory at the front door and places his hands on her shoulders. "He'll be back."

She nods, but she's not so sure he's right this time. Max doesn't know Derek like she does. It's likely he may not recover from his anger and panic so easily this time. He'd been acting so differently; she knew something had to be up, but she never expected it to be a proposal of marriage, and today of all days, on a day when they'd just laid the groundwork for success.

She'd thought about marrying Derek many times, and it was always with excitement, but what just happened didn't match that at all. Not even close, it was the opposite of that. This wasn't the proposal she'd dreamt of. Instead, she felt like a promise she'd held in her heart had been desiccated and now was a shriveled-up has-been. Dead before it took its first breath. A proposal isn't supposed to fizzle out like this, not when she would have happily said "yes". She's been cheated. He's been cheated.

"I'll be here for you, Mallory. Always. And forever. I'm not going anywhere." He kisses the top of her head. "I promise. I will love you no matter what, always, unconditionally."

It's comforting to hear him say this, no doubt, but what she really needs is to see Derek's eyes again and to soothe him into calm assurance because he's clearly doubting her love. Derek is way more romantic than that proposal. That was a knee-jerk reaction. That was not the Derek she knew.

"I...I just can't believe he left like that. Why would he leave? Why would he ask me to marry him and then flee?" She steps back and forth on her feet. She needs to do something, but she's not sure what. "Did he seriously think I'd say no?" Shock has immobilized her, and she stands still, staring at the floor for a minute. She can't even form a coherent thought as she perseverates on the memory of Derek's pained eyes, then him leaving through the front door.

She turns to face Max. His kind eyes are sympathetic and full of compassion. He might not love the idea of her marrying Derek, but he's still not badmouthing him one single bit. Nope. He's just being present and supportive.

"Don't know, honey." He shrugs, then places his hands on her biceps. "Why don't we go out to the backyard and join the others, or somewhere quiet? Whatever you need. Get your mind off this."

"Yeah, but I'm going to try calling him first. We need to talk." Not that Max suggested sex, but for the first time in her active sex life, she couldn't imagine having sex. It shocks her.

Max nods. "Okay. I'll give you a few moments alone." His expression is solemn. "I'll be in the back with the others. Join us when you can." He drops his gaze to the floor just as she catches a flash of defeat on his face. "If you want, that is."

She nods, but it's too much effort to respond. She can't wrap her brain around his continued support in the face of all this. She paces, amazed she's finally spurred on to move. She shakes her hands rapidly as her panic rises to a peak. She tries calling Derek as she watches Max talk with the others through the window.

Derek doesn't pick up, and her heart silently screams in hysteria. She tries three more times, her hands trembling. Then she leaves a message, plus texts him. She doesn't care that she's spamming him, or that she sounds desperate because she is. With his reckless mood, he might be driving like a maniac, and that terrifies her, too. Driving angry and in a panicked state of mind is a really bad idea. What if he gets into an accident?

She fights back a fresh wave of tears as her mind imagines him in his flipped-over car with a gash of blood across his forehead. Her brain won't stop freaking out.

She glances outside at Max again. He's laughing and joking with the others, like nothing is different. He looks happy, not war-torn like her. Instantly, she's reminded of how much Max has hinted at his offer to marry her and take care of her. He's done it so often, it's almost been weekly. This can't be easy for him to stomach, either. Her heart crushes further under this realization. She doesn't want to hurt Max either, but she just did. The two loves of her life, and she can't fully have either of them.

But she never indicated to Max that she'd ever leave Derek; she's never even entertained that thought. An epic filming day, glory and joy have been crushed into chaos. A marriage agreement would have been the cherry on top of a fucking awesome sundae of a day. Instead, she's been handed a pile of rotten rubbish she must somehow magically bring back to life.

She sits on the couch, her whole world layering in deepening darkness around her, choking her with harmless air. What is she to do? She can't poof Derek back. She can't agree to marry Max when she wants to marry Derek. She might as well salvage her friends still being present, and go soak in the hot tub, or she could stay on the couch like a lump of nothingness and cry.

She stands and looks down at her hands. She flips them over and back to palm side up. She could run away and hide in her bedroom, or she could march out back, given that her old friends are all out there having fun with her new friends. But minus Derek, this feels so wrong, but she also doesn't like the idea of being alone right now, either.

She'll keep calling him, and maybe he'll return. She firms up her chin as she dials his number once more.

"Derek, I love you. Please, please, please, please come back. We can talk. We have so much to talk about. Our future is together, never doubt that. I love you. I know I just said that, but I'm saying it again," she says as a big gasp overcomes her. She refrains from sobbing as best as she can, but she can't hide it. "Please, I beg you, Derek. I need you. I need you here. Please, I'm begging you. Please. We can talk alone. I'm ready to do whatever you need, Derek. I want you. I love you. I need you." She loses control, and a wail flies out of her mouth.

Shit. Shit. Shit. She scrambles for control over her emotions. She must show her guests some attention, too, but she's not sure what the fuck to do. Not that she owes them anything, but she's lost, and the only logical path before her seems to go out and join them. That or go lie in her bed and weep.

She dries her tears as best as she can and heads out to the back of the house. She stops just outside the door and watches them. All five are in the hot tub. She drops her robe; they've all seen her naked anyway. Hell, half of them have practically seen inside her body with their faces crammed to her pussy.

They all fall silent as she climbs the steps up to the hot tub. Her cheeks are tear-stained, but her spirit is not broken. With her head high, she proceeds. She can fake this for a bit. She glances at her friends and Max, their compassionate faces reminding her she's stronger than ever with the best support on the planet. She attempts to give them a weak smile, which feels pathetic and fake.

"I'm so sorry, honey," Maria says with so much compassion that Mallory's tears start again.

Mallory gasps and slightly crumples.

Maria slides over and stands out of the water with her arms raised.

Mallory descends fully into the hot water, and it's instantly a comfort, but as she falls into Maria's arms, they are more of a comfort.

"He'll be back," Sam says with confidence and extreme care in his voice. "We know him, right? He'll be back, love."

She nods as she pulls out of Maria's hug. They're right. He'll be back. Of course, everyone knows what happened; how could they not have talked about it?

She crushes her crying fit and stares back at them through blurry eyes. "He's been acting off for a while. I should have been more proactive; I'm just dumb. I thought we were solid. No matter what." Her voice sounds meek and small.

Maria squeezes her hands and maintains eye contact. "Hey, you don't need to justify a thing to us. We love you both," Maria says in a soothing voice. "We're kind of like one big family. We'll see you two through this." She smiles kindly. "I think he just needs to work through some things, perhaps."

"Are we the new adopted kids, then?" Jasper says good-naturedly. "Keeping it in the family is best."

Mallory beams a smile his way, bless him for trying to lighten the mood. "Absolutely, you are! You're in!" It feels amazing to smile genuinely, and she'd love to dwell on the feeling. Jasper's jovialness is exactly what she's craving. It's a blessing. "And, yup. Keeping it in the family," she jokes in agreement.

"Oh, there's a new subgenre for us!" Wesley hoots loudly. "I'd be down. Hot as fuck." He pauses. "Sis."

"Like siblings or cousins, or some shit." Jasper raises an eyebrow as he nods. "Yeah. Right on. I'm in. Next video?"

Mallory smiles. "Oh, I'm sure that's doable in the mix." She snorts. "Isn't it every girl's dream to fuck a fake bro?"

"Fake? Who said anything about fake?" Wesley asks with a knowing grin.

"Role play," Jasper says, nodding his head up and down as a salacious grin consumes his face. "Now we're talking. Fake, but real. Sizzling."

Max raises his hand. "I guess that makes me the grandpa by default."

Everyone laughs as he makes a silly expression.

"DILF looks good on you," Mallory says, finally feeling like joking, too.

"Maria and I would make fantastic fraternal twins," Sam says with a coaxing look. "Eh? What do you think, Maria?"

"Oh. We're the mom and dad?" she asks with a snicker. She falls forward in a guffaw. "I guess we fit that."

Mallory catches her eyeing something inside the house. She startles as she stares, trying to discern what she's looking at. There's someone inside. Her nerves flip to high alert status, confirming she indeed sees movement of someone inside. "Oh!" she exclaims, rising from the hot tub. "Derek! It's Derek. He's back! It's gotta be him."

"Lord, have mercy. Seeing your body like this," Wesley murmurs as she stands on the seat, peering inside. "Nude and wet. Someone take a damn picture, she's a fucking goddess."

She wants to slap him upside the head as she scrambles out of the tub, but that would take too much time. Bad timing, Wes, but she's not stopping to reprimand him.

The ground is cold, despite her expecting it to feel a little warm, and goosebumps erupt across her skin. She ignores the hanging towels and hurries into the house, wet as a dishrag. "I saw something. Might be Derek. I think it's him. I've got to check."

She enters the house dripping water all over the floor, and immediately shivers vigorously because the air conditioning is so cold. "Shit," she mutters as she makes her way across the kitchen tile despite getting water everywhere. She almost falls in her haste. "Derek!" she calls in a desperate tone. "Is that you? Are you back? Where are you?"

She rushes across the carpet. She doesn't care, it will dry. Hurrying to his room, she bursts into it. She glances around and all of his belongings are gone as is his suitcase. "Shit, damnit. Fuck!" She whimpers as she scurries to the bathroom. All of his bathroom stuff is gone, too. "Oh damn, I must have just missed him." Defeat freezes her in place for a moment.

Shaking off her confusion, she rushes to the front door and flings it open, knowing full well she's too late. The warm air is a nice welcome, though. It envelopes her as she walks out. She stands in the drive-through area fully naked as she hears a car roaring away in the distance. "Yup." She shakes her head. "Fuck. Fuck. Fuck." She throws down her fists to her sides in a double punch.

She stares for too long in the direction she heard the car from, half expecting him to come back up the drive. She's the fool. He's not coming back. Slowly, she makes her way to the backyard. She's moving so slowly. Each step takes forever. The cold air conditioning inside drapes her in shivers again as she creeps along like a slug. If only she'd seen him when he came in, not when he was clearly leaving the house. Talk about bad timing.

The faces of everyone as she returns tell her they get what happened without one word uttered from her.

"He's gone," she says. "He came for his stuff." She shrugs, then covers her face with her hands before a sob breaks loose.

AS SHE COWERS BY THE fire, her legs covered in a light throw blanket, she sips a glass of red wine. It's full, robust, and berry-like. It's good. Everyone has left, and it's just her and Max. She hasn't said a word in forty-one minutes, or something like that. She's simply watched the flames flicker nonstop as if in a mindless daze, focusing on their incessantly changing shapes, in which peak is the top, and how thick or thin they are. This was not how she thought she'd end this epic day of filming, a day of glorifying the fantasticness of sex. It was now to be a day tarnished with travesty. The sex parade has fizzled, but the hot memories will persist. She smiles wryly. At least she has that. Which memories will prevail will be told in the future. And that will also depend on her, Derek, and Max.

"I like to see your smile," Max says as he caresses the back of her hand with his fingers. "Care to share what brought it about?"

"It was an epic and amazing day up until that moment. Wasn't it? Right? It went so well. The filming. It was incredible. And, Max, I can't thank you enough for organizing, paying for, and helping direct it. Our success will also be largely attributable to you, Max." He deserves all the credit.

He smiles with a humble expression. "It was all you, though, babe. You're the star here. I'm just some old fat rich guy who adores you and wants to give you the world."

"You've given me opportunities no one else has, or even could, Max. I'll be forever and eternally grateful." She gives him an appreciative gaze, and it's not an effort at all.

"I'd love to comfort you, hold you. Is that something you'd like right now? Or do you want to be alone?" His eyes are soft and loving.

Her heart melts. She crawls closer to him, which causes her blanket to slide off her legs.

He bends to retrieve it and after she settles against him, he snugs the fluffy cloth around her legs.

"I think the threat of a tornado would have been easier to deal with than what happened."

"Yeah, except tornadoes are rarer here. Not saying they never happen, however. You're more likely to drive off a mountain than get hit by a tornado."

She nods as soberness overcomes her, despite all the wine she's consumed. Drowning in her upteen glasses of wine, she should be blubbering on the floor in a messy pile of tears and anguish. But instead, she's in the arms of a loving man who wants the best for her. "I love all the mountains here. It's beautiful."

"I love this part of Nevada, too. The mountains are gorgeous. Just don't drive off one." His tone is joking.

She appreciates his effort as she sniffles, the pains of the day screaming at her in a deluge once again. "Max, my ass hurts." She pouts as a snicker of a laugh escapes her.

He laughs in unison. "Well, it was a target during filming, so I'm not surprised. You got paddled quite a bit."

"Yeah, I'm not surprised either. I might need to set clearer boundaries around the next filming session. They got too carried away with it." She recalls the filming. Derek went hogwild on beating her ass, but it likely won't happen again. If he even agrees to do another film, that is. She suspects there was more than simple kink to it. "Derek was...different today. I'd seen the signs, but I'd thought that us having sex upon his return had put us in a good place. Back in our intimate place." She snorts. "Dang, was I wrong." She hangs her head. "So wrong."

"What would you say to a fireside massage and gentle oral until you orgasm?" Max asks in a soothing voice that's legit full of seductive intent. "Can I interest you in such a thing?"

She laughs. "Gentle? That won't make me come, and you know it, silly." She gives him the look that his suggestion is preposterous.

He laughs with her. "Okay. True. True. But how about a slow start where I start gentle, then suction my mouth to you like a vacuum in the end to make you come hard?"

She snuggles into his side. "That sounds wonderful, Max. You're seriously so good to me. I can't even dream up some of the stuff you come up with." And a big orgasm would definitely make her feel better.

"What if..." he says, but then pauses. "Nah, it might be too crazy to try."

"What?" she asks quickly. Curiosity has her by the ovaries.

"Maybe this isn't a good time to bring this up." His eyes are full of regret.

"No? Well, now you have to tell me because I'm too curious to not hear."

He sighs and makes eye contact with her. He looks like he's about to reveal a big secret. "Babe, what if, after you married Derek, you two moved in here with me? What if the three of us lived together?"

She freezes in place, her brain stalls on his suggestion as she ponders if that would even be possible. Derek might hate it. But then again, he doesn't hate Max. He's been jealous, sure, but Derek has never once said he hates Max. Oh, could they dare? No, this is crazy talk.

"I know it's a wild thought. But you'd be safer living in this state, anyway, honestly. With your job, I mean. Would you consider it?"

She shifts so she can look into his eyes. He seems genuine, and the whole idea blows up her brain. The three of them living together would be incredible for her, but how would it be for either of them? Certainly not ideal.

"You know I never intended to stop our relationship, Max. Even when I married Derek," she insists as she watches his face intently. "Even if Derek and I together like that, married, I mean, I'd never leave you." She falls silent, watching the light of the fire flicker across his face. The idea of the three of them cohabiting is insane, but she likes it. Their families would go berserk over it, especially Derek's.

The world would be her oyster with such a living situation. She'd get the love of both her men, daily, and so much sex it would blow her mind, plus, her and Derek would have financial backing.

"I'd do it. But I'd clearly benefit from it more than either of you." She clears her throat. "I wouldn't expect you to pay for everything for us."

His expression grows skeptical. "I have more money than I know what to do with. It would give me something worthwhile to spend my money on, honestly. And I'm not entirely sure that's right. We'd both get to be with you in our own ways. You'd get us. There'd be no separation between you and us. It would work great for both Derek and me. Seriously, babe. Listen. It would be ideal. We'd be together all the time. It's really the best of everything we could all want."

The full blow of the idea hits her like a shockwave. "You mean, we'd live together as a throuple?"

"Yeah, kinda. Only Derek and I would never have sex, though. We'd have to work out our boundaries."

Her mind immediately flips to a threesome. "But, a threesome? Maybe?" she asks with hope. "I can't not bring that up," she states with a saucy look. "'Cause I'd love it."

He laughs uncomfortably. "Well, I don't know, babe. I'd have to think that one out. Not sure I'm down for that. But we'd be able to have our own time with you, easily, of course. We could come to an agreement." He grins. "Some kind of schedule. I mean. Both Derek and I would work so we'd each be occupied at times, so we'd each have our own time to be freed up to spend alone time with you."

"This is a radical idea." The notion drapes her entire mind in serious contemplation, and dare she admit, excitement. "This actually sounds like a fantasy coming true." She grins deeply. "I'd get fucked. Fucked a lot. By my two main men. Which alone makes me want to do this."

He erupts in a guffaw. "Ah! Exactly right! I'm so pleased to hear this! I'd do whatever you two need or want. Mallory, I know you love Derek. I'd never expect you to leave him."

She raises an eyebrow. "But you hoped, right?"

He shrugs. "Perhaps. But I know that's not reality. You two existed before we even met. But, hear me out, we could make our own reality here, all three of us living under one roof." He caresses her face and hooks her hair behind her ear, his eyes full of love. "I'd foot the whole bill of our life together. Willingly. Happily." He stares deep into her eyes with hope filling his. "Do you think Derek would go for it?"

"Honestly, I don't have a clue. I thought I knew him, but today proved I don't know him all that well. At least not where he's at right now."

"Aww, well, maybe he just panicked today. If he was acting off, maybe he just needs reassurance. And lots of it."

How was Max so understanding in all of this mess?

"I guess." She shrugs, then falls silent as she considers life as a threesome under one roof. "Our families might freak out." She laughs. "No. They will freak out."

"My kids won't care. I know them. They aren't the least bit judgmental." He looks happy and calm.

"Well, Derek's family will flip their lids and shit down their throats! But Derek doesn't really care what they think these days, anyway. They've been such assholes to him. He's kind of outgrowing all that family—I don't know, emotional dictatorship they held over him for so long." She certainly hopes Derek could consider this. Maybe. Just maybe.

"It can't be easy overcoming what he's overcome." He shakes his head, then laughs. "That's an ugly scene to imagine him telling them about us, though kind of funny."

"Oh, he'd have to text it. No doubt. He couldn't be in the same room as them, as he told them. No fucking way." She shakes her head vehemently as a shudder overcomes her. "And, I'm not sure how mine will react. I mean, we don't have to tell them all the parameters of our relationship, though. Right? Granted, living here will bring up questions, but it's not unheard of to rent from people. Plus, my parents have friends who swing, so they aren't exactly unaware of alternative lifestyles." She cringes inside as she lets her fears surface a bit. If they find out she's doing films, however, there might be a few catastrophic eruptions, but they aren't exactly prudes either. Who knows, maybe they'd take it okay. She's not looking forward to finding out.

Max looks skeptical. "Do your parents know about your account? About your success?"

"Nope, nada."

"Aw, okay. I wasn't sure. I didn't want to ask." He pats her thigh. "Hey. How about we get to making you feel better? Huh? You in?"

She nods as she unfolds her body, ready to partake in the pleasure he's offering.

Chapter 2

"Just relax, honey. I want to do what I can to help you feel better. It's been quite the day." His voice is full of the usual compassion and love. He lightly caresses her shoulders, then drags his fingers down her back. He begins to grab firmly at her flesh with his fists, kneading her muscles with a stronger force.

She nods, snuggling her cheek against the soft cushion of the couch. "I wouldn't want to re-do certain parts of this day, but...oh, that feels lovely. Thank you." She closes her eyes as his hands travel her body, working their magic. She sighs. The heat from the fireplace and the comfort of his hands settle her tightly wound nerves and muscles. "Damn, I guess I really do need this."

"Yes, yes, you do. And I'm here to deliver." He leans down and kisses her shoulder. "Some days need aftercare as much as sex acts."

"Yeah. That's quite true," she says in a soft voice. And she needs double the aftercare after this day. "Lay it on me thick," she whispers.

He chuckles softly as he keeps kneading her flesh, creating a sensual feel-good cocoon for her. Soon, her mind and body are at ease, and she enters a floaty frame of mind that helps her rise above the painful chaos of the day.

This is exactly what she needs. Max always delivers. As Max made her a snack earlier, her biggest challenge had been not bursting into tears every second, so this was a huge shift to feeling floaty and loved. Thinking about crying sparks her sadness; however, with feelings of safety and comfort, she lets herself succumb to a sob. It's safe to cry with Max.

Her body curls as the crying fit quakes her body.

Max pulls her into a hug and rocks her, stroking her hair. "It's okay, babe. I'm here. I'm not ever going anywhere."

As her weeping peaks, then wanes, she accepts the comfort he offers. Being in his arms and held against his warm, soft body cradled not just her body, but her heart.

Derek is gone. That's an ugly truth. All her attempts to reach him have failed. It hurts. He's been her daily lifeline to comfort and joy for years, and to have him just take off in a wild, irrational panic is something her brain can't fathom.

"H-he just left like that. How could he do that?" she asks through a sob.

"He's not thinking clearly. He'll be back, honey. I promise you. He'll be back."

The words are comforting; she just needs them to be true.

"Maybe I should try calling him again," she says as she pulls away from his body.

Max shakes his head. "I think time and space will do him wonders. He loves you. That much is obvious." He caresses her face. "Now, how about we get back to making you feel wonderful?"

She smiles at him. "You're wonderful."

"Then let me show you."

She slowly nods and settles back onto her tummy, loving the softness of the cushion beneath her. Crying and finally letting it all out was a relief. Sleepiness wraps around her, but she fights it.

Max resumes his massage, starting at her shoulders, then working his way down to her ass, where he presses his fingers into the base of her spine, then squeezes her flesh, pressing firmly down into her muscles.

She moans as the tension there loosens. The softness all along her front helps her focus on the calmness Max is bringing. It's working wonders.

After he completes a massage across her entire body, he hovers above her ear and asks, "Do you want me to help you come? Or do you want to sleep, babe?"

She awakens slightly from her half-sleep and rotates to her side so she can look into his eyes. "Can I come, then fall asleep?"

"Absolutely. How about I carry you to bed, and we do it there? That way, you can just fall asleep after."

She nods in agreement and allows him to scoop her up. She curls her head into his shoulder, savoring his devotion to caring for her. If there is ever any doubt about where Max's heart is, all she has to do is remember even just one thing he's done for her.

The magnitude of support blows her mind every day. Derek has been similar, but there's something extra in the way Max goes about it. It's like she couldn't ever erase it or lose it. It's as constant as air. His unwavering consistency is something to count on.

Her breathing is slow, and her heart is calm. Finally, a bit of peace. Sliding into an orgasm will be easy. While Max getting his climax during sex, being aggressive and selfish, is a kinky free use turn on, this caretaking of her is equally as erotic. The mix of him is intoxicating.

He places her on her side of the bed, lowering her head gingerly to the pillow. He turns on the lamp to the lowest setting and taps their sensual playlist on his phone. The mood is lulling her further along as he pulls out her favorite sex toys from the drawer in her bedside table. After lighting the candle, he holds up her favorite clit sucker.

"It's a clit night, babe." He smiles kindly at her, but it's the wicked gleam growing in his eyes that launches her lust. "No edging tonight. I'm coming in hot."

She squirms in the delight of his words. "I'm so ready for that," she coos, giving him her best bedroom eyes. "I'm yours. And I love you."

"Just as I love you. Always."

Right from the start, when she met him, Max was all about prioritizing her. She hates to let the thought form in her brain; she fights it, but it solidifies despite her efforts.

Derek is being selfish. Emotionally immature. He's fled and stayed away despite all her attempts to reach out to him. She can't even fathom Max acting that way. She shouldn't compare them. Max's age makes him light years ahead in maturity, but Derek is unhinged. He's spiraled into someone she doesn't even recognize, though she'll take him back in her arms in a heartbeat if he shows up.

This is sexy time, and she needs to get the fuck out of her head. She watches Max settle into place beside her, then kneels over her so he can place the toy at her pussy.

She spreads her legs as the anticipation of him getting her off refocuses her brain onto the present. She wants to be present with Max, so she keeps watching him intently.

He rolls the buzzing toy along her mound with a sly grin. "I'm going to make you come hard and on repeat." He looks giddy.

His desire to make her climax is the ultimate win in arousing her further. She nestles herself against the soft mattress, wiggling her butt into the bed. She's ready to accept every ounce of his focus on her pleasure.

He chuckles softly. "I love this, you know that, right?"

"I know." Her smile is genuine. "And it's the best turn on. I can't wait."

He squeezes out a dollop of lube on his fingers.

The hibiscus aroma wafts up to her nose, and it's so good. "I love that smell."

"Me too." He spreads the gel across her clit.

"Oh, that feels incredible."

"I know," he states.

He continues to rub her, and she doesn't hold back her pleasure sounds. He taps the toy on and rolls through the first two steady state modes, then stops at the highest level of constant. It's her favorite setting. When he presses the sucking toy to her, she groans as she throws her head back in response.

"Aw fuck, that just immediately gets me."

"I said I was coming in hot, and I meant it. No mercy."

He varies the pressure of the toy, then rolls it around in a circle. When he fully presses it to her firmly, she launches.

She grips the bed sheets and yanks as the pleasure sensations ramp up. She mewls and writhes as he works her over with the little humming rose bud.

"Fuck," she mutters.

"Don't stop it. Let it take you," he instructs. "I've got you. I'm not stopping. Going all the way." He reaches to play with her nipples.

She yells as the ecstasy fills her up and spills out of her mouth in angsty sighs. Her body might explode. This toy works its usual magic, and she lets her womanhood sing wild and free. The contractions begin their rhythmic reign over her body. She arches her back as the waves roll out from her center. A full body orgasm transforms her, and the miracle of her body brings on all the bliss.

The orgasm pushes her further, and it's almost too strong. "Shit," she blurts as she considers pushing the stimulation away for a break.

"Push through it. It will get even bigger," he coaches. His tone is urgent and insistent.

The intensity coils tighter, and when he leans over to suckle her nipple, she welcomes the next charge of her impending release.

"Big, big, big," she chants as the titillation fills her. The contractions start, and she curls up on the bed.

He follows her motions, thereby keeping the toy in contact with her sensitive spot.

She squawks and twitches, the pleasure a lovely overwhelm.

He pulls the toy from her body and spoons her from behind. "I'll let you float down, then we can do more, or if you've fallen asleep, that's okay. Either way, I'm a very happy Dom."

The hormones have her woozy, nature's best natural high, and she hugs his arm snug under her breasts. Sleep will come, and she's not going to stop it. The comfort she needs comes as orgasms follow, with his arm holding her. She can look forward to a heavy, deep slumber.

SHE OPENS HER EYES to daylight. A glance at the clock tells her she has successfully slept in to mid-morning, which is a very rare occurrence for her. As she blinks, she focuses on a white piece of paper on her bedside table. She reaches for it and picks it up.

It reads: Once you're awake, take a shower. I have a surprise for you.

She smiles. Such a romantic gesture after the night of pampering he gave her. He never ceases to wow her. She was sad over the fleeing of Derek, and instead of acting jealous, he's choosing to care for her instead. He could be badmouthing Derek up and down to make himself look better, but he's not going there. Not even remotely is he going to do that. As if she couldn't think he could do even better at supporting her, he tops it.

She smiles up at the ceiling as she relaxes back into the bed. It feels so luxurious to stay in the soft warmth. However, this doesn't last long. Her instinct to stay in bed and stew has now been replaced by curiosity and excitement from Max's note. The man might literally be a genius at relationships. Again, she marvels at how it's possible that he's not married to someone. It literally makes zero sense. The only answer is that no woman has ever given him the chance to do what he so happily does for her, every day. And their loss is her gain.

If he were young, she'd worry about him being so devoted to her and missing out on something, but she also wonders if that is ageism. Regardless, he profusely spouts how happy he is all the time, so who is she to judge what happiness really looks like for him? Her role is to ride the flow, not question it.

She rolls out of bed and then sits back down. Ugh. She's moved way too fast for how much wine she had last night. Thankfully, she still has a full cup of water by the bed. She downs the entire thing, lets it settle, then tries to stand again.

"Ack." Ibuprofen might be in order.

This time, she succeeds in rising and staying upright. She meanders slowly to the bathroom with a lingering smile. Max gets her, and once again, he's saving her. Derek is gone, but Max is here.

She pees then slides into a hot shower, her mind full with great anticipation for the day.

Not sure what to dress in, she chooses jeans and a thin, pale pink T-shirt. As she saunters down the hall, the aroma of eggs fills her with a strong appetite.

"Mmmm, something smells delicious," she says as she enters the kitchen.

"And you're looking refreshed, my dear." He grins back. "And very delicious."

She smiles more broadly at his compliment. The man is never stingy with the sexy compliments.

"Thank you," she says. "What do we get to eat?" She peers into the frying pan. "Ah, omelets. My favorite."

"I made my famous rum creamer, too. Grab a cup of coffee and sit down while I finish our omelets."

"Oh, I love your creamer. Yummy." She shuffles to the coffee pot and chooses a dark roast cup and slips it into the coffee maker. As it brews, she hugs Max from behind and runs her hands all over his front side. When she reaches his groin, he twitches.

"Careful, that might interrupt us, and we'll have cold omelets instead." His voice carries a warning, but he doesn't sound serious.

She laughs. "Oh, I don't mind. That's what microwaves are for."

"I have plans, and they include that, a lot of that, but later." He motions toward the coffee pot with his spatula as a chunk of egg flies off. "Your coffee's done."

She leaves him and pours his special homemade creamer into the coffee. The first sip makes her moan. "Mmmm, that is so good. You're a genius."

"Take a seat. It's almost ready."

"How did you know how to time this so perfectly?" she asks as she sits at the table. The bouquet of flowers from yesterday gives off a delightful scent.

"Well, I confess, I left the door open to the bedroom on purpose. I wanted you to wake to the smell of food cooking and coffee brewing." He chuckles. "I might have carried my coffee cup to the bedroom to check on you."

She raises an eyebrow. "Oh, the deviousness," she says with a heckle.

He slides the omelet onto a plate and carries both plates to the table. "An omelet made just how you like it, my sweet babe."

He sits beside her.

"So, when do I get to know the surprise?"

"It will be a day out in nature. I'm going to show you the park I love, and we can hike a bit, then I've packed a gourmet picnic lunch." He strokes her hand. "I can't wait to spend the day with you."

"Aww, you're the most romantic Dom ever." She sighs as her heart beams. Derek's absence is still at the pit of her darkened heart, but Max sure is trying to help. It's working, mostly. But she laments that she didn't text Derek first thing.

"Don't worry, honey. Give him time." He glances up. "He'll come around. He loves you."

"I'm that easy to read, huh?" She slumps her shoulders. The urge to cry thickens in her, and she does her best to squash it.

"We'll have a great day. I aim to keep your brain engaged while we wait."

"How are you so good to me?" Her heart is swelling despite the devastating heartbreak choking her.

"I love you. I will always love you. No matter what you do, I will love you forever."

It sounds impossible, and maybe a bit foolish, but she loves that he's said it regardless.

She lets her happiness show, and he chuckles in delight.

"Now that's the face I like to see. Let's eat so we can go walk around enough to want to eat again. I've prepared the best picnic basket of my life." He pats her arm and looks right into her eyes. "Don't lose faith in Derek, okay?"

She nods as her eyes turn blurry. "Yeah, you're right. I won't."

If only she could keep her mind off Derek long enough to enjoy the day.

ON THE DRIVE, SHE'S mostly silent and very grateful for the lovely music streaming out of the vehicle's speakers. It can't be this hard to be in love with two men, can it? Her life has erupted in so much success and so much chaos that not being constantly consumed by it for once is refreshing. The mountain and the forest scenery calm her. She can savor the simple joy of looking at it.

"I've donated a bunch of money," Max says. "To your hometown's food shelf."

She looks at him sharply. "Well, that's random, but wonderful."

"Nah, not random. I periodically do that, but I wanted to do it where there was a tie to you."

"People like you should be rich more often," she says jokingly.

"Yeah, I want to give more and more. And I love giving to you, so this kind of felt like giving to you but giving to others at the same time." He grins. "Giving to people you might know."

She smiles at him. "You really are a good man, you know that? And I can't say it enough."

"You make me better, Mallory. Without you in my life, I'd probably be head down just making more money, so in many ways, you've saved me."

"Well, it's mutual because you save me all the time, like last night. Like this morning." She caresses his arm. "You can be my superhero anytime you want."

The rest of the drive is as serene as the first half, and she is yearning to get out into nature. The sun is shining, and it's a rare warm day. With Mother Nature smiling on them, it adds to her hope.

They exit the SUV, and she snugs her jacket tight and zips it.

"It's nice out, but still a bit chilly."

"Yeah, but I think it will warm up further. The forecast said so," he says, smiling. "And they're never wrong." He laughs.

She laughs, too. "What universe do you live in?"

He grabs the picnic basket and blanket. "You brought gloves?"

"Yeah, I have these little ones. I have always kept them in my pockets, but I hadn't thought of needing them here."

"Still gets cold here, especially this time of year, in the higher elevation."

"Yeah, I think I'm going to like living here." Her mind drifts to Derek. She wonders where he went. Did he go to a hotel? Or did he drive all the way back home? If only he'd communicate. She pauses and tries calling Derek again.

Max stops and watches her, not even asking what she's doing.

It goes right to voicemail. He will see that she called in a notification. At least then, maybe he will get it that she's thinking about him.

"Okay," Max says as he points to the trail to the right. "We can follow this one. I've been on it several times, so I won't get us lost."

She nods and follows his lead.

The air is crisp, and the scent of the trees and dirt is grounding. She hadn't known she was desperately needing this exact type of outing. At the cabin, she would have dwelled on what just happened too much.

"It's beautiful here," she says softly. The scenery is working magic to clear her mind.

He hikes ahead of her for several minutes, then abruptly stops and turns. "It's always cleared my head to come here."

She can see why. "Yeah. For sure."

After an hour of hiking, they stop for a water break.

"Do you have any ideas for the next video shoot?" He sits on the big rock and motions for her to join him.

"Yes, too many." She takes the water bottle he offers and takes a swig. "I don't want to delay, because I think hitting while the iron is hot with my audience is the best idea. Keep them intrigued and dialed in. A big break of downtime might be what I want, but it's not what my career needs."

"You're very tenacious. And that's why you've gotten this far."

She scoffs. "That's not the only thing that did it." She caresses his thigh.

"I know." He places his hand on hers. "But it would be impossible without you. Money can buy anything, but you."

"Hmmm, interesting. I bet you could buy another woman's desire to make films. Money is very convincing."

"I'm not interested in what money can buy, I'm interested in what money can't buy." His eyes twinkle at her. "And I'm interested in only you."

She shrugs as the feelings of lightheartedness grace her. "These mountains are energizing me. And making me horny."

He laughs in delight. "That's what I like to hear."

"Think your cock would be too cold to be naked?" she asks with a sly grin.

"I'd put it in a bowl of ice for you." He laughs. "It wouldn't be naked for too long."

She jolts back as her eyes widen. "I might need to see that happen, and true." She laughs. "How to kill a boner in one second." She makes her hands shape as if they are holding a large bowl.

He chuckles along with her.

Life might be changing all around her, but he's still the same. "I'd love to give you a blow job in the woods."

"I'd love to rail you against a tree, but if you blow me, we can't do both." He tilts his head as he raises an eyebrow.

"Oh, ye of little faith," she says wickedly. "Just a tiny blow? Then I'll hug a tree for you." She gives him a seductive grin.

"Well, that sounds divine. And I'm not hungry yet, so, yeah. I'd never say no," he states, a burst of interest flooding his face.

She hands him her water and drops to her knees. "This is really hot," she coos. She unzips his pants and draws his boner out. "I see you've cooperated."

"That's not difficult," he says as if it's a joke. "You do this to me," he says, more serious and intensely.

She opens her mouth and falls on his cockhead. Being in nature has her feeling primal. She coasts her hand along his shaft as she sucks his tip.

He caresses her hair. "You're too good to me," he mumbles as his body twitches. "Whew, you'd better stop, honey. I'm about to lose it."

She reluctantly releases him. "Well, that was fast."

"You turn me on, and being in the woods does, too. There will be no tree-hugging if you keep going." He shakes his head as he narrows his eyes. "Though I did pack a toy in the picnic basket just in case."

"You devil. That's perfect." She leans toward him, pressing her lower half to the rock between his parted legs.

They fall into a kiss. It deepens. He threads his hands into her hair, pressing his fingertips into her scalp.

"Fuck, I want you." He cradles her head as they continue to enjoy each other's mouths.

When he kisses down her neck, she leans back slightly, savoring his lips on her flesh. "I want you. Need you to fuck me. Shove it up me until I come."

He pushes her back and leans over to dig in the picnic basket. "I brought your pen. Think you can hug a tree with one arm while I ravage you from behind?"

She releases a soft moan, then a light chuckle. "I sure want to try." She sheds her jacket and places it on the big rock. A shiver runs through her, but she's not letting the chill stop this sexy fun. She adores sex in a forest. "We might get seen. I'd love it."

He grabs her arm without delay and leads her to a tree with a medium-sized trunk. He presses himself against her backside and reaches around to press her sensitive spot through her leggings.

She raises her arm to steady herself against the rough tree trunk.

He humps her from behind as he manipulates her clit through the fabric of her pants. However, this doesn't last long. He maneuvers his hand down the front of her pants and seeks her fleshy nub.

"Mmm, damn," she coos as he arouses her. "You're so good at that." She wiggles in response to his touches.

"You're my little slut, opening up for me in the woods like this, aren't you?"

"Yes, sir, I'm your slut."

"Daddy could buy everything in the world, and never get this." He leaves her clit and grasps her waistband before yanking it down, making her butt bare.

She shivers.

He presses himself against her. "Body heat," he whispers gruffly.

"Yes, want you in me," she slurs. "Fuck me, Daddy. Fuck me damn good." She hums. "I have a warm spot just for you."

"Bet. Now get that toy going," he instructs.

She taps it on and presses it to herself, lurching and crying out at touchdown. "Fuck, that's so good."

He rubs his cockhead along her slit, then runs his fingers along it. "After a minute of that toy," he mutters, short of breath.

She presses the toy firmly and cries out, her body twitching from the intense pulsating pleasure it delivers.

He mounts her and enters, penetrating her swiftly and easily.

"Yes," she says like a groan.

He matches her sound with his own groan and fully enters her. He begins to ride her, making her body bob from his thrusting.

She grunts as she grips the tree trunk with one arm, but falters and slides off, the rough bark grazing her cheek.

He helps her reposition and continues riding her pussy from behind.

After another minute of pressing the toy, she shudders and then partially opens her eyes.

He grunts as he works himself in and out of her in his quest to climax.

Her coiled lust unwraps, and she launches into a nice, hefty orgasm, her body shuddering as the contractions erupt.

As her walls clench on him, his orations escalate. He thrusts even harder, and an eventual bemoan indicates he's climaxed, too.

"Ah, gawd," he mutters.

The increased fluids inside her confirm he's come.

"Mmm, that was perfect," she says as she fully leans into the bark of the tree. Her toy is still vibrating with an audible buzz against her spot. "This was the perfect one to bring." She pulls the toy away from herself and pushes the button to turn it off.

"Yeah, that was my thought." He reaches down and pulls up her pants over her bare bum. "You have goosebumps."

"It was worth it." She swivels and smiles at him. "I love that you are open to doing something like this. That was really sexy. I loved being taken by you in the woods."

"I loved doing it." He fastens his pants. "That worked up an appetite. You ready for the picnic? I brought champagne and strawberries, too, if you just want a snack."

"Oh, that sounds decadent. I love it. Let's start with that. Sex, food, and champagne. You've got me with all three."

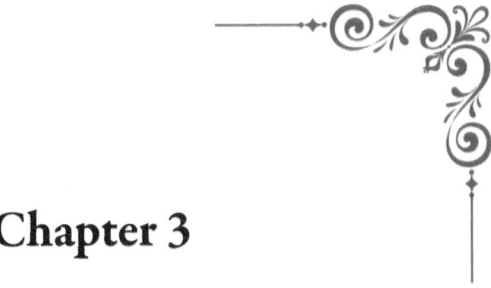

Chapter 3

After a delicious picnic and a lovely hike back down the mountain, the ride home is comforting. A man who wants her to climax, feeds her, and takes her on adventures is a dream come true. Riding the high is a very welcome break from worry.

As they pull into the driveway, the sight of Derek's car sets her to elation, which she desperately wishes isn't false hope.

"Max! He's back!" she shouts as Max parks the car.

"I knew he would be," Max says as he opens his door. "I'll get the stuff, you go on in, honey."

She nods and bolts into the house. She finds Derek sitting on the couch with a very solemn look on his face. "Derek, you're back! Thank goodness. I was so worried about you." She rushes toward him, her arms outstretched.

"Worried enough to go on a picnic with Max?" he asks with a snort, crossing his arms and turning away from her invitation. He nods gruffly at Max, who is carrying the basket in behind her.

"What?" she asks, dropping her arms, taken aback that he'd attack her. That wasn't fair. Her defenses flare. "What, I'm supposed to just sit on the couch and mourn?" She cringes. She's not meaning to fall into his dark mood.

"I've listed the house to sell," he blurts with barely a glance at her.

She drops her jaw. "You've what?" She stands her ground, but feels weak. "What? Why would you do that? And without talking to me first?" Her hands migrate to her hips.

"You aren't even living there anymore."

"I never said I wasn't going back," she says in desperation. Her hope is fizzling fast.

"You need to live in this state with your job anyway," he says, sounding a bit sorry. "I have to go. I just wanted to tell you that. We'll have to make arrangements to move out. Maybe Daddy Warbucks over there can just pay for the movers, and you won't have to lift a finger." He snarls with a lingering look of distaste.

"Derek, why are you acting like this? This isn't you." She wants more than anything to rush toward him and hug him, but he looks so damn hostile. His nasty-toned "Daddy" reference tarnishes the wonderful memory of when they watched that movie together.

"Aaron thinks the house will sell really fast with the upgrades we added. Then we can get our money quickly." His tone is emotionless. "And move on."

Move on? "And do what with it?" she asks as panic fills her further. Is this really happening?

"I don't know. Maybe I'll buy a condo or something." He drops his eyes as his mood seems to go even more somber.

"Where?" she asks in a small voice, dreading his answer.

"I don't know yet, that's the thing." He stares at the carpet.

She's not really okay with selling the house, but he's not wrong. Living here would be safer for her. She's too filled with shock to respond in any sensible way, so she just stares at him.

Max clears his throat. "You know, this is something for all of us to talk about, if you'll allow me into the conversation. It's not my intention to butt in, but I have something important to add." He pauses. Derek doesn't object, so he continues. "I'd love it if the three of us lived here. Together." His expression is pleasant, his eyes are jovial.

Derek shoots Max evil eyes, but then his shoulders slump. He's silent for a minute. "You'd want that?" He sounds like he doesn't believe it for a second.

"Look, Derek, I'm not trying to steal her from you. I just want to love her."

Derek looks cross and folds his arms on his chest. His silence continues as he glares at Max.

"I'm not joking. I have the big house, here." He waves his arms up in the air. "It's just me, and I don't need all this to myself. Seriously, think about this. You can have as many rooms as you want and turn them into whatever you want to. A studio, an office, a workout room, I don't care, whatever you want."

"And you'll pay for it, for her sake, right?" he asks sarcastically as he stands. He gives a short nod of his head. "I gotta go."

She gasps, and a sob escapes her. "Please, Derek, don't. I don't want you to leave," she says through another release of a bitter cry. "Please, at least stay and talk to us."

"Talk to 'us', well, maybe I need to just talk to you, Mallory." He frowns at Max.

"Okay, I'll give you two some space." Max raises his hands. "I totally get it."

Mallory sends a look of alarm his way.

Max shakes his head. "No, Mallory, it's okay. Really, I understand. The last thing I want to do is to come between you two, you know that. Derek, please know I'm all for you and Mallory, whatever you two decide to do. Okay?" He takes a step, then turns back to face them. "I'm just offering. It's for you both to decide." He raises his hands, then brushes them together.

Derek says nothing, but his brows remain furrowed.

"I'll head to my office. I have some work I can do." Max leaves.

Mallory is grateful he didn't look hurt. She feels the hole his leaving creates, and she yearns for him to come back.

Derek sighs and fidgets.

The silence is strangling her. "Please, talk to me, Derek," she pleads. "I love you. You know that, right?"

He softens, and the anger in his eyes melts into a hint of vulnerability. "I don't know what to do," he says in a weepy tone.

"You talk to me, that's what you do. Like you always do." She sits next to him and lightly touches his thigh. He doesn't flinch. "It won't be perfect, living here. We'll have to talk all the time. Create our boundaries." She wants to say and talk with Max, but she holds off on saying that. "We could be happy."

"Can we?" he asks with a sharp look into her eyes. "Is that possible? Here with him?"

"Yes, I believe it is." She drops to her knees in front of him and places her hands on his thighs. "I believe we can be. He wants us to live here with him. He's thought about this. It's not a knee-jerk reaction." She waves her arm around the room. "Look at this place, Derek. It's incredible. He has the room, he has the money, and he wants to share it with us." She stares intently at him. "We can have our dreams come true."

"I can't be bought," Derek states plainly, averting his eyes.

"He doesn't want to buy you. He's not like that." She tries to curb the defensiveness in her voice, but she's terrible at it.

"You don't feel bought?" he asks, as if it were an accusation. "After all he's done? You don't feel that even a tiny bit?"

She leans back and rests on her straightened arms. "No, I don't. I feel his love for me. I feel his generosity and kindness." She sighs. "He's not just a sugar daddy. I love him, and he loves me."

"Well, he doesn't love me. He doesn't even like men." A look of defeat crowds his face.

"It's true he's not bi, but that's okay. You don't have to have sex with him. Ever. We can always be separate."

"I don't want to be sexual with him." Derek has less anger in his eyes, and his body looks more relaxed. "I know you trust him."

"You not trusting him is okay. He's not expecting you to bow down to him. It will take time."

"Let him speak for himself, then." He shrugs his shoulders and guffaws. "I know, I know. I wanted him to leave. I'm not making sense." He drops his head into his hands.

"I don't need you to make sense. I just need you to try and hear me out." She leans forward and sits cross-legged. "And, most of all, I want you to stay." More like need.

"I'd have to get my things," he says as if that's a reason to not come back.

"So go and get them," she states happily, because he doesn't look nearly as miserable as before. "Then, when you get back, we'll all talk. All three of us."

"I need to think about all this." He leans back and shoves his hands in his hair. A look of hope flickers across his face, then it dies quickly into a brood. "My family will freak out. So will yours."

"Who cares?" She shrugs. "It's our life. My life. Who cares what they think?" She scoots to him, hugging his knees and pressing her breasts to him. She gives him a coy smile. "And what if we just said we're renting from him? Hmm? We don't need to tell everyone the truth."

"I don't even know what that is."

"I do. We love each other. Max loves me. We can all live here together happily. You can keep seeing Faye, or anyone else you want, but Derek, I meant it, that we're the nesting couple. And we always will be." She looks directly into his eyes. "You're my home, wherever you are. We are number one to each other."

He stands up. "I can't think. I need to think. I just don't know." His words come out in a rush. He starts to walk, but then stops and swivels around.

She rushes over and throws her arms around him. "And then you'll be back." She nods exaggeratedly. It's not a question. "You don't need to know. You just have to be willing to talk."

He hugs her and kisses the side of her head. "I do love you, Mallory. I'm in love with you." His eyes are brimming with tears. He sounds a bit like old Derek.

"Then stay." She nods while still in his embrace, her heart breaking, but also rejoicing. He hasn't said 'no'. "And I love you. I'm in love with you, Derek. I want you in my life." She doesn't dare bring up the proposal. "You're the love of my life."

He leans back and gives her a kiss on the lips. "I have to go, my love."

At least he used the 'l' word.

He pivots and then walks to the front door. It makes her ache that he goes out without even a glance back.

Loneliness descends upon her as the door shuts. She stares at the closed door for a minute, then goes to find Max.

He's in his office, staring at his laptop with a look of determination. He glances up as she enters. "Hi, everything go okay with Derek? It doesn't look like it."

She bursts into tears and covers her face. "I don't know. He left."

He motions for her to come sit on him as alarm grows in his expression. He opens his arms and envelopes her as she crashes onto him. "He'll come around, Mal. I just know it."

She curls up on his lap and leans against his chest as her sobs continue. Rubbing her head against his chest, she can't get enough of his comfort. Needing him has her feeling desperate.

They remain nestled together until long after she stops crying.

"I guess I needed a good, long, hard cry. Thank you," she says into the fabric of his shirt. "I got you wet."

"That's my line," he says with a snicker and a sly smile. His gray hairs catch the sunlight and sparkle.

She laughs and swats his chest. "You always make me smile." She scoffs. "And wet."

"Good," he says. "Then I'm doing my job."

"You do a very good job," she says as she tweaks his nose gingerly.

He purses his lips toward her, and they kiss. "I don't think I'm going to be getting much work done anymore. Not with you on my lap."

"I can feel that," she says seductively.

A ruckus comes from outside the room, and they both look at each other.

"Derek, perhaps?" she asks with hope.

"He wouldn't be that loud," Max says as he shifts in his seat.

She rises off him, and they make their way to the door.

"If it's Derek, that didn't take long, and I'm happy." She moves into the hallway and glances back at Max.

It's multiple voices, so clearly Derek has brought someone along.

As they enter the living room area, Maria, Sam, and Derek are standing close to one another.

"Ah, my dear! Looking so very lovely as usual. It's so good to see your happy face," Maria says as she strides quickly toward Mallory.

She pulls Mallory into a tight hug and then leans back to plant a kiss on her lips.

She doesn't hide her surprise. "I always love seeing you, too. All of you," she says, making a big show of staring at Derek.

"We contacted Derek and wanted to come and see you all for the day before we head back home," Sam says. "Derek said you were here, so we just came. Hope that's okay."

"Of course," Mallory says. "I'm so glad you did. And we hope you will come back when we host the party for the club."

"Oh, for sure we will be," Maria says as she hugs Mallory again. "Have you got any idea of when it will be?"

"We're thinking about a month from now, so people have time to make travel plans," Max says with gumption. "It will be so good to get everyone together again. We've missed the parties, haven't we, Mal?"

"Yes, and that's the part I hate about considering moving here. But it's just so much safer, and it's beautiful, too." She tries to hide from her forlorn mood, but it settles upon her. She wants to be back home, but it's not practical anymore. She watches Derek as he says something softly to Sam. If Derek goes back home, she fears their relationship will take a major hit. They might even end. She shudders.

Sam nods as he motions to Derek. "We're going to get some privacy in Derek's room." Sam leads the way, and Derek follows.

Derek's expression is swoony as he follows Sam. At least he's not looking gloomy. She's secretly very happy they are going off together. Whether they have sex or not, time with Sam always sets Derek on the right path. He's someone who is wise, and, more importantly, someone whom Derek actually listens to.

Maria grabs her hand and pulls her toward the couch. "We need to chat, too." She motions toward Derek and Sam as they enter the hallway to the bedrooms. "Let them have their time, I want time with you."

Max clears his throat, then says, "And I'm going to pull together some snacks for us all." He disappears into the kitchen.

"So, lots of turmoil still, huh?" Maria asks as she falls back onto the soft cushions. She bounces slightly when she lands. Her eyes are full of compassion.

"Yeah, I can't even seem to process it all. Everything is happening so fast, and I really am not keeping up with it worth shit." She pulls her knees up and hugs them.

"The moment Sam was talking with Derek on the phone, I could see it on his face. After he hung up, he didn't even need to say a word. We just left."

"Maria, he wants to sell our house, and he didn't even talk to me about it. He put it on the market! It's like a knee-jerk reaction. But what bothers me the most is that he just keeps leaving. We have always talked to each other, and he's just like, I don't know...so volatile right now. Like he's legit irrational." She bites back tears. "He's lost it. And I can't get him back on track."

"He's definitely spiraling out of control. I think I'm going to talk to Sam. Perhaps we should stay in town for a bit longer."

Mallory's face softens. "Yes, that would actually be really helpful. To make it cheaper, why don't you two stay here? I mean, Max certainly has the room. I know he won't mind one bit."

"Yeah, we might need to do that. We had to check out this morning. I don't think it will be hard to convince Sam to stay for a bit."

They hear a masculine voice yelling off in the distance.

"Someone's getting happy," Maria says with a smirk.

"Not surprising. And, honestly, I'm hoping it's Derek. He needs it. He's wound up so tight he might break from a simple touch."

Max returns with a charcuterie board and a bottle of white wine. He sets them down on the coffee table. "Be right back with glasses."

"This looks incredible! Thank you so much, Max. You're always so hospitable." Maria is her usual gracious self.

"It's always my pleasure," he says with a slight bow.

Once he's out of earshot, Maria shoots Mallory a glance.

"What's that look for?" she asks.

"You know, I've known Max for years and years, and he's never been this happy. He really needed you in his life."

Mallory smiles. It feels really nice to hear that. "Really? I guess I hadn't thought of us that way." Her muscles relax a bit, and she places her feet on the ground. "I really needed him, too."

"Maybe that's the part that Derek is having a hard time with." She shakes her head. "I know, don't even say it. Derek needed Sam in his life, too."

"Sam is like this spotlight that shows Derek what he needs to see, even when it's right in front of his face."

"It's interesting how we all needed each other, and we fell into this web of one another." She reaches for a piece of cheese, sausage, and a cracker.

"Web makes it sound ominous," Mallory jokes. "Like, is a spider coming to eat us?"

"That depends on your definition of eat," Maria says suggestively, followed by a smack of her lips.

Mallory laughs and dances in her seat. "Count me in."

Maria raises an eyebrow and tilts her head to the right in a quick bob. "Ditto."

They both laugh as Max returns with a tray of stemless wine glasses and a second bottle of white wine. "One won't cut it." He stands the bottle up and begins to open it.

"Max, they've decided to stay a few more days. I offered them a room."

Max smiles hugely. "Perfect. I'll order us some yummy food." He pops the cork on the wine bottle, which he must have used the corkscrew on to loosen it in the kitchen. "You make my life a constant party, sweetheart." He glances at Mallory before he pours wine into all the glasses. "I'd be a lonely old fat rich guy if it weren't for all of you." His belly jiggles as he laughs. "That's not a lie!"

Mallory smiles at him. "I'd let you fuck me even if you were penniless."

Max's expression melts. "How did I get this lucky, huh, Maria? I've never been this lucky in all my life."

"She's a gem. But so are you, Max. I'm very happy for you both."

"And I get to make money from having sex with people I want to have sex with. I think I'm the lucky one!" Mallory chuckles as Max hands her a glass.

"I'm happy to fund that. Your happiness and pleasure. What else can I buy that's as valuable? Nothing." He plops down on the opposite couch and brings the glass of wine to his lips, but he doesn't take a sip. "What else will I do with all this money if not spend it on you?"

"Donate it?" Mallory asks coyly.

"Yeah, I donate monthly. But hon, pick a charity, any charity, and I'll send a big sum there in your name. Tomorrow."

"Really? That sounds fun." Mallory shimmies her shoulders.

"Really. And let's make it a monthly thing. You pick, I pay."

"I think I take the cake. I'm the luckiest," Mallory says in a sweet tone. "It's like a dream." Except for the fallout with Derek, that is.

When Sam and Derek stroll down the hallway, having relief evident on both their faces, Mallory is soothed. Derek so needed that. She dares believe the hope she sees in his eyes. Bless them for coming over. Without them, Derek may have driven back home, or worse, disappeared.

"We've worked up an appetite," Sam says as he guides Derek with a press on his back. "Eat up, boy, you've earned it."

Maria and Mallory smile at each other knowingly. If it weren't for Sam, Derek would not be this happy-looking. She has zero doubts.

Mallory watches as Derek loads up his plate and grabs a glass of wine. Likely, he hasn't been eating well either, which has surely contributed to his sour mood.

They all enjoy the snacks and small talk, and things seem to be returning to normal. With Sam and Maria sleeping here, it's likely Derek will stay, too. This is exactly what's needed.

"So, Max, Derek tells me this is going from a residence of one to three." Sam shifts in his seat as a look of recognition flits across his face.

Mallory looks sharply at Derek. She can't conceal her surprise.

"Yes," Max says, covering his shock much better than she is. "What do I need a big house for, just for me?"

Mallory connects her gaze with Derek's, and they both smile. He chews the food and then gives her a nod.

Sam has worked his magic, and Derek is returning to her. Her only trick now will be to get him to ask her to marry him again.

Or, perhaps, better yet, she should ask him.

Chapter 4

The evening is shaping up to be perfect. Max has meat marinating, Sam, Maria, and Derek are in the hot tub, and Mallory is sitting at the island watching Max as she checks the latest stats of her success.

"I'm just in awe, Max. I can't believe how many people are paying me money for all this. It's legit blowing my mind." She stares at the numbers on her phone, shaking her head. "I never dreamt this was possible." She savors the feeling that things are fixed between her and Derek, but she warns herself not to be too trusting.

"You really are oblivious to how amazing you are, honey. And, it's not just your sex appeal, your beautiful face, it's also your heart, babe." He stops chopping mushrooms. "They can see that in you. It's a genuine glow that you emit. It can't be faked, bought, or reproduced. You are the real thing, honey. And everyone just wants to bask in your glorious beams."

She scoffs. "You build me up way too much. I'm not some golden saint." She shrugs. "I'm just me."

"And 'just' you, is what they all want." His grin brightens. "I can't say it enough. But I can say it again, you just don't see yourself as others see you. You're incredible, but you're also humble. People see that, too. And it's a winning combination." He begins to slice mushrooms again, then glances back up at her.

She raises her eyebrows at him. She's skeptical as heck.

"What? I'm being serious."

"Well, of course, you feel that way about me. I can see that. But these numbers are like unheard of." She scrolls into the pre-order section of her video, and her jaw drops. "Holy fuck, this is the most I've ever made from one video." She raises her gaze to meet his. "And it's the pre-order of what we just filmed."

"Well, then, I need to make sure my guys are working on this so we can blow it up as much as possible." He puffs up his chest. "I was talking with Manny, and he knows a guy who knows a guy in this business, and he's gonna get the skinny for us. We need more kickass stellar ads to really conquer, and they know this field."

She crumples as she gives him a silly look. "Knows a guy who knows a guy? Sounds sketchy."

"It's only sketchy if it's sketchy," he says.

"Who's sketchy?" Derek asks as he enters the kitchen, wrapped in a towel. "I've been sent to retrieve more wine."

"Oh, I've got you covered." Max moves over to the wine fridge and pulls out two bottles. "One is the same as the last, and this one is different. Let's open both."

"I might need to slow down on the wine," Mallory says as she sways on her stool. "I'm feeling it."

"Stay sitting. And you need more snacks," Max says as he points to what's left of the charcuterie board. "Finish it up. All yours."

"I'm full, though," she says before pursing her lips.

"I can help with that in that case," Derek muses. He swipes a few and shoves them in his smiling mouth.

Happiness swirls up in Mallory. Derek looks happy. "Did you try the pepper jack cheese? I know it's your favorite."

He scarfs down his food and reaches for the cheese. "Yeah, I think I ate ninety percent of it." Even his eyes are jovial. "But I have room for more."

She sighs. The aftermath of good cock isn't going to sustain him for long, but she's sure as fuck happy to see him like this. "It is really good."

Max writes something down on a notepad, and she's positive it's pepper jack cheese.

"I'm off," he says, raising his hands with a bottle of wine in each. "Thanks for these. And the snacks."

"My pleasure," Max says confidently

After Derek is outside, she goes to Max.

"You're aiming to seduce him into the idea of living here, and I love you for it."

"Guilty," he says as he wraps his arms around her. "If I can sweeten the deal with spicy cheese and wine, I'm going to."

"You're my hero," she says.

He dips his head, and they engage in a kiss.

The door pops open again, and this time, Maria enters.

"I've come to retrieve you, love. We need your sexy body in the hot tub."

"I'm coming. Was just checking my numbers." She pulls out of Max's arms. "You coming out, too? Or do you need help? I can help first, then go out."

"Nope, I'm good. You go out and enjoy. I have just a bit of prep left, then there won't be anything else to do until just before grilling."

"Okay, you're the best."

Maria grabs her hand and tugs her in the direction of going outside. "You know I'm so ready to make you holler later."

"I know, and I can't wait. I'm on pins and needles, ready for it." She feels a bit woozy as she walks.

"Food first, then untold waves of pleasure," Maria says with determination and assurance.

"Wait, before we go out, how is he?"

Maria goes solemn. "He's good. But I think he's on fumes, honey. Sam is always his boost when you aren't."

She sighs as a sob threatens to erupt. "I hate that I'm not."

"I know. But I think this will pass, but it might take something major."

Her heart sinks. She's right. Derek is just wearing a mask from a good time with Sam, that's all. "Shit. Now I need a moment. I'll be out in five, I promise."

"Okay, take your time, honey. We aren't going anywhere..." She pauses. "And don't worry, Derek will come around."

Mallory swivels quickly, but Derek has already seen her face, so hiding at this point is dumb. But she walks toward the living room anyway. She's taking at least a minute or two to herself. She sits on the couch and tries to calm down. The man who she's been connected to practically at the hip, is deeply lost and her attempts at reconnection have all struck out as blanks. It seems ludicrous. They've been so tight nothing ever came between them. This seems impossible. She fears nothing will help.

But he's here.

He's not gone; he's come back. She needs to seize this opportunity of having Maria and Sam present as the catalyst, then she needs to be the solution. Only she needs to figure out what the fuck the solution is.

She rises and makes her way out to the backyard. The three of them are submerged in the water with steam rising past their shoulders and heads. Three people who are her family in all, just needing Max to complete it.

She walks toward them as the chill in the air gives her goosebumps. She slips off her robe.

"Who needs a bikini?" Sam asks slyly, clearly appreciating her near nudity.

This makes her smile. "I guess I don't." She removes it and hangs it on the rail next to their suits. "I'm not sure why we even bother with suits. It just makes for more laundry."

"True. But I do like how you look in one," Maria states with a seductive gleam in her eyes. "And I adore taking it off you."

"Same," Sam retorts.

Derek remains silent, and it feels more like the lash of a whip. He has always shown his greedy lust for her, and she's adored it. He looks happy, but the mood is a band-aid. His mask will slip when he crashes. She has the urge to plead with him now to stay, in front of everyone, so he says 'yes', but it's not the right time, and she'd absolutely demolish the vibe if she spoke up about it.

Instead, she slides into the water silently and smiles at all three of them.

"I think our video is going to smash." She leans back as the heat consumes her in comfort. "I was just checking the numbers, and the presale is kicking butt."

"That's awesome. I'm so excited for it to go live." Sam appears relaxed enough to fall asleep. "With you in it, it can't not hit."

His compliments always make her feel so juicy and desirable. "This is exactly what I needed," Mallory says. No lie. She's feeling better already. "I want to strike while the iron is hot, though, and start planning the next one."

"Yeah, makes sense," Sam says.

"Is Max joining us?" Derek asks.

His question makes her cringe inside. It shouldn't.

"He's coming," Maria says. "I just saw him pass by the kitchen window, and he was shirtless."

Derek is still wearing his happy mask, which means his crash will be harsh. It isn't going to be pretty or easy. He's put himself in a prison he knows the way out of, if he follows the light. But it's never that easy.

"I'm going to use the bathroom," Derek says as he rises out of the hot tub.

This seems a bit too convenient.

"Avoidance isn't a solution, son," Sam warns.

"I just need to piss. I'll be right back." The annoyance in his tone is almost undetectable, almost.

Max opens the door and steps out. "Whew, it's brisk out here." He walks to the hot tub and sheds his suit. He climbs in as Derek climbs out.

Max looks guilty.

For fuck's sake, Mallory sighs.

Derek disappears into the house.

"Is it me?" Max asks with a head shake. "Scratch that. I know it's me."

"He's taking a piss," Maria states with a raise of both eyebrows. "So, if he doesn't return, we'll know."

"I'll go fetch him if he doesn't." Sam leans back and puts his hands behind his head. "Don't worry, Mallory. I talked with him earlier, and trust me on this. He's confused and lost, but deep down he knows you two are solid."

She nods, and her emotions swirl up again. The ups and downs of her emotions are getting exhausting. "It could be so good. Amazing really. If he lets it be."

"Yeah, and I think he knows that," Sam says. "He just needs some time."

"So, when is dinner?" Maria asks in a light tone.

"Seven," Max states. "This is my favorite marinade. You will love it."

Derek returns, with a blazing rod of a hardon.

"Well, welcome back with that," Sam says appreciatively. "The bathroom trip was good to you, I see," he says in a jovial way, lusty suggestion practically dripping from his words.

Derek beams a proud smile. "It's been so long."

Maria giggles in delight. "You are a treat, my love."

Mallory is able to grin, too. "He's always had that delicious ability to pop one in an instant."

He climbs into the hot tub, his hard rod of a cock bobbing like a fat wand. He moves toward Mallory with clear intent and descends upon her, settling on her lap. They erupt into an embrace and deep kiss instantly.

The kiss is so satisfying, with his hungry mouth on hers, the urge to weep rises in her, but thankfully her lust beats it to the finish line. She kisses Derek back deeply, her muscle memory for their intense intimate link snaps into place in a hot minute. She moans as he begins to thrust his swollen meat against her torso.

As he kisses down her neck, she drops her head back, making her back arch. "Yes, Derek. Please," she pleads in a desperate, sensual voice. "I need you."

He grabs her head fiercely, and they fall into another intense lip lock. He kneels on her thighs. His cock is so close to her mouth as he thrusts against her; she moves to try to take his cockhead in her mouth.

He taps her head upright gently and begins to thrust into her cleavage. There will be no oral.

She presses her breasts together, and he rides her, making the hot water splash up erratically.

Derek grunts as he pumps, increasing the motion of his hips as he rocks Mallory's body.

She's sure he will come again any second and spill his seed upon her breasts, or more likely, shoot it onto her face. But after a few grunts and an angsty, lusty growl, he steps back and motions with his hands for her to spin.

"Want you doggy," he says gruffly.

The others are silent as they watch, and their eyes on them are so hot as fuck. She rises and turns around, presenting her ass to her lover.

He grips her hips and shifts his hips so his hard cock slides against her vulva. She loves it. She's ready to scream, wanting him inside her so badly.

He taps his firmness against her clitoris, and then he rubs.

She twists slightly, the cold air jarring her into a slow rise. Her arousal ramps up higher as Derek presses his fingers deep into her hips, guiding her back onto his cock. He pokes his tip at her opening, but doesn't enter her.

He reaches under and rubs her sensitive spot at the perfect pressure, and she squirms.

"Fuck," she mutters as she writhes in place.

"Beg me," he asserts.

"Please, Derek, please."

"Who?" he demands.

"Daddy, please, Daddy."

"Ass out of the water," he commands.

She obeys and leans forward so she's more out of the water. She shivers, but she's not stopping this delicious train.

He presses her clit even more vigorously, and she's about to launch, but he pulls back.

"Not yet, not until I'm in you and I say." His dominance is blaringly bright as a beacon.

"Fuck yes," she murmurs. This gets her heart beating faster, and her breath coming quicker. "Fuck me, please, Daddy. Put it in me. I want the real thing."

He penetrates her and begins to ride her backside, slamming into her wet goosepimpled flesh. The water splashes up as he fucks her fast and furiously. Her nipples are hard as bullets. The cold is harsh, but she ignores it.

He grunts and holds her hips firm, pinning her in place as he plummets his cock deep into her cunt.

She accepts his pounding, his rams sending scrumptious reverberations through her pelvic region.

She could come with ease.

"Get it, get it good," he instructs in a breathless voice.

She's holding up her body to stabilize herself firmly with her arms. Bending over further, she rests her head on the frigid deck boards so she can reach under herself and rub.

"Good girl," Derek says in a strained voice.

She rubs her fingers around her swollen folds, and she soars into the bloom of her orgasm. The intensity of the sensations tips her over the edge, and she free-falls into the burst of her climax. Her body twitches as she gives into the swells of pleasure her internal contracting walls gift her.

Derek responds with a deep growl, a desperate grunt, and then a series of wild, beating thrusts against her bottom, enough to match the force needed to bust down a dam. He groans in satiation as his nails indent her flesh.

"Fuck," he mutters. His tone is primal.

The wetness increases, and the motion of him slowly going inside and out of her makes squelching sounds.

She pants as a shiver wracks her body.

He backs up and pulls her by her hips back into the warm water.

She needed that.

He needed that.

And having the rest of them watch was fucking top-notch.

She reaches up, and he falls into her embrace.

They hold each other in the hot water and don't move for more than a minute.

No one says a thing.

"I love you," she whispers.

"And I love you," he responds.

Her world has returned, and Derek has come back to her.

The water bubbling sound fills her ears as steam rises up. She closes her eyes to savor his arms around her, then reopens them.

He caresses her hair and then leans back. Holding her face in his hands, he plants a kiss on her lips.

Without a word, he settles into the seat next to her, then pulls her onto his lap.

As she snuggles in, she catches the faces of Maria and Sam. They both have endearing looks on their faces, Maria, possibly even a bit weepy. This may not be a total fix, but it's a far better scenario than Derek leaving and not coming back. It's a step in the right direction. A big step.

"Hi," Mallory says as she meets Maria's eyes.

"Hi. That was beautiful and extraordinarily hot," Maria says softly.

Mallory beams a smile her way as Derek squeezes her arms.

She can't see Max's face, but she doesn't need to. She's secure in where she's at with Max.

No one speaks. The moments don't fly but instead dwell. Being present in Derek's love and the loving gazes of her best people, her worries dissipate like the steam rising, fading into the reality of the air. Air that's cold and unfeeling, but takes the warmth as if unaffected. But that's not possible. Heat is transformative, and whether it's hot sex with her man or the warmth of his arms, her heart feels safe.

She breaks the silence. "Derek, remember when we drove to Maria and Sam's house that first time and we were terrified?"

"Yes. We almost didn't go."

"And look at us now. We have these incredible people in our lives."

"Yeah, and I wouldn't change it for the world." Derek caresses her elbow with his thumb under the water.

Her heart is wrapped in comfort and warmth. She's not trying to be too right that it puts him off. "Neither would I." She rises and looks him directly in the eyes. "And I wouldn't want to live this life without you in it."

All the success, all the newfound power she has, it literally would not be the same if Derek weren't by her side. She has a strong urge to ask him to marry her right on the spot, but then again, even though she wants to solidify it, she doesn't want it to happen this way. They need to be alone. Even saying 'yes' right now isn't right. Baby steps, and one of them at a time, is how she must proceed.

"I don't want to do life without you either."

Good. It's settled.

She twists so she can see Max. He looks happy, and that gives her a bit of relief. "So, when do we eat? I've worked up quite an appetite after that."

"Soon, in fact, I may get out and do the next steps. You all have a few minutes if you want to take them." Max rises, water dripping off his nude body, and he steps out. He quickly grabs a big towel and wraps it around himself. "Dang, that's cold."

"I want to shower," Maria says. "I'm going to get out, too. Then I can help with whatever you need, Max."

Sam follows, which leaves the two lovers alone.

"I'm sorry." Derek meets her in an eye lock.

"I'm sorry."

"I have been a bit irrational. I shouldn't have listed the house without talking to you first."

She sighs. That's really the least of her concerns. "It's been a bit crazy. But, in truth, if we move here, we don't really need the house." She watches his face closely.

He shifts his gaze to the water, then up to the sky as he leans back.

"Would you consider it? Living here, I mean?"

He says nothing as he scans the sky.

"Why not accept the offer of someone who is wanting to make our lives easier? Better?" She stares at him despite his averted eyes.

"Yeah, I suppose that's one way to look at it." He stares at his hands.

"What if you just took this gift? You could work on your dreams instead of working a shit job you hate."

He nods slowly. "That's true. But I'm not doing things in his favor. I don't want to be indebted to him, Mal." He brings his gaze to meet hers. "If I do that, I will be in a place where I feel like I owe him. And I don't want that. I'm not comfortable with it."

"I'm okay with all the gifts he gives me." She touches his arm. "And you've benefited from those gifts through me for a long time now."

"Thanks," he says sarcastically. "Not helping."

She sighs. "But it's true, isn't it? I mean, my making more money has helped you. You can't deny that fact."

"I'm just trying to figure out how to be okay with all this, you know? I don't have any false beliefs like I have to provide for you to be a man, but, at the same time," he says before pausing, "he can do for you what I cannot. And that stings. I want to help you."

"But Derek, you do help me. But perhaps in different ways. And that's not bad. That's good." She softens her eyes, hoping he sees all her compassion.

"But from what I see, he can support you in those same ways on his own. Which leaves me where...why do you need me?" His look of desperation hurts her heart.

She scoffs. How is it possible he's thinking this way? "Need you? Yes, it's true I need you, but Derek, I love you. I want you as my life partner. That's what the real truth is. It's…Max will never be, and never has been, a replacement for you. Nor a fill-in. You each fulfill me in different ways. In my perfect universe, I get you both. Every day. And I'm luckier than both of you for it." She smiles sheepishly. "And I realize I'm being selfish. But I'm also not afraid to ask for it." With every fiber of her heart, her will is screaming at her to be bold, be daring, but to be tender, and to ask for the impossible. "I will always want you, wherever I am, whatever I'm doing."

"I like to spoil you." A little sly smile erupts on his face, and a sparkle appears in his eyes.

"So does Max. See, I'm the lucky one." She raises her hands and gives a slight shake of her head. Her heart is smiling. He's more himself than he's been in a long time.

"You deserve it."

She slides to sit on his lap. "You're a strong person. You have a big heart. You might think needing you is more important, but to me, wanting you is the most important."

He collects her to him in an embrace, his eyes a shining aura of lust, love, and spark.

"Now that's what I yearn to see." She kisses him on the lips.

Their peck on the lips gets interrupted as Max sticks his head out the door.

"Not to interrupt you too, but I wanted to give you a heads up that I'm about to come out and throw the meat on the grill."

"Oh, okay. Thanks, Max," she says. She returns her attention to Derek. "We good?"

"Very good."

"I loved how you just took me in front of everyone like that. It was really hot."

"It was."

More than anything, she's happy he had the confidence and the drive to do it. "Anytime you want to take me like that in front of others, count me in." She giggles.

His sexy smile twerks her libido into a swell of lust. But it's time for dinner.

Chapter 5

After her shower, she enters the kitchen. Sam, Maria, and Derek are munching on appetizers while Max is manning the grill outside. The smoke billowing off the grill floats above him as he flips the meat. He shuts the lid and turns to come inside.

He looks happy. There's a spring in his step. She likes that.

"Almost ready," he says as he enters the house. "It's looking good."

"It smells incredible," Mallory coos. She often gets glimpses of how she'd imagine Max would be, so miserable living his life all alone, and it solidifies for her how good they all are together. His kids reach out, but that's not like living with someone. And his aloneness makes it crystal clear to her why he joined the club in the first place.

Living so far away from the home base of the club will be the hardest part of their new life, but they will have each other. She's hoping that doing the collabs for filming will be a good enough substitute for missing all the parties and group play. Plus, they can travel there from time to time. Her brain keeps fixating on Max's idea of hosting a play date party, and her dream of it only gets stronger day by day. If only everyone could travel, that's the question. Max has the room, so they could likely accommodate everyone, with many sharing beds, of course. She smiles at the thought. It sounds deliciously fun!

"It won't be long now," he says as he pulls the potatoes out of the oven.

She peers over his shoulder as he sets down the pan. "Did I mention how I love your new obsession with cooking?"

He chuckles and turns slightly, leaning in for a kiss. "Once or a hundred times. I've always loved to cook, but cooking for just one is no fun."

"Well, those look incredible."

Max beams a smile even bigger. "Olive oil, a packet of dry Italian seasoning, seasoned salt, and dried rosemary leaves. It's an experiment."

"It looks and smells wonderful." She hugs him from behind as he loosens the potatoes from the pan with a spatula, the scraping sound hints that they will be nice and crispy on the outside.

She leaves him as he begins to scoop them into a bowl. "These all need to go to the table?" she asks as she scans the dishes on the island.

"Yep," Max says over his shoulder quickly.

"I'll help," Maria says, grabbing the salad bowl.

Derek pops two more mini beef sticks in his mouth, then chews as he grins. He snags the bread bowl and carries it to the table. He's all shiny with smiles, too. Max has already set the table and lit two long candles in the center.

"This is looking like we are royalty here," Maria says in astonishment. "Max, you surprise me."

"He's full of surprises," Mallory gushes.

"I guess so," Maria muses as she goes back for more dishes of food.

Sam raises his hands. "I'll be on drink duty. What does everyone want with dinner?"

AFTER DINNER, THEY all lounge around the living room, sipping their drinks.

"Absolutely incredible meal, Max. Thank you," Sam says. His eyes shine with admiration. "I think I need to take a few cue cards from you."

"I won't complain!" Maria blurts. "I'm ready to eat whatever you make. I'm honestly tired of cooking." Her expression falls into disgust.

"I'm ready to take up the hobby," Sam says with a tilt of his head. "We need to eat every day, right?"

They cuddle together on the couch. They are so good together.

"I'm feeling so lucky," Mallory states. "Our little family is more than I could have ever asked for."

Max motions for Mallory to come sit on his lap. His eyes tell her he agrees.

She moves over and settles across his thighs, leaning back into his shoulder. The only problem with all this is that Derek is left all alone on the love seat by himself. He doesn't have a frown, though; instead, he's leaning back with his belly pushed up.

"I'm a big fat pig," he states as Mallory continues to stare his way. "I may never move again." He pats his belly, which is anything but fat.

"I'm so happy you all enjoyed the meal. It was wonderful to have a group to cook for." Max squeezes Mallory's shoulder. "And I have brownies with raspberry syrup for later."

"Raspberry syrup?" Mallory's eyes light up. "The one you made before using real raspberries? Oh, I love that one!"

"Yup, that one."

"Oh, wait until you taste it, Derek. It's to die for."

"Can't wait," he pats himself again. "But I'm thinking once my stomach is settled, it's time to fuck."

Mallory bursts into laughter. "You're a delight. And I'm in."

"I need to wait for this ball in my stomach to stop stretching me first," Maria says, her arms framing her body. "I feel roly poly."

Derek's switch to contentment suits him, but Mallory fears it's just a temporary state with Sam being present. If only Maria and Sam would move in, too, but they'll never move away from their kids. Five people living here would be wild, but honestly quite doable.

"What if you two stayed for a whole month?" Mallory barely had the thought before it flew out of her mouth.

Sam's face erupts in amusement. "Well, the whole, we-might-smell-like-dead-fish-long-before-that thing."

"No, I'm serious. Right, Max? It would be okay, right? We could have sex, make some films, party a lot, and eat lots of good food. It would be good for all of us."

Sam brightens.

Maria's face softens. "I love your sentiments, honey. But maybe we could consider that in the future, we have several things we have to get back to. However, I would like to try that sometime. Especially to get away from the weather for a bit. What do you think, Sam?"

"Might be a welcome long getaway, yeah, but maybe next month or something?"

"Yeah, right now would be impossible." Maria and Sam exchange glances. "We'd just have to plan it right. There are some things we can't miss back home."

"Yeah, but doable, in the future for sure," Sam states. The sparkle in his eyes puts hope in Mallory.

"It would be so epic," Mallory says, not hiding her desire for it one bit. "I'm always hungry for more of you two."

"You're welcome to come anytime," Max says as he caresses Mallory's hair. "My house is your house. It's an open door."

"No time like the present for some spicy fun, though," Sam suggests with a sly grin. "I'm always ready to pop a boner and go." He smirks and glances down at his lap. "This talk is getting me there already."

"Mmm, I like that," Mallory says with a soft coo.

"A little group fling before we have to fly out is exactly what I was hoping for," Maria says in a seductive tone. "Something to get us to last until next time. I'm feeling my stomach settle enough to get pounded." She smiles wickedly.

"That's the perfect idea to end this night." Mallory stands up with raised hands, then approaches Sam.

He opens his arms as she descends, settling firmly on his lap. She's perched and ready to engage. He wraps her up in an embrace and gropes her backside. They fall into a loud, mouth-smacking kiss.

"Well, shit. I was already horny, but now I'm on fire." Maria rises and approaches Derek. She copies Mallory's lead and plants herself on Derek's lap.

They kiss deeply. Derek slides his hands under Maria's clothing, and soon, he's lifting off her shirt. This breaks their kiss for a second, but they go back at it hot and heavy once Derek tosses the shirt away. He unlatches her bra and slips it off, tossing it in the same direction as the shirt.

"I'm not patient," Derek states with an intense look.

"Neither am I, and I appreciate that in you."

They engage in lip-locked oral pleasures again.

Mallory turns her attention back to Sam, and they continue to kiss, though both of them are still fully clothed. Sam grunts, squeezing her bottom in a forceful grab.

She squawks and squirms.

"Yeah, just like that, honey," Sam coaches. "Grind into me. So so so very, very good."

She dances in his lap as she dives back at his mouth.

He chuckles, then slides his hands into her clothes, cupping her bare ass cheeks. He grunts as he presses her firmly against his pelvis.

He breaks the kiss and slides her pants down over the hump of her ass. She pops up, and he bares her lower half so she's half-nude. "I guess I'm not patient either." He reaches for her shirt and tugs it off, then moves to remove her bra.

"First one fully naked," Mallory hoots, shooting her fists in the air. "I get the prize."

"Come here," Sam retorts quickly. "Need that naked bod on me right now, and I'll give you a prize you won't forget."

She resumes her position and wiggles her bare pussy mound into his hardened cock. "Mmmm," she hums.

"Want you," he mutters into the flesh of her neck before he kisses her. He nibbles her flesh and then sucks hard.

"I want you, too," she slurs, dipping her head back. She catches sight of Max, and his cock is out, and he's stroking. He's left out of the action for the moment, but is taking care of himself. His expression is hungry and wanton. It tweaks her desire higher with him watching.

She'd love to have both older men loving on her, but getting Max to join such a threesome is always a challenge. She can understand it; he has an aversion, and it is what it is. He's reluctant to somehow bump into a man sexually, which is so not his thing. He's often told her he'd rather wait until she's had her fill of a man, then come to him. But she can hope for more someday.

Sam drives his attention down her neck in a series of ardent kisses, then he takes her nipples into his mouth, each in turn. He suckles and then nibbles her with firm lips.

She squeaks as he uses his teeth on her tightened nubs.

He lets the nipple slide out of his mouth slowly. "Love your wrinkles and bumps, honey." He re-consumes her nipple, pressing on the middle of her back to keep her in place.

"Max, come join," she urges as she tries to make eye contact. She can't resist at least pointedly inviting him, on the off chance he might try it. She only gets a look at him for a split second as Sam moves her.

"No, honey, I'll wait. Make me next, though, huh?" Max sounds gruff with lust.

"Yes, Daddy," she whispers with a quick glance and grin. Her clit is buzzing, ready for more direct contact.

While Sam is dining on her tits, she checks on Maria and Derek once more. He's ramming his cock into her doggystyle like he's chasing his orgasm, as if a wolf in top breeding season. He's grunting and pounding her, making her tits swing wildly and her head bob. Her chin juts out. He's being so rough, she's flopping in front of him as if she's no more weight than a folded piece of paper. Her sounds are primal and arousing as fuck.

"Wow, look at them go," she purrs into Sam's ear.

"Want to join that?" he asks, his voice thick with desire.

"Yeah, that would be hot." She slides off him. "Let's do it."

She walks toward the two of them, then gets a burst of urgency as she rushes, making her breasts and ass cheeks bounce as she scurries.

"Wait for us to catch up," she pleads.

Maria tries to look back at her, but Derek's ramming her so relentlessly that it's difficult. Her face twists through slight grimacing and pure pleasure.

"He's got me," she says in a strained voice.

Mallory bends over, placing her hands on the couch cushion so close to Maria's that they are touching. Mallory wants this badly and is so pumped it's happening.

Her hip bumps Mallory as Derek doesn't slow his forceful thrusting one bit. Mallory feels like a part of their fucking, and she loves it.

Sam wastes no time. He reaches under Mallory and accosts her clit. He rubs her, and she dances along with his motions.

She giggles. She's so ready.

"Love that, honey. Get yours." Sam rubs harder.

Her panting rises as do her sounds of pleasure.

"Please, fuck me, before they lose it. I want to be fucked in tandem." She knows Derek will stay hard, even if he comes, but she's in a rush to feel her body getting rocked while in contact with Maria's.

"Your wish is my command, sweets," Sam asserts.

He lines up his cock, but primes her hole first with some external fingering, then some internal pumping. After a few jabs of his fingers going in and out of her hole easily, he penetrates her lips and enters her body.

Both of them groan in satiation.

Sam gets down to business tout suite and drives his cock into her with strong force, gripping her hips tightly for leverage.

Mallory looks toward Maria, and their eyes meet. Both are being jerked back and forth rapidly, their bodies banging against each other.

"Enjoying the ride?" Maria asks breathlessly.

"Yes, you?"

"For sure," Maria says with fire in her eyes. "It's the best."

"Mmmm. Always," Mallory retorts quickly before she's gripped by a swell of pleasure. She moans and grunts, trying hard not to advance to her climax yet. Her eyelids fall shut as she arches her back.

"I've come five times," Maria says between puffs of breath. "Derek once."

It's too hard for Mallory to answer as her trek toward her peak soars, and opening her eyes is impossible. She manages to stave off climaxing. She's not ready to go there yet, plus, she loves it when Sam orders her to, so she's going to try her hardest to control her orgasm from launching.

"I'm filming," Max announces. "This looks really hot, I gotta."

Her eyes pop open as the pounding keeps going, and the skin smacks fill the room as do all four of their grunts, groans, and sighs.

About five minutes into the duo doggy fuck, Sam stops moving, but keeps his cock inside her.

She pouts, her lip protruding as she glances back at him.

Their eyes meet.

She questions him with her gaze.

"You first," he whispers as he withdraws from her pussy.

She swivels and sits on the couch, spreading her legs. She writhes as he drags his tongue down her skin from belly to mound.

He leans back for a split second, his eyes are zoned in on her pussy lips. Diving into her womanhood, he suckles at her folds, flicking her bean, taking every loose piece of her flesh in his mouth. The stimulation is driving her arousal high. He sucks all over her folds without any reprieve.

She thrashes on the couch as he has her pinned. "No mercy?" she asks in a desperate tone when he focuses on her clit.

He increases the force of his suction.

She climaxes like thunder, her moans merely a prelude to more. She grips Maria's arm, digging her fingernails into her flesh as the orgasm rumbles through her body.

Maria catches her in an eye lock and her body twitches, too, her sounds and exaggerated body shudders indicating she's climaxing as well.

Derek quickly whips Maria's body around and positions her on her back, mirroring Mallory.

The men continue to eat the women out side by side until both women have come again.

Then they switch.

Derek services Mallory while Sam takes care of Maria. After another round of big orgasms, Sam returns to Mallory and slides inside her, going hog wild with his thrusting until he spews deep inside Mallory's womb.

The four collapse on the ground in a heap, and Max ends the video with a close-up of all their sweaty faces.

"That was seriously hot as fuck," Max says as he drops his phone to his side. "That will bake the cocks on your account real good."

Mallory laughs. "Now it's time to bake you." She glances at Maria. "Care for a Max sandwich?"

Maria laughs. "Oh, I'd love one."

They both stand and move toward Max.

He gives them a look of sheer delight. "Oh, I'm in trouble now, double trouble." He smiles widely as the women circle him like predators, then come in close in a double embrace around him.

Mallory grabs his head and pulls him into a kiss while Maria dances against his backside. She drives her hands right into the front of his pants. Mallory steps back a bit so she can stroke Max.

Max grunts. "I won't last long like this."

Maria keeps stroking him, wiggling her body into his back.

Max grabs for Mallory's breasts and bounces them in his hands as she kisses his neck. "Oh, I'm gonna." He jerks his body, and Maria releases him.

Maria slides his pants down to his knees, and Mallory bends over the couch, giving him a nice target.

"Fuck me, Daddy," she demands. "Pump me up. Fuck me good, you horny old toad."

This gets everyone to laugh, including Max.

"I needed that, so I didn't lose it." Max taps his cock along her slit, then spanks her clit with his hard shaft.

"Please," she begs. "I want you to come, too."

Max coasts into her pussy easily and bumps her butt in a series of pounds. It doesn't take but a minute, and Max is grunting and arching in ecstasy.

He slows his pelvic gyrations and rests on her back. "That was long-awaited and so very good."

He stands up and pulls her into a hug, his eyes lit with twinkles. "Cuddle?" Pulling her to sit on his lap on the couch, he nuzzles his face into her hair. "You always take such good care of me."

The other three lay huddled in a heap on the other couch, their bodies entangled, their faces aglow with the beautiful aura of just having had fabulous sex.

An epic end to the perfect evening.

Chapter 6

"What the hell, Max?" Derek is irate; his hands shake, making the single sheet of paper in his hand flop.

"Derek, I was just trying to help. That's all," says Max.

"But why not ask me? To do it without even consulting me." He scoffs. "It's insulting."

Mallory rushes over as she ties her robe. "Hey, hey, hey. What's going on?"

Derek waves the paper in his hand, then slams it down on the island. "Daddy Warb...ucks." He makes a disgusted face. "Strikes again. Stay out of my business, loser," Derek blurts as he waves and then smashes the paper back down on the counter. His gruff hand motion has created a tear in the paper.

Mallory picks the document up. It's Derek's car bill, and it shows a mass sum was applied to pay off the entire loan. "Whoa." She raises her head to catch Max's attention. "You did this?" She can't keep the astonishment out of her voice. "You paid this?"

"He can buy you, but I'm not for sale." Derek points at his chest sharply before he pouts. He turns abruptly away, his eyes ablaze.

"Hey, he doesn't 'buy' me." Mallory frowns, wishing she could still see his eyes. And she's not for sale either!

"I'm sorry, Derek. I overstepped." Max's apology is full of regret; his tone of voice is demure. "I won't do it again."

"Derek—" Mallory starts.

Max interrupts. "I thought it would help since you aren't working yet."

"Well, then, ask me. I'm not your damn child," Derek retorts. His anger spills from his eyes in daggers. "Money doesn't fix everything. But what would you know about that? You just wipe your money over things and think it fixes it." He twists his body back and forth rapidly. "Money isn't magic!"

Derek grabs the bill and throws it away in a huff.

"Derek, he truly is helping you. Helping me. We had that loan together. Think of it that way," she calls after him. She wants to say Max wasn't always wealthy, but that won't help matters so she stays mute.

"Not good enough, Mal." He throws his arms in the air and heads out the front door, grumbling the whole way.

"He'll cool down." Max rubs his temples. "I wanted to surprise him. I never expected him to react like that." He sighs, looking sheepish. "I'm so used to taking care of you, I guess I shouldn't have extended that to him."

"Hey, I appreciate you doing it. I have money, so I could have paid it, but as always, I appreciate your ever-flowing generosity. Derek will get used to it. I mean, he's gotten used to living here, right? And not paying anything."

"Yeah." Max's worry dissipates as he pulls her into his arms. He smiles down at her. "You're incredible, you know that?"

"Oh, well, I think you are. I'm kind of mad at him for reacting that way when you're literally saving us a monthly bill."

"I'd happily pay all of your monthly bills. As I've said, I don't need this much money. I'd rather use it to make the lives of the people in my life better. You save me every day from myself, and that's worth more than any amount of money. I'd be a lonely old miser like Scrooge without you."

"I don't believe that. You're generous, you're not hoarding money. You just make a lot."

"I used to hoard it, but not anymore." He kisses her on the lips. "Thanks to you. You help me be more generous."

"Derek's being a spoiled brat. I mean, who complains about someone gifting them enough money to pay off a loan? That's ludicrous."

"He's probably mad because I did it on my own accord without involving him." He looks sheepish. "I opened his mail." Max steps back and shrugs. "His manhood might feel threatened. I can understand, and I should have thought of that."

"His tantrum is a dick move. I'll be chatting with him when he returns."

"Don't be too hard on him, babe. This is a huge transition for him. You and I have our dynamic down, but he's likely feeling a bit lost."

"I suppose. You're being more generous about this than I am." She opens the fridge and grabs the creamer. "He could be a bit grateful for fuck's sake. You are feeding us, providing shelter, and he's being a child. You know, he is. He agreed to stay here, and then he throws a tantrum about being given the money he needs." She puts a coffee pod in the machine and pushes the button. "It's stupid." She rolls her eyes.

"Maybe, but I'm willing to cut him some slack."

"You don't have to," she says sourly. As her coffee brews, she tries to shed her dark mood. If anyone had ever given Derek this much money in his life before, he'd have been jumping for joy. When it's Max, he throws a stinking hissy fit.

"I have faith he'll come around." Max spreads cream cheese on his bagel. "Hey, good news, my guys have the video fully ready, clips for advertising, and graphics. We are set to launch the full pack."

Her mood is instantly lifted. "Oh, that's very good news! Did they send it yet? I could post it for the first level of subscribers." She rubs her hands together. "Oh, I can't wait to hear their reactions! This is so exciting!"

Mallory knew that with Sam and Maria gone, Derek's mood would shift, but he's getting to be a bit much. His mood swings are awful. She'd slept in his bed last night, and they'd had sex three times, and that still hadn't put him in a good mood. Something needs to happen, and she has no clue what that is, but this can't go on. At least now she has the film distribution to occupy her thoughts.

She watches Max study his coffee cup. "Can I suck your cock while you enjoy that coffee?" She slithers her body close to his. "As a thank you."

"You don't owe me that, but I'll always take your mouth on my cock." He allows her to press her body to his. "I need to sit for this."

"Pick your seat," she muses as she steps back from him. "Coffee and a blow job. Every man's dream way to start the day."

"I thought that'd be pussy."

"Yeah, this is the second best, you're right." He settles into the captain's chair at the table. "I heard you two last night. I can't say I wasn't jealous." He looks good-natured as he talks, despite admitting his jealousy. "I'll never interrupt you, either, but if you ever ask me to watch, I'll never say no." He laughs as she dives for his crotch. "Text me."

"That sounds like a plan," she says as she yanks his pants down to expose his cock. "Coffee and dick. Best breakfast around."

He pulls out his phone and taps on the video.

She disrobes and moves between his legs. "Mmm. Good idea. A nice little video we could post as a teaser for the film's release."

"My exact thought."

She drops onto his cock, taking his tip into her mouth, loving how they use their sex life for promotion of her longer content.

She coasts her hand along his shaft, chugging up and down as she sucks. Her tits swing as she bobs on him, and his groans egg her on. Recording turns her on, too, and she looks right into the camera as she sucks him off. The camera is loaded with voyeurism potential, and she's playing it up.

Max gasps and twitches as she takes him deeper. He grips her scalp with one hand, grunts, then releases his load down her throat. He's shaking, so the video will be unsteady, but that's hot and a great POV for watchers.

She gags, but gets it down, still trying to suck. She keeps her eyes on the phone and keeps sucking as his cock softens in her mouth.

"Uh, shit. I needed that." He caresses her hair.

She pops off his cock then says into the phone, "Hey all, the first tier of subscribers will get the full video in one hour. Stay tuned!" She does the cliché finger swipe across her lower lip. Her fans eat that up.

Max taps his phone. "Off. I'll send it to you. And thank you, that really hit the spot."

"My pleasure," she says as she wipes cum from the corner of her mouth. "Who needs breakfast?" she asks jovially. She takes a swig of her coffee. "I love that we can just make content like that on the fly."

"Yeah, me too. I never knew I'd turn into such an exhibitionist."

"You ever worry about your business partners finding out?"

He laughs. "You have no idea what they do. And a few know and applaud me. Those guys are letches, big time pervs. No one will be offended. Trust me." He gives her a knowing look. "If it's ever a real problem, I'll just retire."

"Hmmm. Somehow, I believe you." She smirks.

She takes her coffee to the living room and settles on the couch to post the video to all her subscribers across the platforms that will allow it.

She has an appointment in two hours to get her hair done, which is the perfect amount of time to post everything. It's payday, in a big way, and to celebrate, she wants to do something big. Her brain has been swirling with ideas to try to make Derek's proposal more than a bad memory, but with him pitching fits like this, it's not the right time. He needs to be in a healthy, well-adjusted position for her to propose, and he's nowhere near that yet. No matter. She can wait. Besides, she wants it to be special and fun, not weird, awkward, and seeming forced. But she's got it in her head that the best way to fix it all is for her to ask him to marry her. It's all about timing.

She sighs as she watches Max enter the room.

"You working today?" she asks as he takes a seat next to her.

"Yes, I have a meeting in twenty minutes."

"Okay. I have my hair appointment, then I might go shopping."

He reaches for his wallet.

"No, I want to spend the money I made today. It will feel like a triumph." She smiles proudly.

"Okay, I can understand that." He still pulls out his wallet. "I've been meaning to give you this, though. Just keep it in your wallet, honey. No limits. I like being your sugar daddy. It makes me feel macho." He flexes his bicep and makes a silly face.

She laughs. "You're impossible. But I love you."

"I love you," he says with an even goofier expression. Then his tone falls serious. "Money means nothing to me. You mean everything. I can't say that enough."

"Oh, I get it." She leans forward. "Hey, I was thinking we have lots to plan. A party for the club and a new film. Maybe the three of us can have a meeting later? If Derek is over his tantrum, that is." She rolls her eyes. "Seriously."

"Yeah, I'm in. I love planning with you. I have a few ideas. We can all brainstorm and then set some preliminary plans. Do you have creators in mind you'd like to work with?"

"Yes, I do. Several, so we have options. I started a list in my notebook so I'm ready to move to the next step of asking them." She glances at him. "It won't be cheap."

"It shouldn't be." He grins. "But Sugar Daddy can pay, so let's make it big. Now give me some real sugar before I head off to my meeting." He rises and plants a kiss on her forehead, then their lips meet in a quick peck.

"I want to suck you off during a meeting sometime. Would you let me?" she asks as she bats her eyelids at him rapidly.

He laughs. "Yes, but I'm not a very good actor."

"Good." She adores the idea of pushing him to climax in front of his peers. It's a deliciously naughty dream of hers, and if the men end up knowing, all the better. It's the two women Max works with regularly that she worries about, so maybe it will need to be the right audience.

"I'll see you later today. Love you, bye." She watches him turn.

"Love you, bye. Have fun."

THE DAY IS SHAPING up to be fantastic. She loves her new hairdo and got to unload all her secrets to her hairstylist, who might as well be her therapist. She loves living vicariously through Mallory, being that she is stuck in a monogamous relationship with a jealous vanilla hub. However, she is really enjoying mom life, so in many ways, Mallory is living motherhood through her.

Her stylist lamented today about how she never even acted on her bisexual yearnings, and how she regrets it, but she had met her husband right out of high school, so she hadn't had much opportunity to try it out. Plus, she hadn't even felt safe acting on her sexual whims back then. Her comfort with it all is coming too late for real life, so she hangs on to every juicy detail Mallory spills.

The looks they got from some of the surrounding patrons were priceless, but the staff always give her a knowing smile with a spark of interest twinkling in their eyes. Many women she encountered cheered her on and secretly wished to live the life she was enjoying. She's lucky, and she doesn't need anyone to point it out.

She enters the store and scans the layout for the undergarment section. She makes a beeline for it. New lingerie is something she had on her list to buy with big success. She also wants a few new outfits, and then she'll stop by the local sex toy shop for a new clit sucker or two. A woman could never have too many of those around the house.

A sheer tight dress and a strappy number find their way into her hands, it's basically all straps and nothing else. Once in the fitting room, she relaxes. This is a show just for herself. Her mind drifts to her hairstylist again. She had once told Mallory a story where her husband refused to believe that lingerie could ever be for a woman to enjoy on her own. What a fucking tool! Talk about a sexist patriarchal view, for fuck's sake, that's asinine! She shakes her head, wishing her stylist could leave the fucking misogynistic loser. But she's now trapped with him, having had kids together. Mallory also knows this will never be her fate.

That is one thing Mallory is very happy about, not having to live under. She does like kids and wouldn't be opposed to having some in the future, but too many women she knew got trapped in marriages because they had kids with men who turned out to be restrictive, controlling, and manipulative. They wanted out but couldn't fathom the harm it would do to the kids. So, they stayed in misery.

Of her friends, very few were truly happy with their partners, except those in the club. So many ignored the red flags, feeling happy instead that they had a man who wanted to marry them. Such a foolish view, but society does that to women. More discernment is needed on a large scale with young women and deciding who to marry, or if to marry at all. She'd gotten lucky in that department, too.

She spins to view her body in the mirror. Yup. This is hot. Max and Derek will like it, and so will her fans. It's a winner. She tries on the next one and decides it's ideal as well.

As she leaves the store, she gets a text.

Glancing at her phone, she sees it's from Derek.

Derek: When are you home?

Mallory: Not for an hour or more likely two.

Derek: Okay. See you then.

Good. Derek is back. Hopefully, he's in a better mood.

She shops around the mall, visiting several clothing stores before deciding it's time to visit the sex toy shop.

The drive to the store is quick and uneventful. At the store, there are only four cars outside. Probably two are the workers, and two are likely from customers. She's only ever seen one or two workers there at a time. Upon entering the store, the familiar sight of multicolored dildos and toys fills her scan. Lingerie racks are half full, and she regrets not waiting to buy some here so she could have supported this small shop instead. Next time, she'll buy an extra toy or two to compensate. For once, she's got the money to do it!

She recognizes the young girl behind the counter from her last visit. She appears to be in her early twenties, has a nose ring, and long, straight brown hair. Her look is very innocent and girl next door, aside from the nose ring, and that she works in a sex toy shop.

"Hey," she calls in a friendly voice.

"Hey," Mallory parrots.

"Can I help you find anything?" She is perched on a stool and has a clear cup of greenish fluid on the counter in front of her.

"My clit sucker died, and I need a new one. A really good one. That one had the strongest suction I've ever found, and I need to replace it." She scoffs. "I'm a bit devastated."

"Oiy, okay. That's not good. We'll get you set up." She makes her way toward Mallory and stops near the clit suckers. "We can open them and try out the suction."

Mallory laughs. "Really? I didn't think you'd allow that."

She smiles. "On your hand. Nope, we don't take used ones back. But you can feel the suction on some other part of your skin."

"Thought as much, but I was tempted to hope for more."

She smiles back, which turns into a smirk. "I understand."

She snags a few toys, then leads Mallory to the checkout counter. "I'll just unwrap them and let you feel them so you can make the best choice."

Mallory searches the wall behind her. "Oh, what's this one?"

Another woman enters the store. She has a shock of pure yellow hair up the middle of her short hair. She's heavy-set and has multiple earrings going up the curve of each ear in addition to a nose ring. Her shirt matches her yellow hair streak, and she has baggy jeans on that might fit two of her.

"That one is put out by Playbuxx, but they rebranded it into a smaller brand name, and it's the same toy. It's good, but it didn't do well until they rebranded it." She nods, her confidence in her words apparent.

"Oh, then can I try that one too? It's a sucker as well, right?"

"Yeah, plus a dildo. And it bends." The yellow-haired girl scoffs. "But it doesn't fit many women in dual. The fucking moron designers should have measured the distance between the G spot and the clit better. It's too far for most women's anatomy is what I've heard." She snorts. "Men."

"Ah, okay. Got it. Not a one-size-fits-all."

The first salesclerk unwraps a sucker toy and turns it on. She presses it to the fleshy part of her lower thumb, then shrugs, but nods as if indifferent. "Mediocre."

Mallory lets her press it to the lower part of her thumb. "Decent, but this is hard to judge. I've only put suckers on my clit," she says with a light laugh.

The other clerk smiles and nods. "Most are that way."

The young woman unwraps the next one and puts it on her flesh. Then inverts her hand so the toy hangs by sucking her skin into it. "Better."

Mallory tries it and nods in agreement.

"One more?" she asks. "But we can certainly try as many as you want."

"Okay, great." Mallory notices a person coming out of the back room where the DVDs are kept.

The next one she presses to her flesh, and it's a much bigger, and therefore, heavier toy. It hangs easily off the loose flesh beneath her thumb. "This one is stronger." She taps at it, and it remains hanging while suctioned to her.

Mallory tries it on her skin. "Yup, this one is better for sure." She sees movement behind her and glances back.

"Oh, my God. Mallory?" It's the old man she saw a glimpse of. "I'm your biggest fan in the world!" he exclaims. "I can't believe this! I can't believe I'm this lucky to see you in real life!" he says shakily. "In person." He visibly trembles.

She spins to fully face him as her heart pounds enough to make her faint. Astonishment fills her as she gazes upon the man. He clearly knows her from her films and is so excited.

He's practically kneeling in front of her. "I've watched everything you've made, every video, every picture. I'm on my last breath, waiting desperately for your video to launch. I ordered it on pre-order. I couldn't wait, so I came here to try and fill my time up with other stuff, stuff not even remotely of your quality."

A fan. A real, true, legit fan in person! Her first recognition in public!

Elation bursts inside her, and she gives him her biggest and brightest smile.

He shrinks down further as his face bursts into further excitement. "I thought you lived in a different state. To see you here is...mind-blowing!"

"Oh, I'm so thrilled to meet you. You're my first fan I met in person like this!" she gushes. "Can I give you a hug?" She opens her arms.

He rushes into them so eagerly.

When he steps back, his face is so bright with joy that he seems to be emitting light. "I got to touch you. I will never forget this day for the rest of my life!" He turns to the salesclerks. "Don't you recognize her? She's famous!"

Both women look at her, but don't seem to recognize her.

"Awesome!" says the first clerk. "That's exciting! I'll definitely look you up. And can I have your autograph?" She reaches for a pen.

"Oh, me too," the old man says in an urgent tone. "Please. Let me find something." He begins searching his pockets. "Oh, I know." He moves over to the magazine rack and takes the first one within his reach. "Sign this."

Mallory's excitement over being spotted in the wild has her brain moving slowly. She searches the counter for a pen. "I don't have a pen."

"Here, use this one," the clerk says, handing it to her.

The old man hands Mallory the magazine. A nude woman is on the front. She has large tits and a sultry expression. Her pussy is shaved clean. "Sign her tits." He winks. "Mark it right across a nipple if you can manage it."

"Sure thing." She wishes she had some pics in her car she could sign for him, and makes a mental note to add some.

She signs a paper for both clerks, too, who now both have doe eyes for her.

"Gals, you need to check her out. She's the newest and hottest thing out there. She's incredible!" He runs a quaking hand through his hair. "I am in awe." He stares at her for twenty seconds. "Could I be so bold as to ask for a picture with you?" He looks apologetic.

"Oh, of course! I'd love it. And post it and tag me. I'll share it on my story."

The gentleman hands his phone to the clerk and puts his arm around Mallory. She takes several pics, then hands the phone back to him. His touch is light and respectful.

"Thank you," he says with gratitude in his eyes.

"And hey. Big news. The video is now live, so make sure you check it out." She watches his face blossom into delight.

"It is? Oh, I need to get home and watch it. Before my wife comes home from the grocery store, thank you and I'll never forget this day."

The yellow-haired clerk checks him out as the other one tends to Mallory. "So, do you want to try more or do you like one of these?"

"I think I'm going to take the last one. I'm curious if it will fit my anatomy."

"It's the most expensive at $165.99," she warns.

"That's okay. I'm spending money today that I just made on presales of my new film. It's a celebratory spend."

"Nice. That's really awesome. I have so much respect for someone like you. Doing what you want and making a business with your own sexuality. You're so empowered. I've often dreamt of it." She blushes.

"Well, you should try it out. I never in a million years expected mine to take off the way it has. I'm literally making so much money, it's now my job, and I'm doing what I love."

"That's really incredible."

She pays for the toy and forgets all about her plan to buy extra stuff until she exits. She should have just bought all three, but it's too late now; she's on a mission to get home and tell her men the exciting news that she got recognized in public! She's on her way to true celebrity fame-dom!

Chapter 7

Mallory opens the front door of the house, and the sounds of skin on skin smacking hit her ears. Grunts like someone in pain fill the air, too. The sounds keep going at a rhythmic pace. By the time she enters the living room, the groans are undoubtedly familiar, and the sounds are unmistakable.

She blinks and jerks her head back in shock. Derek is across Max's lap, and his ass is bare. Derek's flesh is reddened, and Max lays slaps on his butt cheeks in a series of hard, rapid hits, making them jiggle. Derek cries out as he raises his head back each time from the impact.

"What the hell?" she asks meekly, more out of astonishment than anything else.

"Oh, hi, Mal," Max says, looking happy.

Derek doesn't move a muscle.

She frowns slightly as confusion fills her.

Max pushes Derek off his lap. He scrambles to stand and pulls up his pants, shame filling his face.

"I'm confused," is all she can manage.

Max smiles at her as if he's offering her a buttered muffin. "We were going to tell you."

"Tell me? How long has this been going on?" She needs to sit down, but doesn't move a muscle.

"A few days, I guess," Derek says. He looks guilty as heck.

"A few days? And no one told me?" She can't shake the shock of walking in on Max delivering a hard spanking to her boyfriend.

"Yeah, it's just between us, so we didn't say anything, but we also didn't mean to hide it from you." Derek sits down on the couch with a grimace. "It's no different from you and him doing something together or me and you." He shrugs.

She knows this, but stares at them slack-jawed.

"It's no different from you spanking me," Derek states defensively. "Well, it is different, I guess. Max is dominant; you are just playing dominant."

"Are you two having sex?" She drops her arms at her sides. "I mean, I don't care if you are." This would shock her even more than the spanking.

"No. We aren't having sex." Max stands and walks to her. "Can I take your bags? Take a seat so we can all talk." He scoops up her bags.

Mallory lets Max lead her to the couch. She sits.

"Spanking is different when there's no sex with it," she states as if they must know this.

"Well, there's a bit of sex. It's sexual for him." Max points at the cum on his pants. "I'll have to change again. That means more spanking for soiling me." He looks sternly at Derek.

Derek nods, looking sullen.

"Okay, I'm all for kinky stuff, but someone needs to start talking." Mallory's brain is working too slowly for her patience.

"It's not sexual for me, but it is for Derek, and if he comes on me, and I have to change my pants, it means extra punishment. Another hard spanking." Max wears a harsh expression, and it jars Mallory as if she's just been woken up. She's not used to seeing him display this kind of hardness.

"It's no different from any Dom/sub dynamic. As you know, babe, not all Dom/sub relationships are about sex. Some are sexless."

She stares at him. "But I've never actually seen this." She pauses and stares at Derek, then back at Max. "So, you're his Dom now?"

"One of them. With being away from Sam, he sought me out." Max gazes at Derek. "And I was happy to oblige. Sam knows. We talked."

"So let me get this straight. This all happened before this morning, as in before the you paying his car off tantrum fiasco?"

Max nods. "Yes."

"I can't believe you two didn't tell me." The shock wave hasn't settled inside her yet.

"We were going to. We were just...figuring things out for ourselves first." Derek drops his head back. "It's hard to explain, Mal. You'll think it's weird."

"I'm happy to listen, if you want to share." She's happy he and Max have made more of a connection, but she never would have expected it to be this. Not in one million years.

"You know my dad always spanked me. And hard. Like he beat me. Brutally." He drops his shoulders. "And he hated that I liked boys, too. So, he whipped me to try and hit it out of me."

"Yup, I know all of that." She nods slowly, remembering his sickeningly horrific retellings of the incidents.

"I need someone to correct me. And it's a kink, but it's not only a kink. It's a trigger for me to get hit by a dominant, so when you spank me, it's just not enough."

"I see." She purses her lips, not offended one bit. "That makes sense. I can understand it."

"I asked Max to spank me for the first time a few days ago. We talked about it for hours and came to an agreement. It's asexual for him, and he gets his aggression urges met, and I do get turned on, but we have a predetermined set of rules in place for the scenarios. Rules I know and agree to, as does he. Then we just started with the first spanking." Derek shrugs. "And it's helping me. It's...me claiming and reframing the kink I was given, well, that was shoved down my throat." He pauses. "I mean, I never came when my dad spanked me, though. That's where it gets confusing. I was never turned on when Dad did it. It was the exact opposite. And I was terrified."

"It's no different from any Dom/sub dynamic, it's just that we are a sexless one." Max clears his throat. "We have a set of rules, and when Derek breaks the rules, I give him a spanking. He gets his correction swiftly."

"Kind of," Derek says as his face flushes.

"Right." Max gives a nod to punctuate and sends her a knowing look. "And he's in control this time with a safe word and rules, not like when his dad was hitting him."

"I know all this, but honestly, you two have succeeded in shocking me, when I didn't think I was shockable." She gives a light burst of laughter as she twists her head to the side. She peers beside Max and widens her eyes. "Is that the heavy wooden paddle I see?"

"Yes, that's for when he comes on my pants. Which he will have a licking coming for after we're done talking here." Max's soft eyes are brutish and uncaring as he raises his eyebrows and nods toward Derek.

He smashes the paddle into his left palm, the heavy thud sound carrying throughout the room. This is a side of Max she has not seen, except for maybe a tiny, microscopic glimpse of when they've fallen into the her-getting-used-by-him kink scenes.

"That one hurts," she says demurely, a cringe overcoming her.

"Yes," Max states without emotion. "It delivers the message. Nice and solidly." He whacks it against his palm again.

Derek flinches.

"So, I will have to get used to you just pulling his pants down and spanking him around the house randomly?" Mallory knows all about this kink, so why is her comprehension of this as difficult as wading through cement? She can't quite process it all.

"Yes," Max says definitively.

"Okay," is all she manages.

"I've done many BDSM acts throughout the years, even a relationship or two." He clears his throat. "I know what I'm doing."

"There's so much more about you that I don't know." She places her hands on her thighs and looks back and forth between the two men. "Well, I guess this doesn't include me or concern me if you two have figured out your rules and boundaries." She leans back onto the couch. "I'm glad you're getting what you need, Derek. And I never knew you thought I was such a lame duck spanker." She laughs at herself. "I'm not nearly as strong as a man, that's true." She stares at them, still aghast.

"It's just different, Mal. Your spankings aren't bad. It's just that Max's are more effective, and I have no wiggle room for questioning. And I know he's a dominant man, so there's that." Derek stands up and pulls his pants back down. "You can stay and watch or leave. I'm not offended either way. I know I'm gonna get it good."

"Good boy," Max says in a stern voice. He pats his lap. "Get over my lap now like a good boy. Take what's coming to you."

Derek lies upon Max's lap, his face already in a strained grimace. His flesh is red, and it won't take much for it to blister. Mallory really hopes Max doesn't go that far.

Max raises the heavy paddle and smashes it against Derek's ass.

Derek's back arches as he yells out in anguish.

Mallory flinches as Derek squirms in recovery. She might not have the stomach to watch this, but she can't deny that it turns her on a little, too.

Max hits him four more times in rapid succession; the wallops are loud and brutal. After the fourth hit, he stops.

"You're done. Now stand up and pull up your pants."

Mallory releases her held breath. Finally. She couldn't have watched much more if they had kept going.

Derek rubs his butt gingerly as his face changes through a myriad of painful expressions. "Thank you, Daddy."

"You're welcome, son. Now behave or I'll be at your butt again. And I won't hold back for her sake."

Derek nods somberly.

The realization hits her like a ton of bricks that she and Derek are now sharing a Dom. She has the urge to comfort Derek after the spanking, so she crawls over to him.

When she reaches him, she kneels before his bent legs. "Can I give you head to make you feel better?"

Derek looks at Max for permission.

Max nods.

Relief floods Derek's face as he nods. "You can."

Domination from Max in the trickle down through him, domming Derek. Nothing could be hotter.

She rises up and hovers over Derek's thighs.

He moves, and his pained expression changes to more pain as he shifts. He unveils his fully loaded cock for her and wiggles it.

"I'm going to change," Max says. "I doubt he has any come left, but suck him dry if he does."

Mallory takes him in her mouth and tenderly sucks his cock's tip.

He gently caresses her head as she blows him. After a few minutes of sucking, Derek's grunts intensify. He shifts his hips so that he fucks her mouth a little, and within thirty seconds, he's coming inside her mouth.

She gags, swallowing his cum, and then slides off him.

"Whew, that does help. Thank you." Derek's look of relief is worth the gag.

"My pleasure."

"Uh, fuck. That hurts," he says as he maneuvers his cock back inside his pants. "Every move hurts."

"Well, this is certainly a new development in our little group."

Derek sighs as he nods. "I didn't see it coming. But I got the urge, and as you've always encouraged me to act on my urges, I did it and asked Max. And he was receptive to doing it."

"So, now you need his permission to be sexual with me?" She cowers at this and doesn't plan to agree if that's the rule they've agreed upon.

"No, it won't be like that. It was just because you were offering to make me feel better when I was supposed to be feeling the effects of the discipline. Like it was still inside the discipline bubble."

"Ah, okay. I get it. That makes sense. And good, because I don't think I'd like it that way."

"Me neither." He grins sheepishly at her. "I'm a weird fuck, aren't I?"

"No weirder than me!" she exclaims. "You need it as long as you need it. I'm not going to try and change your mind."

"Yeah. It oddly makes me feel healthier. As I said, it's hard to explain."

"I think I sort of get it. We're victims of what has happened to us in our past. The crazy part is, what your dad did to you brought on this kink, and he'd be mortified if he knew." She laughs. "It's kind of funny, though, to imagine him finding out."

Derek joins in her laughter. "Yeah, that's spot on..." He pauses. "Oh, and the other thing is, we have an agreement that he will also give me daily maintenance spankings in addition to the punishment ones. So, you will see him spanking me for no apparent reason other than to enforce his dominance over me." He shrugs. "I don't know how long I will crave this, but I'm finding it to be pretty hot." He shivers. "And helpful."

"Yeah, I understand how that dynamic works. It will be interesting around here, that's for sure." She smiles. "Our life is never boring! But I crave that."

"Always," he agrees. "Same. We're a match there."

Max returns looking all fresh and happy faced, like she's used to.

"So, babe. Tell us about your day. It looks like you found some things." Max picks up and hands her the bags.

"Yes, I did. And you'll never guess what happened. It was the best thing ever! Someone in public recognized me and asked for my autograph!"

A slow grin breaks Derek's lips open. "That's really cool, Mal."

Max rubs his hands together, a huge grin on his face as well. "You're coming into your fame. I love this for you."

"It was just, I don't know, hard to explain. Sort of validating? Satisfying? Special?"

"I can imagine. And I predict it will happen more and more." Max moves closer to her. "Let me give you a hug. We'll have to celebrate by giving you some orgasms in a bit."

She melts into his arms, trying not to look at his hands in a different way after what she witnessed. "I'll never say no to that." His chest is comforting against her body, as is his squishing belly. "I'm pretty niche for a famous person, though, and I was in a sex toy shop. It wasn't like I was at the grocery store."

Max chuckles as he cradles her. "Got it." He rocks her back and forth. "Come on in here, Derek."

She is impressed that Max is inviting Derek to their hug. Maybe the spanking practice is changing something between them. Dare she hope it's some sort of positive connection?

Derek nestles up behind her and wraps his arms around her, and since they are close, his arms go partially around Max, too.

Derek's breath on her ear is a welcome addition. She's snug as could be between her two men. This hug is not something she expected to ever have happen, so glee fills her.

Feeling an overwhelming sense of giddiness as their hug keeps going, she has never felt closer to both of them. Admittedly, finding out about their new spanking dynamic had her feeling left out, after the freaking shock wore off a bit. Which was kind of strange because it's not like she wants to be spanked like that herself, nor does she have the desire to ever spank Derek severely like that. She's really only okay with spanking associated with kinky sex, control, and domination in association with sex, and yet their ritual is sexless. That's totally foreign to her.

"Well, I have to break up this comfort party, unfortunately. I have an urgent meeting that popped up, and I need to get to it. But I promise, those celebratory orgasms will be a part of our day."

He steps back, releasing her from his firm embrace. "You deserve all the recognition. You're a powerful sex goddess, and the world is falling in love with you."

His words always build her up. No one empowers her more than Max.

He leaves, and Derek remains wrapped around her backside.

"I want to talk more about this spanking business," Mallory blurts, effectively busting up the sweet, intimate moment.

He releases her and slowly makes his way to the couch. "What about it?" he asks in a grumpy tone.

"Derek. I know you," she says, taking a seat next to him. "This spanking thing you two are doing, I'm fine with it. What I'm not fine with is how there's no aftercare. You aren't accepting any comfort from Max to deal with the stress of the spanking?"

"I don't need that."

"Bullshit," she says adamantly. "That's not how this kind of stuff works, and you know it."

"I don't want to cuddle with Max," he says with contempt. His eyes are angry and clouded over.

"I have a proposition for you. It will pull me into your dynamic, but I think it's a needed part of it. And the three of us need our dynamic." She pauses as she looks directly at him. She places her hand on his thigh. "What if I'm the comfort after the spanking?"

He looks up at her sharply with surprise in his eyes.

"I think it will make what you're doing even better."

"How would that work? You aren't always here when he's been spanking me."

"Well, is that because you're only asking him to spank you when I'm not around? What if you waited until I was home? Or he only did the maintenance spankings when I'm here, since those aren't reactive to your misbehavior. Then I could be the comfort piece for those, at least."

"I've been using alone time, and sometimes masturbation for comfort." He holds his chin high as a proudness moves across his face. "I've been taking care of myself for that."

"Okay," she says, nodding. "I understand. And that's good, but are you open to trying what I suggested just to maybe see if it works even better?"

"Mal, he hits me really hard. You've seen my ass. I'm not sure I want you watching that." He grimaces as he shifts in his seat.

"I can be in a different room, like a bedroom. And you come to me like we could have it very orchestrated. Because you're right, I may not tolerate that brutality very well." She shrinks into the couch, remembering how she felt just now watching the hard spanking.

He hunches forward on his thighs, his arms bent at ninety-degree angles. "It's weird. It's like he's Dad-like to me, but he's obviously not my dad. He's nothing like my dad. And the only thing I'm managing to figure out is that it's like helping me process what my dad did to me because I'm in full control. I can say no."

"Right. I get it. Using a kink to heal, that's a real thing. I've listened to therapists and psychologists talk about this on podcasts. It's like a brain processing thing. Sort of a reframing of past hurts and traumas."

"Oh, I have past traumas, that's for damn sure. Like truckfuls of it." His face falls into a grumpy state.

"And think about this, Max has shifted into a caretaker of sorts for you, so he's become more so-called Dad-like to you. Maybe subconsciously, that's what's going on?"

Derek nods slowly as the aha moment takes over his face. "Yeah, that really makes sense, Mal. And I perhaps chose Max because he really poses zero threat to me..." He pauses as the thought seems to solidify in him. "I'm safe with Max. Geez, Mal. You're a genius. This is all making way more sense to me now. I think you've nailed it on the head."

She rubs her thighs as relief fills her. "So, you'll try my idea?"

"Yes, I'm all for it. I can't imagine Max disagreeing."

She nods rapidly. "He won't disagree. I know him."

He smirks and scoffs. "I was thinking of going to see Faye. I think perhaps I was craving some comfort."

Mallory's shoulders slump instinctively. "I won't lie. It hurts that you didn't automatically think of me for that." If there is any evidence that their relationship is now different, and not in a good way, it's that.

"Yeah. Wow. I didn't even register all this. Not one bit." He doesn't look sorry.

"We have work to do on us. That's what I see. But now that we're talking about it, I think we can start. Right?" She stands up, hope energizing her. "How about we start right now? No sex. Let's just cuddle and watch a movie. I'll make some popcorn, make us some peach iced tea, and get a big soft blanket. You pick the movie." She takes a step toward the kitchen. "Just like we used to do all the time."

He reaches for the remote. "I like that idea very much. I'm in. I don't need to see Faye. Luckily, I hadn't texted her yet."

"So, you would have driven that far just for a hug?" Mallory is aghast. Their relationship really is in the dumps.

"Yeah, I guess I would have. Insane, right?"

"Not really." She tries not to let this hurt her too much, but it doesn't work.

"We would have had sex, though, too. I'd have likely stayed a few days. She's been asking me to come."

"You should go at some point." She needs to be as supportive of him as possible, even if it's super hard.

He gazes at her with gumption, steeling his eyes. "I will. But I think you're right. Our relationship needs some repair first."

The feel-good vibes flood her, and she dares to believe more than a glimmer of hope is brewing, an inkling of their relationship is legit being rekindled. "I'll be right back. Won't take me long." She's grateful Max is still in the meeting. This is ideal timing, and with him around, it may not have progressed to this bonding. But yet, she couldn't have excluded Max if he were present either.

She busies herself in the kitchen getting things ready for their movie date, as a bright light fills her every lonely crack. Cracks that had been missing the spots Derek usually filled to overflowing. Back in their old house, it had always been only the two of them, except when they went to parties or when one of them had a date. It was always the two of them taking on the world, comforting each other, and fucking their brains out until they were spent panting wet messes. It had been glorious. And she hadn't realized until now how much she'd been truly missing all of that. Things had gone a bit awry, and that had largely been in part to the separation she'd had with Derek. Never again. They could never let things go this far again. It's tragic and wrong. They need to live in the same house.

Chapter 8

The movie is in full swing when Max reappears. She and Derek are cuddled under a blanket like two peas in a pod, and the empty bowl of popcorn sits beside them.

Mallory meets Max's eyes as Derek pauses the movie.

"I'm sorry to interrupt your movie, but I'm running to the store. Does anyone need anything?" He looks pleased, and this tickles Mallory.

Max really does have her best interests at heart.

"Deodorant and shampoo. Shaving cream and black socks. Large." Derek shrinks a little, caving into Mallory's body. "Is that okay?"

"Of course," Max says immediately, without a hint of gloating. "I will get whatever you need, Derek. Always." He shifts his eyes to her.

"I need more face powder. You know the one. Tampons, the multi-pack like you got last time with the ultras. And I was kind of wanting new sparkly eye shadow." She smirks. "Any. You pick."

"It will be my pleasure to shop for all of that. You always get me to new parts of the store, and I love it."

"You really are the best," she says. "Will you also get some aloe gel? Like for sunburn?"

He pauses as an odd look takes over. "You planning on sunbathing in this weather?" he asks as if it's a joke.

"No. I want to try it on Derek's ass."

Derek releases a burst of laughter. "Aw, shit," he mutters, his face turning red.

Mallory thinks it's hilarious that he gets embarrassed more by that than when Max was spanking him.

Max's eyes widen, and he chuckles a little. "Yeah, that might help. I'll add it to the list."

"We also have a new plan...for things. If you have a moment, it will be really fast."

Max looks at her intently, then gives a single nod. "Okay. Shoot."

"Can you keep the daily maintenance spankings to when I'm home? I'm going to be waiting in the bedroom, and I'm going to give Derek aftercare after you are done."

Max's eyes pop. "Okay. Well, I can certainly comply with this plan. Derek, you're on board with this?"

He nods vehemently. "I really am. I've been doing it myself, but I think she has a point. It might be even better with the addition of her in this role. She's so good at it." He looks sheepish, but calm.

"Yeah, I know we aren't exactly the cuddling man duo."

Mallory suppresses her giggle. This is serious stuff.

Derek presses his lips firmly as if in thought. Then he speaks. "Yeah. And I've never even yearned for that, to be honest. With you, at least." He pulls the blanket snug to his chin. "And I also knew it wasn't your thing, so I never asked because it didn't feel right."

"It's settled then. I like this development." Max raises his hands, his eyes softening. "We might just get our trio figured out yet."

Mallory has hope, and the hope on all their faces makes it even more real for her. Their version of a throuple might work after all. It's clear. Derek craves correction from an older man, and without Sam around, he's been missing it. It's literally been fucking with his brain and moods. Not that Max could ever be Sam, though, that's a far cry, but this setup might work. And if Derek wants sex after or a blow job or something, she can provide the sexual piece that Max has no desire to do. She can fill in the gaps with things she wants to do. It's a win-win.

She's pretty sure Derek would be sexual with Max, but Max has always made it clear that he's heterosexual with zero bi curiosity.

Max leaves, and they get back to their movie. But she can't resist sharing. "I'm proud of you. After everything, you are accepting help from Max. And strangely, the spanking is somehow part of it. I didn't really get that until now."

"I don't think I did either." He gives her a silly, perplexed look that falls into a settled grin. His demeanor is more proof that he's all good.

She snuggles into him close and tight to his body. "Okay, you can play it now. Unless you have more to say."

"I'm good."

They watch the rest of the movie in mostly silence, but laughing together here and there, making the usual comments people make while watching a movie together. The warm fuzzies are on steroids for Mallory, and by the look on Derek's face, and the return of the happy sparkle in his eyes, he's on the same elevated plane as her, or nearing it.

The one thing she's dreading, though, is when their families find out they are in a throuple. But part of her wonders if they ever even need to know. As far as they were concerned, she and Derek were just living and renting from Max. Her family might be okay with it all, but the judgment may still come, and she's not so sure she even cares to bother to defend herself to them.

This part of her life literally doesn't concern them. But Derek's family will raise holy hell, likely even with them living with Max. But he's also having less and less contact with them, which honestly is not a bad thing. They are mostly toxic people. They just bring him down. He doesn't need them in his life.

"Hey, we should surprise Max with a dessert or something. We could bake. Like we used to." She sits up, and the blanket falls.

"Yeah, that sounds like a good idea. What does Max like?"

She laughs. "Every sweet on the planet."

"Okay, well, let's see what we've got, and maybe we can make something."

He stands up and reaches for her. "This feels really good, Mal. You know, you do know me."

She falls into his hug. "Yes, I do. And you know me." She leans back to look into his eyes. "I want you to promise me something..." She pauses to give him a look as genuine as she can. "That you'll tell me when you need something. Just like you used to, I feel like you stopped."

"Yeah, I will. And you, too. You tell me. Anything. Everything." He steps back and drops his gaze to the floor. "But I think Max takes care of all you need. You really don't need me anymore, Mal." The defeat he shows breaks her heart.

"Oh! No! That's so not true! Not at all! I totally need you and want you. I need to hammer that into your thick skull, I see. You're a totally different person from Max. I get different things from you than I do from him. Besides, you and I gel in a different way. We need to get into that more. Live in it more. Like be present together." She shrugs. "Like we are now. That's healing. That's what will bring us to where we should be, to where we used to be." She hadn't meant to make it sound all about what she gets, but she also needs to move on because this is hitting a chord in him.

"Yeah. You're smarter than me, but I already knew that." He smiles at her and reaches for her hand. "Let's go make something. I'm ready to make and eat it." He grins big.

Once in the kitchen, Mallory starts pulling out supplies one by one, then starts playing some music on her phone.

Derek looks delighted and dances around the island.

"This is going to be fun. Just like we always used to do." She gives him an excited look back.

"Yeah, we need to do this more often. Feels like us again. Feels good." He approaches her and hugs her from behind. Rocking her, he says, "You are a very special woman, and you are so special to me."

"Aww, you're melting me. You're special to me, too. I love us." The thing is, their 'us' never left, Derek did. But she's not bringing that up now. No way.

After a little dance to the song, he breaks the embrace.

"What's first. Put me to work." He raises his hands in the air. "Command me, O' Commander."

She points to the recipe. "You want to start pulling out the ingredients? I'll look for the cookie pans." Well, she doesn't need to look; she knows. As she's digging in the cupboard, an idea for a massive collab event erupts in her brain like an explosion. Then another magnificent idea fires. What about Derek being an organizer for such an event? He will do better if he has a focus, something to own that he can work on. It will promote her and give him a project. This is brilliant! She beams a big smile his way. "I just got the craziest idea!" She gazes doe-eyed at Derek, her exuberance practically ballooning out of her pores. "What if we did a huge collab event and you were the organizer?"

He freezes in place, and his jaw drops slightly. "What? Me? I'm not so sure I'd be good at that. I have no experience with event planning."

"Why do you say that? You'd be fantastic. This would be such a perfect fit for you! My mind is already going crazy with ideas." She shakes her hands as more ideas tumble into fruition of collabs, new films, and fan interactions. "Okay, hear me out on this." She raises both hands.

Derek places his palms on the island. "Okay. I'm listening."

"What if we planned an event, a meet and greet for fans with multiple stars and talents, vendors, podcasters, authors, and studios?" She stops talking to squeal. "We let people book the studio for collabs while they are in town so people can also make content while they come to the event." She covers her mouth, then her ears, then extends her fingers out straight, framing her face. "Like, this could be epic! Since they would all be in town, and together, the combos of collabs could be huge and unlimited! And they can use our studio as a safe place to do it." She throws her hands downward.

"Well, yeah, but that will be limited by time for usage of the studio," Derek says as a spark of excitement starts to glimmer in his eyes. "But I could see how that could be stellar. Imagine the number of films that would come out of such a setup."

"True. And get this, Derek, with Max, money is no object." She clasps her hands, shakes them, then spreads them apart rapidly. "We can shoot for the stars and catch so many constellations it will blow the industry wide! It will be the event of events, and history will be made! Everyone will be talking about it for years to come for how productive the time will be."

He laughs with great jubilation, the joy reaching his eyes, making them glow bright. "You are a visionary, Mal. You always have been. I'm buying into this."

"See, these are my thoughts. Geez. My mind is fucking racing right now. You run the whole thing, like you'll be the CEO, Max pays for it and supports us, and I do the social media, podcast interviews, and appearances to drum up interest. You and I could meet with fans during the event. Then, whoever among us attendees wants to film can, but we only take one recording time slot, maybe at the front or back, so as to leave the others open for people to rent for their collabs. We could hire helpers and security at the house, and it will be the central hub." She taps her forehead. "People will have to be extremely efficient, though, many are used to having an entire day to record, so this will be a challenge. But I think it's doable."

"Do you think Max will go for this?" He gives her a slightly skeptical look. "I mean to offer up his home to so many strangers like that?"

"Well, I'll likely know them, or know of them, or my friends will know of them. This is a tight-knit group. Plus, if we have a security team here, what could go wrong?"

He laughs heartily. "A lot!"

"Well, then we'll deal with it. We could make everyone sign a release form. Max has lawyers on his tab for that kind of stuff. It will be easy peasy, and we won't even need to worry about any legal mumbo jumbo."

"This is brilliant, really brilliant, Mal."

"What's brilliant about her?" Max asks as he enters the kitchen, carrying multiple bags. His tone is happy and interested, as usual.

"Wait until you hear her idea. She's incredible." Derek beams, his expression the poster for a partner's pride.

"I have this idea, and it's pretty big," Mallory gushes, her face flushing. She raises her hands and then presses them to her sides. "Really big."

"I like big!" Max sets down the bags. "Do tell." He looks at her with alertness, his mouth dropping into an O of awe. "I always love it when you get big ideas. They are always a stellar success."

"This idea is really, really big, I'm not kidding, and it will need all three of us to pull it off." Mallory jumps. "It would be incredible!"

"I love seeing you like this," Max says with energy.

"What if we hosted a meet and greet with content creators, vendors, studios, stars, all that...and then..." She pauses talking as her excitement builds, then says, "We offer the studio up for collabs for people to film in it because everyone will be in the area. We could charge for the use of it, but keep it at a low cost just to keep it affordable, but to ensure we only get serious filmmakers."

Max's face erupts into a shining grin. "I love it, babe! This is an epic idea! This house needs lots of fucking, more fucking!"

She loves her freedom to speak and doesn't hold back. "We'd need money. Use of the studio. Lawyers. Your team." She states it boldly, not shrinking back one bit.

"Done," he says with a wave of his hand. "I'll make it happen. With extreme pleasure. I'm honored to be a part of another one of your dreams, honey."

"Oh, I knew you would be!" She releases a holler of elation and throws her arms around him. She peppers kisses all over his face and then jumps into his arms to straddle his middle.

He catches her in a cluster of laughs and exclamations. "Oh, well, I'll say yes to anything to get this kind of reaction," he says in a lighthearted, jovial way.

He twirls her, then lowers her down after a minute.

"And Derek can be the CEO. You don't need more to manage, and this gives him a job." She shoots Derek a confident look. "He'll be great."

"Yes, that's a great idea," Max states, meeting Derek's gaze. "And I can be your consultant."

"Yeah, I'd like that." Derek looks happy, truly happy.

Her heart might burst. She's the luckiest woman on the planet! "So, you're okay with people traipsing in here? Vetting them first, of course, will be a necessity. But mostly I'd seek out those I already know. Use referrals. The community will eat this up, I just know it!"

"Well, we have lots to plan, then. A club party and now an event. We will be busy in the coming months. Have you thought of a timeline yet?" Max tilts his head as his happy, amused grin grows bigger.

"No, but maybe the three of us can have a meeting soon, and hash one out."

Derek nods. "I'm free."

Everyone laughs.

"Unemployment does that."

"Sorry, funny, not funny," Mallory coos with sympathy.

"No, it's funny." He points to his face. "See, I'm laughing." He laughs. "Really funny!"

"I'm game for whenever," Max says. "But it seems you two are up to something here. Something I might like." He raises his eyebrows, and his curiosity makes it to his eyes.

"You will definitely like it. We're making some cookies, and I have a hankering to make some kind of sweet bread, too." Mallory clasps her hands in front of her, then flicks them apart.

"I'm enthralled, excited, and already salivating." He begins to unpack the food from the bags. "I like seeing you two in my kitchen like this..." He pauses, then does a double-take with his head. "Scratch that. Our kitchen."

Mallory senses a swell of love spinning like a funnel cloud in her heart, wild, out of control, and natural as natural can be. This man continues to amaze her. "You really always know the best things to say."

"It's a gift. Maybe. Hey. I'll get this stuff put away, then I'll get out of your hair so you can do your magic." He swiftly places things into the fridge.

Mallory measures out flour. "Did you find the brown sugar, Derek?"

"Yeah, it's right there," he says, pointing. "I'll get the eggs." He opens the carton and sets it on the counter. "Um. I'll be right back. I won't be long."

"Okay. Nature calls?"

He looks sheepish and shrugs. "Sort of, something like that."

She gives him a quizzical look.

"Mal," he pauses for a long second, "I need a spanking."

She stares at him aghast. "Right now? In the middle of making stuff?" How can this possibly be? He hasn't even done anything that could be in need of punishment.

He stares at the ground and pushes his slippered toe back and forth. "Yeah. I just need it."

She wants him to elaborate. She flicks her gaze at him for a quick flash of a disgusted look, then chastises herself. Judging him is not going to help him. Softening her gaze, she relaxes her shoulders and sighs.

"Okay. I'll be here for you when you're done getting your ass beat." She suppresses the urge to roll her eyes and gives him a weak smile instead. Maybe she should have chosen different words; that was not supportive of her. "I mean, I'll be here for you after."

"You can watch if you want. Or, not. I get it." He rubs his ass with both hands.

She can't pretend this isn't weird. They all just had a very happy moment together talking about collaborating on something positive, and he gets the urge to have his ass handed to him in an impromptu spanking? She shakes her head as she watches his covered backside leave the kitchen.

"Makes no sense to me," she mutters under her breath.

She adds the sugar, the baking soda, and the salt. Her mind is reeling, wondering about what the two of them are doing, and against her better judgment, she creeps along the hallway, closely hugging the wall. She doesn't want to be seen, but her curiosity has her snooping. He did invite her to watch, though, so it's not fully peeping uninvited if she gets nosy. As she gets closer, she hears the slapping sounds of Max hitting Derek's butt. It sounds harsh, and Derek is yelling out with each hit. It's fucking an enigma to her how this has developed, and how Max, who is beyond sweet to her, is voluntarily reddening her man's ass flesh to welts and bruises. It's mind-boggling.

She slides her hands along the wall as the slapping sounds escalate into deafening smack sounds and frequency. It must be the finale with a barrage like that. She smirks. She stifles a giggle because that phrase makes her think of a fireworks finale.

"Thank you," Derek says with relief in his voice.

Mallory freezes in place. She wants to hear this, but she sure as fuck doesn't want to get caught. Her heart pounds as she considers bolting down the hallway back to the kitchen, where it's safe.

"My pleasure. Anytime you need it, I'm your man."

"You like this." Derek doesn't sound angry.

"I do. But it's about you." Max sounds nurturing and caring. "Not me."

"I needed it." Derek sounds relieved.

"Care to elaborate on why?" Max asks, wonderment filling his words.

"No."

"Okay. But I'm always available if you change your mind and want to talk through anything."

"I almost came on you."

"I know."

Mallory's jaw drops. This is the most bizarre fucking shit.

"I'm glad I didn't. You'd have hit me more."

"Yes."

"But if you want more, I can do that."

"Yeah."

After twenty seconds, the sound of spanking erupts again, and Mallory shudders. The pain must be excruciating with the sounds Derek is making. With harsh spankings every day, how does he even heal?

He groans like he's coming, and she straightens her body quickly, bracing for Max's anger.

Derek moans.

"Damnit, Derek." Max sounds angry.

The spanking sounds louder, and Derek's shrieks magnify. Likely, Max is using a paddle.

"Now." Smack. "I." Smack. "Have." Smack. "To." Smack. "Change." Smack. "Bad." Smack. "Boy." Smack.

Mallory can't shake the severity of having heard each word brutally enunciated by a merciless, harsh wallop. She stares in astonishment, frozen in place as she tries to fathom that it just happened.

Derek cries out with hysterics, his sobs tumbling out in desperation. Her heart aches, and she wants to hold him.

She lurches forward, ready to stop this senseless assault. She must stop Max! But as she reaches the doorframe, Derek's cries stop, and she halts her movements. She really shouldn't get involved in their consensual dynamic like this. She might wreck what's helping Derek, help that she can't deliver that Max can. She needs to shed her judgment, pronto.

"I needed that." Derek sighs.

"Are you still having trouble coming?" Max asks.

"Kinda. But this helps. I needed the release, so thank you."

"Anytime. But I do need to change."

Mallory's shackles rise. Is Derek having trouble orgasming? What the fuck? This has never happened to him...that she knows of.

She twitches. They will be coming! She races down the hallway, her heart pounding. Arriving in the kitchen in a flash, she tries to slow her heavy breathing. She busies herself with stirring the powders together as Derek saunters in.

"You, okay?" she asks quickly. Her nerves are a crackly mess.

The look of relief on his face is obvious. "Yeah. I needed that."
He shakes his head and looks sheepish. "You must think I'm insane."

"I think perhaps you are going through some things, processing."
She stops stirring the powder mixture. She's stirred it too much, and
the cloud above the mix swirls in the air. No. She can't understand
what he's going through.

"I think I am. Max is helping, though it may seem like he's
hurting things. But it's not like that." He looks intently into her eyes.
"I can assure you."

"You don't need to justify to me. I'm not a kink shamer." She
raises her arms. "How can I make you feel better? A hug? Cuddle?"
She trips over nothing and falls into his arms. She smirks as she gazes
up at him. "Oops." She laughs. "I guess I've ruined the seduction. I
was going to say blow job next."

He laughs, and the joy in his eyes erases some of her fears about
what she just witnessed.

Derek is okay.

"It's still sexy. But no, no blow job. Just you in my arms is all the
aftercare I need right now." He squeezes her around the shoulders.
"Maybe someday I can share everything. Once I figure out what it is."

"At your comfort. I don't need to know anything other than that
you are okay."

"I'm better than okay." He grins. "I'm outstanding."

"Good."

He lifts her chin and kisses her on the lips.

"Now, let's make some yummy stuff for Max."

"We are halfway there already." She points to the bowl. Derek's
response to Max's question rolls around in her head, setting off a
series of mini alarms. She's never once witnessed Derek unable to
climax. In fact, he's always been quite the opposite, with multiple
ejaculations even being easy for him. She's not going to press him for
anything and upset his happy mood. "Let's do it."

"Tell me what to do next." He raises his hands and pushes up his sleeves. "I'm ready to get dirty."

Chapter 9

Mallory dips her head back, as if urging Max to grab her hair in a ponytail hold.

He takes the hint and grasps a fistful of her locks and wraps his hand tightly in them, all the way down to her scalp.

She coos instead of letting the yelp in her gut out. "Fuck me, Daddy War...Bucks."

Max chuckles softly as he yanks her hair again in a brisk tug. "With extreme pleasure." He gives her right ass cheek a smack.

It sends a ripple through her pelvis, and her clit thickens. She can't help but think of him spanking Derek, and it rages her lust a notch higher, which is a surprise. She sinks into it, though, as Max pounds away into her hole, making lewd squelching sounds.

"Mine. You're mine, you sweet young bitch," he says with a grunt and a strong thrust into her. His squishy belly fat bounces off her ass as he rides her pussy deeply from behind.

She grunts as he slams her against the edge of the bed, her chin jutting out and her whole body rocking back and forth with his movements.

"Take that cock. Gonna suck my oozing tip after I come, you wench?" he asks gruffly.

"Yes, Daddy," she murmurs. "Take my hole as yours, and I'll suck the remnants out of you."

"Good girl," he mutters in a strained voice while continuing to plow into her.

The peeking sun through the part in the curtains nails her in the eyes, and she closes her lids, dropping her head down because she finally can.

With her eyes closed, she can savor the sensations more, and she inches closer to her climax. Her curiosity has her craving a harsh spanking from Max, where her entire ass is beaten red. Now that she knows Max does that to Derek, she kind of wants to try it out. Just once. But she's unsure if he will do that to her. It sort of seems like it's just something Max would only be willing to do with Derek. She's not afraid to ask, she's afraid of his 'no'.

"Uh, fuck," she spits as he ramps up his bulldozing of her insides to a frenzied level.

With each rebound of his body, he seems to knock it up a notch in force. Which means, he's close.

"Selfish fuck this time. Take it," he says through his panting. He tugs harder on the wad of her hair in his fist, and her head tilts back, her chin jutting out again. He thuds himself against her at a maddening rate.

She's ready to burst as she whimpers.

Within thirty seconds, he slows his movements, skipping the last slow savoring slides that he usually does. He pulls out of her and swats her ass hard. "Suck my tip. Clean me out, babe."

She swivels and drops to her knees, swiftly taking his softening cock in her mouth. She sucks on his spongy flesh, drawing out any leftover cum that she can. Tasting herself on him mixed with his juices swells the eroticism for her. She's very pleased.

He caresses her hair, and her eyes fall closed as she keeps him in her mouth. It's not an aggressive blow job, but more of a suckling of comfort for her.

Her body jostles with jerks of arousal as he very lightly pumps his hips into her face, weakly moving his softened cock in her mouth. It's lost its firmness for a face fuck, and is waning quickly.

Saliva mixed with cum drips from her mouth to his thighs. She sighs, digging her fingers into him as she drags her tongue around his soft penis inside her mouth.

"Good girl. That's a good girl. Daddy likes it." He reaches for her face gently and holds it between his hands, ensuring his cock doesn't leave her mouth. "Like a good cumslut. That's it. Right. Yeah, nice and slow." His voice is tender and caring, with notes of lush aftercare intent.

"Mmmm," she hums as she inhales the scent of the remnants of his cum on his shaft.

"I'll get you off now."

She loves him using her just like that. It's not a secret. And since his kink cabinet also includes such acts, they often fall into such scenes together, like magical bliss. Derek had instructed her to come to him once Max made her come. The morning is promising to be a legit fuck fest for her between the two men.

"Get on the bed and spread your legs for me," he instructs. "Going to make you so desperate to come that you beg me with everything you've got." He smiles wickedly at her as he descends between her spread legs.

"Yes, Daddy. I want that. Yes, please." His obsession with her is one of her strongest kinks, and always has been. She hadn't thought it could grow, but she was wrong. It's like simply seeing the look of lust on his face and hearing his words of intent alone, hurl her damn near her climax all on their own. Desire and displayed passionate intent are the best foreplay.

"You look good on my cock. And you took my cock so good, baby doll." He caresses her flesh.

"I love taking your cock," she says as she watches her own tits rise and fall as she breathes heavily.

He shoots her a seductive stare as he nudges his face into her pussy. "Mmmm. So wet. Love eating you out when my cum is oozing out of you."

The proper old white guy who loves to eat his own cum out of her pussy, and it's never a wasted act because it drives her want for him higher every time. She's pretty sure his old crusty colleagues would razz him to the brink of hell if they knew he did this regularly.

When he accosts her clit with a strong suction, the ricochet of elicited sensations ping-pongs through her body like bolts of lightning. She twitches as he voraciously roots his nose into her clit as he pushes his tongue into her slit. She grips his hair and grunts as he gnashes on her external swollen bits like he's a man starved, a beast feasting.

She launches with ease into a climax that carries her into a double-peaked orgasm. Her sounds fill the room as she twitches and writhes from his incessant stimulations. He pushes two fingers inside her and bangs her in an aggressive finger fuck as he seals his mouth around her clit. After a few minutes, he pulls his fingers out of her and grips her thighs with such strength she almost begs him to back off.

The domination breaks her. She bucks, and the clenching erupts inside her, squeezing her muscles together around nothing inside her empty vagina. She often finds her orgasms hit hardest when she's got nothing inside, like they are desperately trying to touch something to announce the intensity to, but incessantly fail, so they get bigger in their pulsations instead. It seems as if the muscles amplify the contractual punches when they have only themselves to bounce against. It's pure orgasmic heaven. She has no clue if that's a thing, but it makes sense. Sort of like ripples in water, the muscles contracting amplify the orgasm for her. She gasps and tries to push him off her.

"Too much," she says, wincing.

He goes at her harder with his mouth.

She screams and swats his head.

He wedges his face so forcefully into her and packs so many fingers into her slit in unison, she can't tell how many. It's like he's almost fucking fisting her.

She yelps, and he goes even stronger, forging his way into her folds as if he's rooting out food from her cunt, grunting like a pig devouring.

She digs her fingers into his scalp as the launch of the impending orgasm sends a wave of terror through her. This is going to be big!

Helpless to the sensations, she undulates her hips up and down, rising off the mattress as she moves. He follows her, tracking her movements with stealth. She's desperate to reach her apex, but she's also hankering to shove him off because it's just too strong.

"Ugh, ack, oooohh," she slurs as her orgasm seizes her body. The contractions are so strong she involuntarily makes primal sounds as the ginormous constrictions take over. "Too much," she says, pleading. "Please," she begs. Desperation fills her.

As she peaks again, she hits his head and forcefully punches him. He's got her pinned. She's stuck on the wild ride; her efforts have no effect. After another earth-shattering blast, she begins to descend in height.

As her sounds settle back to calm, he follows her pattern and slows his motions of stimulating her.

She's silent as the aftershocks travel through her, making her torso twitch. Finally, she says, "Holy. Fuck."

He leans against her thigh. "That was outstanding, seemed really big."

She sighs and can't move a muscle other than to say, "It was. Ginormous." She takes the calm and allows her descent to continue. "Were you fisting me? The girth sent me, whatever it was that you were doing."

"Yeah, I had five fingers in, and a few times my knuckles went in, too. You seemed to respond well. Did you like it?"

"Yes, it was like...it gripped me. I had no choice but to surrender to the bliss. It was divine."

"Perfect, I love that."

"My turn?" Derek asks from the doorway. "Watching all that has me with a raging boner. I need to fuck you, Mal."

"Can we fuck here, Max? Would you mind?" Normally, they go to Derek's room or hers, but she has zero desire to move.

"Go for it. I'll go shower." He motions his hand toward Mallory's nude, strewn body. "Next for the pussy pounding. She's well primed."

"Saw that," Derek muses. "Very nicely done."

Being talked about this way by them always turns her on like she's their sex toy to share.

"I'm wasted on hormones," she says softly, in a slight, jovial tone.

"Good, I'll use you to wipe up my cum then."

"I don't need to come, I just came so hard it wiped me out. Just fuck me until you do."

"I'll decide that," Derek says firmly.

"Atta boy," Max says as he zips away into the bathroom. He turns on the water immediately and starts humming a song.

It makes her smile. Them working together to fuck her into orgasmic ecstasy is hot.

Derek commands her attention, though, and swivels his fingers. "Ass up, head down, bitch. Time to move."

The dirty talk rejuvenates her, and she turns over, pertly presenting her raised ass for him.

"Nice," he states. "A good wet hole for me to use. I should thank Max."

"You're welcome," he calls over the hum of the shower.

He slides into her with zero foreplay, not that she needs it at this point. He thumps his cock into her pussy, smacking her bottom, making it jiggle at an alarming rate. It's zero to one hundred as he jackhammers himself into her relentlessly, using her. He's ruthless in his pursuit and bashes himself into her as fast as the crack of a whip.

He stops and reaches for something. Clearly, he brought a toy.

Her nerves erupt as she contemplates what he brought. He drags the soft fabric feeling toy along her flesh, and she imagines it's a rope or a flogger. The toy leaves her, and then he brings it down harshly against her, beating her four times rapidly in a row.

She screeches with each blow, though they don't really hurt.

He drops the toy and grips her hips with extreme pressure, then he drives his cock into her like a stallion.

He growls, grunts, then he jerks against her backside. Her insides feel sloshy with more cum as he slows his pumping.

"I'm serious. I don't need to come, Derek." Her body is exhilarated, and she's satisfied.

"I need you to," he retorts angrily.

"Oh," she says. This is about something, and whether it's about him or her, she's ready to acquiesce. She's never yet said 'no' to an orgasm.

He flips her over and readies his hand over her clit. He spanks her clit several times in a brutal beating.

She gasps, grasping the bed sheets. Her body revolts in jerky movements with each hit. He stops and presses her rose clit sucker to her swollen clitoral head. Her body lurches upward from the strength of the toy's sucking. She cries out and bursts into an uncontrollable crashing of another big orgasm. He keeps going, and her body is brought to climax two more times. The overwhelm is the familiar woozy feeling she seeks, a dopamine OD, and he blissfully knew exactly how to drive her to it.

He plucks the toy off her, and it makes a pop sound as her flesh gets freed. "I love it when your clit goes inside the little hole."

She's panting, but grins, still unable to speak. She's spent and ready to fall asleep, even though it's morning and she slept a good eight hours last night.

"That was incredible," she says in a low, sleepy voice, her whole body throbbing and tingling. "Unmatched."

"Good." He collects her body to his and spoons her from behind. "You can sleep if you want."

"I might," she says dreamily. "It's very tempting right now."

"Fucking you to sleep is a goal," he says softly into her ear.

As she drifts off to sleep, she hears Max enter the room.

"Need it?" Max asks.

Derek moves away from her, but she's too sleepy to protest.

"Yeah, my room, though," he answers quickly, kind of hushed.

That's the last thing she hears before she drifts off, loving every sensation her 10,000-plus nerve endings in her clitoris gifted her.

When she wakes, Derek is wrapped around her again, snoring lightly.

Chapter 10

Mallory zooms into the kitchen, her hair flying up as she moves. "Oh, this is serious. She's got a notebook!" Derek says from his perch against the counter, a steaming coffee cup in his hand.

Max leans against the counter a few feet away from Derek, his arms crossed over his chest, and a big, beaming smile on his face.

"Whatcha got cooking there, babe?" Max asks with a tilt of his head.

"Plans." She plops down at the island and opens her notebook. "I've made a list of stars, content creators, talent, sexuality vendors, and sex therapists to contact about the event. I know them, but I know there are more I can find, so I'm starting to mine social media for suggestions of people."

"You know what I love about you, babe? You are so tenacious. You get an idea, and it's like you are on fire." Max moves toward her and takes a seat. "Honestly, it's hot."

She grins at him for a split second, then she drops her eyes back to her notebook. "Well, I am an Aries." She flashes him her pearly whites, then flinches. "Oh, and I just thought of another." She jots down the name.

Derek grabs a croissant and sits on her other side.

"First meeting starting now," she declares, glancing up at both of them.

"This is going to be fun to watch. I'll do whatever I can to support. I can see that with the three of us, this event will be a huge success." Max taps his forefinger on the surface of the island. "I have just the person I'll ask to be your assistant. She's perfect."

"Oy!" Mallory exclaims. "I get an assistant? I've never had an assistant before!"

"Well, you're getting one now. And Derek, if you find you need one, too, let me know."

"Okay, but I'm doubting that. I literally have nothing else to do, being unemployed."

Max looks up at him sharply, his brows furrowing deeply. "Unemployed? I thought you were CEO-ing this event? That's a job."

Derek scoffs, then releases a curt laugh. "Oh, I am. But it's not all that."

"Max thinks otherwise." Mallory smiles sweetly. "You want to tell him?"

Max nods. "Yeah. So, Derek, you are now on the payroll as CEO of this event under one of my companies. This means you will be making $250K a year at this moment, should you choose to accept this offer of employment from a fat old man with too much money." He grins sheepishly.

Derek's jaw drops, and he almost loses his croissant in his coffee mug. "What? Are you fucking being serious right now?" His eyes widen, and a glimmer of pride unfurls. "Two hundred and fifty? I've never made nearly that much ever in my entire life."

"It pays to work for a generous boss." He winks. "Who also spanks you."

Derek's jaw remains down, and his expression doesn't change.

"Wow, this is sounding like an erotic novel or adult film," she says with a snicker. "It's an idea. Workplace spanking and employee makes $250K with his butt." She snickers.

"Only no sex," Max asserts with a stern look.

"For you, maybe!" she insists. "Not in the version of my film!"

"True. At least not that way for me, but great idea for a film." He claps his hands. "What do you say, my man? Want to be the CEO of my newest little endeavor with Mallory at the helm alongside you?"

"Only I'm not a CEO," she says. "No thanks."

"Um...yes...hell yes." The shock hasn't left his face as a sly smile begins to surface. "I can't believe this is happening. I had assumed I'd be working for free, with all you are giving us with the house, food, and everything."

"Don't forget I can spank you if you fuck up," Max says in a joking voice.

Mallory slaps his bicep. "We know!"

Max laughs, and then Derek joins in.

"That's incentive. Except it's not." Derek slaps his hand down on the hard surface. "Hot damn. I'm making six figures plus!" He straightens up, extending his neck to peacock his new status. "I might need to go shopping for some new clothes."

"Absolutely. And I have a company credit card for you to use."

"What? You're too good to be true." Derek watches with saucer-like eyes as Max slides a blue credit card across the slate toward him.

"I just woke up in my dream," Derek states aghast.

"A wet dream," Mallory says as a giggle overcomes her. "I love that sex jokes are a part of our first meeting."

"It's definitely a wet dream," Derek says as he takes the card close to his eyes to examine it. "Just seeing what privileged looks like close-up."

"Be smart or I'll..."

"We know!" Mallory interjects loudly with exacerbation.

Max belly laughs, leaning back as his chuckle rumbles over him.

"If you can't joke about it, it's too vanilla," Derek says while pocketing the credit card. "This is going right to my wallet after our meeting."

"So, we need advertising, food vendors, and drink vendors. I'm thinking beer trucks? A winery vendor? Or a cash bar." Mallory writes down all three, each on a separate page. "I'm thinking we sell tickets and collect email addresses. That way, we can create hype by sending emails to keep people interested, and then if we do another one in the future, we have our attendee base already set up."

"Smart. I like these ideas, honey." Max stares at the ceiling. "I've never been to one of these events. Do they ever have interactive aspects like a roaming performers or character actors? I'm envisioning someone who dresses up and acts out a part of a character or is a tasteful imitator of one of the stars? Or even like an act, such as a contortionist or juggler?"

"Wow, you having never been to one is going to give us fresh ideas to liven up the event. I never even thought of those. Well, I have seen a few content creators do this if it fits their brand, but they are usually playing the part of themselves." Mallory writes the idea down furiously in her notebook. "I never thought of hiring extra actors for that. This is good stuff!" she exclaims. She falls silent as she stares at the paper. She's brainstorming how to find such people, and maybe putting out an ad calling for them is the best idea.

"I need a notebook myself," Derek muses.

"We can cover that," Max says with a wink.

"Mal, you know the social media stuff, so you and your assistant could be in charge of that. Plus, you will likely be making video promos and stuff, I'm guessing." Derek takes a sip of his coffee, then sighs. "Mmm, that's a good cup of joe."

"Yeah, for sure. I can do a few video clips. My fans like to see me, even with clothes on," she says in a joking tone.

"You're beautiful both ways," Max muses as he reaches to squeeze her forearm.

"Aww," she coos and raises her shoulders as she scrunches. She taps her pen on the paper. "We have so much to do."

"Advertising should be a big push, even starting now." Derek looks like his old self, and Mallory is delighted. This is exactly what he needs. A purpose, and not just a purpose, one with pay.

"I could get spanked by a rich old white guy in a video, clothed, of course." Derek stands up and waggles his butt.

"Clothed?" Max asks, perplexed.

"You two are seriously obsessed with the spankings," she says, shaking her head.

"It's new. It will wear off," Max protests, holding his hands up. "We've got a shiny new squirrel, and it dances its tail in front of us constantly." He chuckles. "Literally."

Derek gets up and shakes his booty while cracking up.

"How can you think this shit is funny? It's your ass that gets whooped!" Mallory asks.

"I can't explain it other than to say I need it. It's like...I don't know. It centers me. Resets me." He shrugs. "Like it focuses me. I get this urge for it that overcomes me. And I feel incomplete until I have it." He looks at Max. "It's like the blast of suddenly feeling horny. It's just there all of a sudden." He gives Max a silly look. "Sorry, I'm not trying to sexualize it for you."

Max shakes his head and purses his lips, but doesn't look pissed.

Mallory raises an eyebrow while slowly shaking her head. It's way too late for that. "Whoever said kinks aren't pervasive was clueless," she says with a playful dance in her seat.

"They are required for daily breathing," Derek insists.

"All that you've said I've read recounts from submissives saying, so you aren't alone in what you feel. BDSM acts between the right people can heal." She stands up and moves toward the coffee pot before turning back. "And even if you were alone in that view, that would be okay, too."

"Like now. I have the urge." Derek meets Max's gaze, then drops his eyes downward.

Mallory tries to peek at his crotch as he squirms. Most likely, he's turned on, but she's not going to point that out. What happens between them is between them. She's not intruding on their dynamic.

Max points at the hallway. "We can go. Right now."

"No. We're doing the meeting now. I don't need it that badly. It's just an urge."

Mallory glares at him. "What did I say you should be doing about your urges?" she demands while blinking slowly.

"I should pay attention to them. Or you'll spank me."

Max erupts in laughter. "You've said that, Mallory?"

"Yes, and I have! For a long time now, I have," she exclaims. "But I've been replaced by an older man, clearly."

"Twice over," Derek states with a sassy wave of his hand.

"And Sam, yeah," she says, leaning back slightly and crossing her arms loosely over her chest. "Well, you both are way more dominant than my attempts ever have been, so I get it."

"Let's go," Max says and grabs Derek's arm.

The two traipse off down the hall, and she hears the door slam. Alone time this time, apparently. No matter, she doesn't need to hear anything. If Derek needs her after, he knows where to find her.

She keeps adding to her notes as she gets a text.

It's from Maria.

Maria: Sam is in the hospital. He fell while skiing. He's okay, but I wanted you and Derek to know. He's pretty banged up.

Her heart drops to her gut as she draws in a gasp.

She texts Maria back: OMFG, is he okay?

Maria: He is. I'd call you, but I'm at the hospital, and everyone is loud.

Mallory: Okay. I understand. Call when you can. I'll tell Derek. Tell Sam he's in my prayers.

Maria: Will do. Thank you. It was so scary, Mallory.

Mallory: I bet. Hugs to you, and I love you.

Maria: Love you too, hon.

The urge to go back home rises in her. This is awful. She's not sure how Derek will react. He's so close with Sam, second only to her. He will be freaked out.

After a few minutes of staring at her notebook and praying, she glances up when Derek appears. He looks like a raging bull.

"Need to fuck you. On the couch, ass up, head down. Now." He points toward the living room. "Get moving, slut."

Rather than stop the train of his lust, she obeys, choosing to save the news about Sam for after he's railed her and come.

Derek follows her hot on her heels and roughly removes her pants before bending her over in a rush. He doesn't even bother taking her shirt off as he leans over her backside and reaches for her clit. He rubs aggressively, and she slides right into her arousal easily, as usual. Worry about Sam is there, but she can sink into this sex act for Derek's sake.

He preps her hole with two fingers until the slide in and out of her makes sloshy sounds.

He lines up his cock and penetrates her with the determination of a bull. He grips her hips and fucks her in a wild frenzy, his sounds all wild and primal sounding.

She loves his brutishness, his passion blazing hot, reckless, and urgent as he ravishes her. Her arousal is climbing. Shoving himself into her in a barrage of obliterating hip thrusts, he grunts right through to the bursting of his cock inside her. He only slows because she shifts, so they aren't lined up perfectly anymore.

With him done, she's ready to tell him. She doesn't need to come; this is too important to delay. "I have some news." She turns around and faces him.

The look of confusion on his face has distorted his O face into shock. "What?" he asks quickly.

"Sam has been in a skiing accident, and he's in the hospital."

"What? When?" The alarm on his face erupts. "And you just let me fuck you like that? What the fuck, Mal?" He runs a hand through his hair as he takes steps backward.

"I wanted you to finish. I didn't want to separate the flow of your energy. If I had told you, it would have gotten stunted in you and festered." She boldly stares at him. "You needed the aftercare, and I was going to give it to you, no matter what."

"I have half a mind to spank you for that. And I should." He shifts his weight from one foot to the other, as if he's deciding whether to take action or not.

"Maria just texted," she says, ignoring his declaration. "If you need to spank me, I'll let you use my butt."

Max enters the room. "What's happened?"

Mallory draws in a deep breath. "Sam had a skiing accident, and he's in the hospital."

"Oh shit. Is he okay?" Max is out of breath as he settles into the easy chair. He mops his forehead with a tissue, taking away the wet look of his flesh.

"Yes. Maria is with him."

"Good. Is it bad?" Max looks from her to Derek and back with concern.

"I need to go." Derek leans forward as if he's about to spring up. "I can't just sit here. I need to see him."

"Maybe Maria can do a video call." She pauses. "Or if you want to go, I totally understand, Derek." She's not going to stand in his way.

"Yeah." His phone rings, and he answers it. "Maria? Is he okay? Can I talk to him?" He rushes from the room.

"Well, this day is taking twists and turns I hadn't expected. I hope Sam will be okay. Derek is so attached to him." Worry floods her, worry for Sam and for Derek.

"Yeah, I know he is." Max relaxes back into the soft back of the chair. "That was a workout. He wanted me to chase him and then smack his ass wildly. That's not easy for an old fart like me." He guffaws. "I may need some cookies now for energy."

She laughs. "Now I wish I had watched." Her spine goes rigid as she wrings her hands. "He shouldn't be driving while distraught. Maybe I should drive him."

"Or he takes a plane. That would be much faster and easier. He could take a lift to the hospital."

"Yeah, but he has no money for that." She puts her hands on her thighs. "Not yet."

"I mean what I've been saying, hon. We're a family, and if he needs to fly home to check on Sam, I'm buying him a ticket. I'm covering all his expenses."

Derek appears in the living room, his face strained and looking shocked.

"I got to video call him. He's okay, he looks okay, but he has to go to surgery. His shin bone is shattered, and he needs hardware put in place." He looks back and forth between her and Max. "I'm so worried about him." On the verge of tears, he remains motionless in the middle of the living room.

"I'll call my travel person. We'll get you on a flight as soon as possible." He pulls out his phone. "Don't worry. This is the easy part."

"Should I go too? I'm worried about him as well, and Maria could use extra support, I'm sure." Mallory caresses her hands. She wants to be there for all her loves.

"But Mal, I thought you had a collab scheduled for tomorrow?" Derek asks with a glance at his phone. "I have it on my calendar."

"Yeah, I do. I could reschedule." She shrugs.

"No, don't do that. This is an important one, and you already have people who have preordered it. I think you should go so as not disappoint them. I can go for both of us and be there for them. You're on fire right now, and I'd hate to see you lose momentum." Derek stands up and rubs his thigh as he looks between Mallory and his phone. "They know, Mal. They get it."

"But family comes first." She bites her lower lip, fretting at the thoughts of Sam and Maria hurting, but she's not there as well to support them. It instantly festers like an infected wound.

"Let me do this, Mal. I have no obligations, whereas you do." He nods. "I got this. Let me."

She shifts in her seat. "Okay. You're right, but I'm right."

"Yes, and yes," Derek says with a nod. "But I can represent and be their support in person, and you can support from here. Video calls go a long way."

"They aren't hugs," Mallory says, pouting. Why is he discouraging her from going? It feels ick.

Max puts his arm around her shoulders. "Honey, I think Derek is right on this one. And think of this, if his status changes, I'll get you a plane ticket in a flash. No matter the cost."

It's true his unlimited funds make everything easier; even a last-minute flight that would likely cost a damn fortune is doable.

"Let me check in with her and see how Sam is doing before I decide." She calls Maria, but there's no answer.

The two men follow her to the kitchen, where she paces. "I don't like this. Not being able to be there for them, this hurts." Her emotions swell, and tears threaten to break free. Why the fuck is she being so damn emotional? He's not on his deathbed for fuck's sake.

A text comes in from Maria.

Maria: I'm in with Sam and the surgeon. They are explaining things. Don't have long, but Sam is okay. Surgery is planned for tomorrow.

Relief floods her. He's not in imminent danger. "How will I be fucking tomorrow knowing Sam is in surgery though? I will be so distracted, I might not be able to perform."

"What time is your collab scheduled for?" Derek asks, his eyes are soft and full of compassion.

"It's at 1 p.m., so maybe the surgery would be over by then?" She raises her left shoulder and tilts her head to the left.

"Maybe. What did Maria say?" Derek caresses her bicep.

"The doctor is there right now, that's why she didn't answer."

"Maybe we will know more soon, and can make a better decision then," Max suggests. "In the meantime, how about I make us some grilled cheese sandwiches and soup?"

Mallory nods, though she's not a bit hungry.

"Oh, I'd love that. I'm famished. And I love your grilled cheese." Derek rubs his belly.

"That's because I use loads of butter," Max says with a wayward laugh. "There's nothing low-cal about them."

"Well, I'm on board for them anytime you want to make them. I'll take three, one for the road." Derek stretches, then turns. "I'm going to go pack."

"I'll have her make the flight arrangements as soon as we know if Mallory is going or not. I assume you'd rather wait and take the same flight?"

"Yes, for sure." He disappears down the hallway.

Mallory releases a slow, tight exhale as she checks her phone for the tenth time. "When will she text back?" She stops pacing and meets Max's gaze. "This is seriously excruciating."

"Don't worry so much, honey, your worrying won't change a thing. Just focus on taking action on what's needed, and know that nothing will stand in your way if you have to go. I'm sure your colleagues will understand if you explain you need to fly out."

She nods, chewing her lip, and puts her right hand on her hip, palm out. She begins to pace again. After ten minutes of incessant pacing and the delicious smell of grilled cheese sandwiches filling the air, her phone buzzes.

"Hello," she says, unable to hide the desperation from her greeting.

"Hi, hon. Sam is doing okay. The surgery is set for tomorrow at 8 a.m., and he's fully doped up on pain meds. He's asleep. He's fully aware and understands what needs to be done surgically."

Relief fills Mallory. This is at least something good. "I'm happy he's comfortable."

Maria says, "Yes. And he knows I've been conversing with you two, and he's very grateful for the support."

"We were thinking of flying in to support you two," Mallory says meekly, as if she's giving an apology for having moved out of the state. It feels like that anyway. Maybe the move here was a bad idea.

"No, don't do that. I'll keep you both informed. No need to drop everything and fly here. Plus, you were telling me last week about that incredible collab. Has it happened yet?"

"No, and that's the problem, it's tomorrow. But you two mean way more to me than some dumb collab."

"Honey, listen to me. I appreciate your devotion and interest in being here, but it's just not necessary. You've worked hard to score that collab. Just do it. I'll keep you posted and as up to date in real time as I can." She falls silent. "Sam is strong. He will be just fine."

"Derek is flying there," she says plainly, fighting the hurt that's brewing from Maria shutting down her need to go there. "He's already committed to it."

"Okay, that's totally fine. And great! I mean, I'd never say no to either of you coming back. We love it when you come back."

"Right, me too."

"Sweetie, you're feeling bad. I can hear it in your voice. It's okay to stay. Derek can be here, and you can be there. Sam will know all this. I'll tell him when he wakes, okay? And I'll call when he's up, so you can talk with him. That sound good?"

She nods but remains silent as the fighting of her tears makes talking too difficult.

"Hey, it's okay. Sam will be okay. And it's okay for you to stay, even if Derek comes." Her tone is motherly, caring, and so damn full of understanding that Mallory wants to curl into a ball and not move. "We love you."

"I love you guys," she manages though restraining her tears.

"Talk soon, okay?"

"Yes," Mallory says.

She draws in a deep breath after the call. She just needs to get herself okay with all this, and that's going to be the hardest part.

Chapter 11

Mallory wakes to an empty bed. Max must have had an early meeting, which means no wake-up sex, especially since Derek is gone, too. No matter. It might be for the best, given her filming later. She resists the urge to masturbate. It will go much better for her to be ripe and horny for the filming, especially with her mind swirling with worries about Sam.

She glances at the time. He's now in surgery. She had thought about setting her alarm so she'd be awake at the start of the surgery, but then she realized that was stupid. She couldn't do anything about it, and if something came up, Derek would have texted her anyway.

Shooting days are usually exciting, but the joy is seriously dampened today. Her only hope is that his surgery will be over before she spreads her legs to get fucked this afternoon, so she can focus. She might need something to calm her otherwise, nothing a drink or two couldn't fix. She'd never been one to feel she needed meds, but with her gut churning, her body apparently has other ideas.

She hops out of bed and moves toward the shower. The good news is that sleeping in has energized her, and she will need all the energy she can muster for today's shoot. There will be four men who will be fucking her relentlessly, and two are known for rougher sex. Being juiced up on lots of sleep is a good setup. She'd taken a melatonin, which she rarely does, and it gifted her the ideal night of sleep in preparation. She needs to add that to her prep regime before filming every time.

In the shower, she allows the hot water to stream down her as she does nothing but stand there. A morning of pampering herself is exactly what she needs. As she slowly considers starting the process of washing her hair, Max appears in the bathroom with a breakfast tray.

"Damn, I missed you. I had an early call, then I wanted to wake you with breakfast in bed."

She wipes the steam off the glass and peers through it at him. "Oh, that looks incredible. I can get back into bed!"

He laughs. "Okay. Unfortunately, I have to drop this and go. I have another meeting. Derek is at the hospital, by the way, and he and Maria are in the waiting room. There's been no word yet on Sam's status."

She frowns as she watches the shampoo foam stream down her breasts. Derek was supposed to be texting her with updates. She's being left out of the loop, and she doesn't like it. "Oh, he texted?"

"Yeah," Max says, then hesitates. "He didn't want to wake you, honey. Not on your big day."

"He told me he'd let me know," she says sourly while watching the suds go down the drain.

"Text him that you're up. I'll be in my meeting anyway, so I'll pass the torch to you." He kisses the glass as he looks through it. "Looking delicious. If I didn't have a meeting..." His phone rings. "Ah, shit, I gotta take this. Enjoy breakfast, babe! Hugs and doggy fucking thoughts!" And then he leaves.

"Thanks for getting me hornier than leaving," she calls after him sarcastically, not even knowing if he's still in earshot.

She finishes her shower and then crawls back into bed, adjusting the pillows behind her back for optimal support. She texts Derek that she's up.

No response.

She pulls the tray over her lap and digs in. A plump omelet overstuffed with veggies, cheese, and ham, a thick piece of toast with homemade strawberry jam, orange juice, and coffee with Max's special home-curated rum coffee creamer looks like heaven on a tray. She digs in and happily eats. She knows some who never eat before a shoot, they wait until after, especially if they do anal, which she doesn't. That's definitely not her. If she doesn't eat, she can't think or function. Again, she thinks about how lucky she is that she gets to be picky and not cave to do acts she has no desire to do, and that's largely because she has the financial backing from Max. It's a luxury many in the industry don't have, or think they don't have.

The silence is intolerable, though, so she puts on some music.

With a full belly, she leans back and checks social media. She has so many responses to do, it's overwhelming, so she switches to checking emails. That's no better.

She gets out of bed and adds oil to her hair, then carries the tray to the kitchen. Leaving her skin bare is the plan, so the crew can do her makeup on site. It's a weird thing to go on set with no makeup on. She never liked going out in public with only a washed face, but now, every filming or collab she goes to, she walks into the place with a bare face. This makes her feel more naked in public than being naked in public!

She will do a few things to her hair, but they often do her hair on site, too. So, curling it now makes no sense. Plus, she doesn't know the look they're going for yet. They may want her straight-haired. They always have a plan, so she just goes in plain Jane so they can pretty her up. It's odd having everyone see her pre-being-made-up, however.

She tightens her robe as she snags a decaf coffee pod. Sliding it in the slot is oddly satisfying, and she chuckles at herself. 'Fill the hole' seems to be the theme of her day.

Her phone buzzes as she's pouring more of Max's famous creamer into her mug.

It's from Derek.

Derek: Phone reception is spotty here, so I'm sending a text. I'll head outside and call you if I don't see a response. He's out of surgery, but in recovery, and doing okay. We haven't seen him yet, but the surgeon came to talk to us, and she's happy with how the surgery went. She's confident it will give him the best outcome.

Her body sags with relief. He's out already. That has to be a good sign. A sigh escapes her lips, and her muscles loosen, which alerts her to how tightly she'd been carrying herself. Being on edge is not the way to have a stress-free pre-work environment. She'd taken to the ritual of literally doing nothing on filming days, other than the bare minimum.

"Thank God," she slurs.

She types back: Good. I'm so happy to hear this. Thank you so much for telling me. I was so worried. Let me know when he wakes up. I'd like to talk with him if I can before the shoot.

Derek: Will do. Love you.

Mallory: Love you.

She carries her fresh cup of coffee to the couch and settles in, intending to either listen to a podcast episode or watch a movie.

At the midway point of the movie, she stretches. Still no sign of Max. He must be in the thick of a heavy workday. She meanders to the kitchen to make a mug of tea.

As she pops the mug of water in the microwave, a sense of calm comes over her. She's in a sweet spot. Derek seems better, and Max is incredible as always. She's making enough money that she could support herself living, even if she were suddenly alone. This is a place she didn't think she'd reach. And her business is growing. She steels herself to the counter by gripping it firmly with both hands as thoughts of her future fill her head.

Perhaps soon will be the time when she can think about proposing to Derek. The thought sends her heart aflutter, and a rush of excitement erupts in her. What a wedding they would have! All the friends from the club could come, all her coworkers and their partners. It would be a big party!

But then there would be Derek's family. They'd be the pearl clutchers who'd scan her side of the chapel with disdain. Though if they actually knew many of them were porn stars, that would say something about their hidden habits, and they'd be outed. Maybe Derek spills that spicy stars will be there, so many of his family won't even come. Hey, why even invite them?

She shrugs with a smirk.

She wasn't going to worry about that now, but part of her wants two weddings to keep the haughty glares from Derek's judgmental family from marring her big day. Her family will likely be okay with the guest list, even if they do recognize a few of them. But her family is the polar opposite of Derek's.

Her family is generous, liberal, accepting, and supportive, and his family is hardcore corporal punishment, prison style, and evangelical Christian. She's all for Christians if they are progressive and nonjudgmental. She believes there's a God, but not one who is assigned a human gender, and mean. God isn't a human for fuck's sake!

Maybe that's where Derek's spanking fetish comes from, his family. It's likely the root of it. He even admitted as much. She'd recently gotten a request from a few fans who wanted to see a video of Max spanking Derek on her site. Derek had posted something, and fans fell on it like a piece of cheese in a den of rats. She'd also made a tiny little comment about him getting manhandled and spanked by Max, and some more of her fans picked up on it, because they pick up on everything, they miss nothing, and they are die-hard fans who request more and more of her, and increasingly Derek, too.

They are willing to buy everything, and they tip well. She's very lucky to have them; many creators end up with loads of people who only buy deals or who expect stuff for free. So, she needs to ask Max and Derek if they'd do it. She'd film it, of course, with Max headless. But that means she'd have to watch all the ugly parts where Derek cries out in pain. Or, they just don't go that far for the film. This might be a challenge.

After snuggling with Max over lunch, where she ate nothing because she was still full from the omelet, she hops into her car to head to the studio. She's not happy that they haven't called back about Sam. She was hoping to talk to him before the filming.

The drive is uneventful. She dances and sings to the music, and after forty-five minutes, she arrives at the mansion.

It's glorious. An absolute fucking dream. The white, thick pillars are tall and smooth, looking firm and taut like the bodies of Pegasus. The gardens are straight out of a magazine, rich with blooming colors, complete with sparkling water fountains. She's never been to this place before, but she's heard a lot about it. It's supposed to be epic inside and owned by one of the biggest names creating adult films today. She couldn't believe she passed the interview process and got selected. She had joined the audition on a whim and never expected they'd choose her.

The owner is a retired security roadie for popular bands. His company was one that all the big-name singers and bands sought out because they were so good. He was so successful, he retired, then out of boredom, he started filming adult stuff. The man has one successful business after another, and she can't wait to meet him.

Mallory shivers as she drives up to the parking lot. She's nervous to meet him. Everyone says he's a nice guy, but most rich people are assholes, and nice guys aren't usually so nice, so she's not counting on their reviews of him. Though, she has to admit, Max is a legit nice guy and he's beyond mega rich. But he's an anomaly.

She slides out of the car and stops to stare at the massive home before her. It should be illegal to have this much money. But then, this is also his place of business. She shakes her head as butterflies spin in her stomach. She's usually not so nervous meeting people in the industry. In her experience, they are the most down-to-earth, understanding, caring, and non-judgmental people she's ever met. This group will likely be no different, but tell that to her butterflies.

She gathers her bags and walks toward the house. There are several other very expensive, nice cars parked in the lot with hers, making hers look like she's a boring suburban mom more than anything.

Before she even reaches the front door, it flies open. Out pops a butler. Of course, there's a butler! She chuckles. He's legit the part in a tuxedo and holding a tray with a drink on it, as if she's walked onto a movie set. Well, there is a studio inside. She giggles louder; she can't help it.

"Mallory, I presume?"

The man has an African accent of some sort and sounds very regal and proper.

"Yes, I'm Mallory."

"Great to meet you, my dear. Jax is inside waiting to meet you. But first, you will visit with a few people. Please follow me."

The butler enters the house and waits for her to enter, closing the door behind her. The white marble everywhere is blinding. The stark contrast of the pictures of nudes with dark backgrounds along the wall is attention-grabbing. The naked people are of all different sizes and shapes, some being thin, some with voluptuous figures and melon-sized tits. As she walks on, the poses of single nudes change into people fucking and group scenes. She recognizes a few major player porn stars in some of the images. The pictures change to a showcase of boob jobs as an investment as she walks along. She likes her naturals just fine.

"Some of Master Jax's work is on these walls. Like a shrine to his great erotic mind."

Mallory nods, her thoughts stalling on what she's looking at. "Wow," she muses. There's not much more to say.

She's seen pictures of Jax. He's a tall black man with big biceps and a jovial smile. He doesn't look like he's loaded; he doesn't dress like it either. Every picture she's seen, he's in gym shorts and a T-shirt, often with images of old TV sitcoms logos and cartoon figures on them.

As she's led deeper into the house, there are more and more people milling about, and a few are already naked. It's half a nudist colony. The butler ushers her into a room that's basically like every professional salon she's ever had her hair done at, and this is inside the house!

Her eyes go wide as she gazes around. No one is in the chairs, but several look set up and ready to be used.

"Jax spares no expense," the butler states as he sweeps his arm across the expanse of the room. "Just have a seat, and someone will appear shortly. I've notified them that you have arrived." He hands her the drink.

"Thank you," she says. "It was nice to meet you." She takes a sip. "Mmm. Good!"

"Likewise," he says all professional-like, but there's a twinkle of interest in his eyes. "Your images online don't do you justice. You're even more stunning in person."

She blushes and giggles. "Wow! Well, thank you! I have no makeup on." It was such a lovely compliment, but his demeanor made it extra poignant.

"To my point exactly, my dear." He winks.

The butler leaves, and she scans the room. It's incredibly stocked and elegant, as nice as any high-end salon she's ever been in.

She checks her phone as she waits, sips the drink, which is calming her nerves. The chair is super comfy, and the music playing relaxes her. This is the environment her nerves require.

A man with purple and yellow hair appears and scuddles over. He's short with freckles on his pale cheeks, and moves with an air of exuberant flamboyance. "Mallory, my lovely. It's so good to finally meet you. I'm Spencer and I've been studying your look for a week now and I have some exciting suggestions to fall right in line with your style, but also make you dazzle like cum on the tip of a big cock." He picks up locks of her hair as she giggles. "I've been dreaming about playing with this hair of yours. It's as thick and lush as it looks. I can't wait!" He covers his cheeks as his eyes fall partially closed like he's about to orgasm. He runs his fingers through her hair. "Heaven! Just heaven!"

She melts into the chair as he massages the back of her neck. "Oh, that's incredible," she coos.

"I have plans for you. Big plans," he says, finishing with a low-neck press. "What can I get you next? Water? Juice? Hot cocoa? Cider? Bubble tea?"

"Water would be wonderful." She raises her glass, then drains the rest.

"I'll be right back," he says and disappears quickly.

A group of loud people go by the door but are gone in a flash.

Before she can start to worry much more, he reappears with a tall glass of water filled partially with ice.

She takes it and takes a long drag. After a sigh, she says, "I needed water, I guess."

"Oh, you were parched, honey!" he exclaims as he fingers the ends of her hair. "Oh, so very nice. Strands of perfection. You take good care of your hair."

He finger-combs her hair as he rolls his eyes and shakes his head while making a decadent face, like he's tasting something chocolatey rich. "So good! I can't stop touching it. I love my job!" He rolls his eyes with a decadent expression.

She laughs. He is delightful.

"Though you are getting makeup second today, so we'd better get started. Have you washed? Yes? No?"

"Yes," she states.

"Yes, thought so. Jax wants you in curls. He said next time it will be straight." Reflected in the big mirror, his expression is one of serious contemplation. He strokes his chin with his fingers.

She beams as she focuses on what he said, *Next time.*

Her phone buzzes, and she glances at it. "Oh, my friend who just had surgery..."

He motions forward with both hands. "Take it, by all means. I'll just comb you while the iron heats."

She taps into her phone. "Hi, Maria," she says, unable to keep the angst from her tone. "How is he? Is he okay? He's awake? What's happening?" she asks breathlessly in a rush.

"He's doing well. He's awake. Pain is controlled. And yes, he can talk."

She releases a big sigh. "Well, that's a relief." She hears Derek in the background yelling something. "What's he saying? I can't understand him."

"It sold."

"It sold?" she repeats the question. "What sold?" Then it hits her. The house. Holy shit!

"Here's Derek," Maria says.

"Hi, the house sold. Can you come here and sign?" Derek sounds happy.

"Hi, and whoa. Seriously? That fast?" She watches as a woman comes in with a tackle box-looking kind of thing, only it's shiny and pink.

"Yeah, it sold two days ago," he says, though he doesn't seem a bit upset.

"Holy shit. Why didn't you tell me?"

"Forgot." His tone is cavalier and almost whimsical.

"You forgot?" she asks aghast. "Have you been drinking?"

Derek laughs. "No. Why?"

Spencer returns from where he had disappeared to, and he begins to curl her hair. He looks both amused and intrigued.

"Yeah. Sorry. I don't know. A lot has been going on, and I spaced it," he says a bit more subdued. Then he goes silent. "Sam wants to talk."

"Okay." She falls mute as she waits. Two days? What the fuck? Spaced it? She can't fathom.

"Mallory," Sam says in a weak voice, a tone she's certainly not used to hearing from him.

"How are you? Are you okay? I can't believe this happened. You're such a good skier. How?"

"I caught an edge." He falls silent for a short bit, then speaks. "Lost control."

She grimaces. "Ouch. Are you sure you're okay? I don't want to stress you out. But it's so good to hear from you."

"Yeah, I'm doing okay. Just sleepy and weak feeling. It's been a bear waking up from the anesthesia. But I'm making progress. They said I might get some broth."

"Mmmm, yummy dinner," she says sarcastically.

She watches as the woman opens her case. There are trays of makeup visible.

"Yeah, this has been quite the shit to deal with." He coughs.

Spencer rotates and fidgets with the curling iron.

"I'm sorry, Spencer, I'll hurry and finish up."

"No worries, hon. Just trying to stay on schedule is all." He has zero annoyance in his voice.

"Okay, you need to rest, and I need to be curled and go through makeup, so we should hang up. Thanks for calling through. I needed to hear your voice, Sam."

"Same. Love you. And go have so many orgasms you can't walk, and they'll need to carry you out of the studio. You'll do amazing, as you always do."

"Thanks, love you, too."

She hangs up.

"I like the sound of his voice," Spencer says, raising his eyebrows. "Not trying to eavesdrop, but his voice carried." He smirks, then raises an eyebrow. "A playmate of yours?"

"Yeah, and his voice, yup, it's epic. He's a total sex god."

"Mmmm. Has he been in any of your videos, my dear, where I could see him?" His interest is clearly piqued.

"Yes, a few. The most recent one is out to preorders and releasing to others soon."

"Sam?"

"Yes." She smiles. "He's a bisexual dominant."

Spencer pumps his fist in the air and glances upward. "Yes! Thank you, Jaysus!"

She laughs along with his jubilation. "He's incredible. I'm not lying. And he's older, a very sexy older gentleman."

"Double thank you!" He rolls his gaze upward, then quickly returns it to her hair rolled into the curling iron. "There are many blessings upon me today."

He continues to add curls.

She watches the makeup artist look at her, then back at her bin, over and over again. Finally, she says, "I'm Candace. I'll be doing your makeup once Spencer is done. I have a dramatic look planned for you to go with the film's cocktail party theme. After I do up your face, you can walk down the hall and visit Miranda in wardrobe. She's waiting for you to appear."

Spencer stops his cleanup and stares directly at her. "Now, do you need any shaving done before I leave?"

"Okay, I understand," Mallory says quickly to Candace. Then she looks at Spencer, "And no, did that all this morning, but thanks for asking, Spencer."

He nods and steps away with a wave. "Okay. Good luck, hon, you'll be fabulous!"

"Bye, thanks, Spencer. It was great to meet you."

"Likewise. It was my pleasure." He leaves the room with another wave of his hand.

Candace has perfect makeup. She looks like a glamour model herself, a big-bodied one. She's gorgeous. She'd make an ideal film star herself. She busies herself lining up eye shadow, brushes, foundation, and powder puffs on the counter. Then she starts pulling out lipsticks and holding them up to her cheek.

Spencer approaches her on his way out the door. "She's truly an artist. You may not even look like yourself once she's done. But then, you are gorgeous to begin with, so this will just be a fun, different look on you, but no less beautiful than the bare naked you."

"Bare naked, I'll be that soon, too," Mallory says with a wicked chuckle.

"Ah, yes. And an erotic work of art, as well." Spencer plays with her curls, tugging on them, teasing them with his fingertips. "Close your eyes, love," he coos. He spritzes a mist all over her head and locks. "Perfection."

She opens her eyes and tilts her head back and forth to see the sides and movement of her curls. "I love it!"

"You're up, Candace."

Candace seems all business and not even a little bit chatty. "Look up," she commands. She smears some oil beneath Mallory's eyes, dabbing it at the creases.

"What is that?" she asks, out of curiosity.

"Hemp seed oil. Keeps you dewy-looking without being too greasy. Love the stuff."

"Hmmm, I'll have to check into some."

"I swear by it. Use it every day myself. It's cheap." Candace holds up a few different bottles of foundation to her cheek, chooses one, then begins to apply it with a sponge. "This might feel a bit heavier than you're used to."

Mallory holds still and lets her mind wander.

The house has sold. The house she and Derek had was a place of so much joy, so much sex, and where they made so many meals together. The many nights of cheap dates, making homemade dinners together, then watching movies, then falling into bed as randy as dogs in heat, fucking until all hours of the night. Then crashing to sleep in until noon. All the holidays, the birthdays, and the boring Tuesday nights float through her brain.

Selling the house feels a bit like those times are being whisked away. She hadn't expected to feel so emotional about it selling, but then again, she hadn't even been a part of it going on the market. She chastises herself because she wants to live with Max. There's no point in keeping the house if both she and Derek will be living with him. But her heart isn't catching up with her brain on this one.

She tries to shove the mood-shifting thoughts from her head as Candace moves in close to work on her eyes. She gets right in there, works a bit, then steps back, cocking her head to and fro. She's very tuned into her work with an intense gaze never leaving her face.

The music beat picks up, and Candace dances in place. She smiles at Mallory, and Mallory grins back. She loves seeing her frolic a bit.

"Almost done, sweets." She finishes the last touches on the lipstick and then moves away from the mirror. "Take a look."

"Wow!" Mallory stammers. She looks like a movie star from way back. "I can't believe it!"

"You're beyond stunning, my dear. Now hop down the hall and get that sexy bod into a cocktail dress. The set is ready for you."

She gives Candace a grateful look. "Thank you so much. I could never have done this to myself. This is really sexy and fun."

"Go knock 'em dead." She waves the brush in her hands toward the door.

Chapter 12

M allory enters the room that has the sign "Wardrobe" over the door frame. The word is in cursive with curly painted lines all around the edges. No one is inside, so she takes a seat on the loveseat along the wall. There are racks and racks of clothing, a raised platform in front of a three-way mirror, like she's seen in bridal dress shops.

The same music is being piped into this room as was in the salon. She leans back and sighs. This prep experience is so far one of the most fun collabs she's been to. Hopefully, the filming goes well.

An older man with white hair and olive skin pops into the room. He has a clipboard with a stack of papers in one hand and his phone in the other. "Mallory, correct?"

"Yes," she replies, fidgeting with the fluffy cuffs of her robe.

"I'm Bill. I handle all legalities. I have your signed contract here. Everything is in order. Thank you for submitting your test results. We are very strict on following our regime on that, so thanks for cooperating. The male talent has all been prepped with your boundaries, dos, don'ts, and safe words. Jax himself oversees this because it's very important to him that consent for all of his talent is an enthusiastic yes, or it's not happening. He's very respectful of every talent's boundaries. Like the man will fire someone on the spot for not taking this shit seriously, he doesn't care who they are. I've watched him do it."

He raises an eyebrow as a warning look befalls his face.

"He'll be the next person you meet after wardrobe, just before you enter the film studio, which is where his office is, so stop in there before you enter. He's very anxious to meet you." He winks. "Don't worry. You'll do fabulous, honey. You're a pro."

Bill flips through his papers.

She tries to push her jitters from her mind, but since he noticed her precarious mood, it makes her more nervous. At least her worries about Sam's surgery have been settled. But her mind keeps drifting to Derek and his erratic behavior. He's going through so much and not cluing her in, and that hurts. They've both always been there for everything for each other, nothing hidden. Things are so different now, and she doesn't like it.

Bill hands her a slip of paper. "Give that to Jax when you see him. It's just confirmation that we've talked. Now, do you have any other questions or concerns about filming, payment, the release schedule, aftercare, or anything at all?"

She shakes her head. "Nope. I'm good to go."

"Okay, I'll leave you and send Miranda in. There's a help yourself bar over in the corner; help yourself to anything you desire. Miranda is running behind, by the way, so you might want to grab a refreshment. You'll learn that Jax runs things very differently." He nods knowingly.

"Okay, thank you. And good to know."

Bill leaves.

She walks over to the bar and assesses it. She's not sure if she wants anything. A drink would be welcome to calm her nerves. Just one. There are drink recipes on cards laid out on the bar. She scans them. One is for an old-fashioned, one is for sex on the beach, one is for a butterball, and the last is a lemon martini.

She smiles; she gets to play bartender. Not worrying about lipstick, she chooses the butterball. Hopefully, she doesn't mess up

Candace's work, though she guesses Candace will be on standby during the filming for touch-ups.

She mixes the drink and perches herself back on the couch. Taking a sip, the liquid spreads a calm through her body. It's tasty, smooth, and delicious.

"Ah," she says to herself.

She leans back and keeps sipping. Having downtime is both good and bad. The time to chill is valuable, however, and the drink is seriously helping her frayed nerves, but her brain is slipping back to Derek. She wants to marry him, but he hasn't even brought up his proposal, not even once. It's like it never even happened. She maintains her plan to ask him, but at the right time. It's not the right time yet. He's still floundering, but over what exactly, she wishes she knew. She considers texting him, but doesn't want to get interrupted by Miranda appearing, so she decides not to.

After ten minutes of waiting, she has an empty glass and feels significantly more relaxed than before the drink.

Miranda enters the room. She's a medium-height woman of Asian descent. She has jet-black hair, smoky, made-up eyes, and deep red lipstick. She has a little black dress on and red heels that match her lips.

She smiles at Mallory as she rushes over. "I'm so sorry I got detained. They had a wardrobe disaster on the outside set and needed my immediate assistance, but now I'm all yours." Her demeanor is harried, but she seems to calm quickly.

"This is a very busy place," Mallory coos. She never expected it to be so elaborate or bustling.

"Jax takes filming days very seriously and packs in as much as he can. He likes to film in intense bursts. But then there's mass chaos to deal with at times." She shrugs.

Mallory gives a single nod. "I get it."

She walks across the room. "Come over here. I have a deep maroon velvety cocktail dress for you. It's going to be an ideal match for your hair and makeup. Candace, Spencer, and I work together to plan a look for each of the talents, so we are all very coordinated in what we do."

"This is all so organized and impressive. I never expected this. In fact, on some shoots I've done, I've done all this myself."

"Welcome to the big leagues, my dear. Now, right this way. Let's get you nude and dressed, so you can get nude again!" she spills with a lighthearted laugh.

She presents the dress to Mallory. "Sultry, huh?"

Mallory widens her eyes. "Very. I love it."

"Let's see how it fits. I have a backup if it's not right."

Mallory strips without shame, a sly, unapologetic grin on her face. "A bonus of this new life, I'm no longer worried about being naked in front of others."

"You shouldn't be." She raises an eyebrow.

She helps Mallory put on the dress. "Oh, yeah! It's stunning. Have a look." She waves her hand toward the platform and the mirror. "I have your shoes right here, too."

Mallory moves to the platform and steps up; she's thrilled with the dress once she gets a glimpse of herself. She rotates to see all the angles. "I love it! It's incredible."

"It's perfect. Here's the shoes." She hands Mallory a pair of shiny silver heels. "I'm not even going to have you try the other one on. This is smoking hot."

Mallory slips her feet in and prances around the platform. "I feel so fancy."

"You are a star. Now let's get you to Jax. Everyone else is ready, so you just need your quick visit with him, and things will get underway."

Mallory nods and leaves the room, making her way carefully down the hall in the tall heels. She hates heels and had to practice walking in them for hours to be able to tolerate them. But now she has the muscles for it and can do it mostly with ease, for a little while anyway, not all day. But it's become part of her routine to wear them around the house to keep up her ability. Thankfully, she won't be on her feet the entire day because they will be in the air so much. She snickers at the thought of her heels whipping in the air.

She approaches Jax's office and knocks. There's a picture of a king's crown on his door.

"Come in," a deep voice calls. "It's open."

She slowly pushes the heavy door, carefully peering inside.

Jax is standing behind his desk, and walks around it with his arms raised. "Mallory, it's so good to finally meet you. I'm Jax, as you've likely guessed. I've been eagerly waiting for you. I'm a big fan. Huge." His smile is genuine, and his eyes are kind and interested. "Gargantuan."

She blushes. "Thank you for commissioning me. I'm very excited to meet you and to be here." His reputation precedes him well. He's very amiable.

He takes her hand and shakes it. "Have a seat here so we can chat."

She sits in the plush chair, while scanning the room in a quick, high-level glance. It's opulently decorated with professional boudoir portraits all over the walls, plus autographed photos of NFL and NBA players. He has crowns everywhere, images, stickers, statues, and real-size crowns perched on shelves. He is wearing simple clothes, gray athletic shorts, and a dark blue T-shirt with a cartoon chocolate chip cookie on it.

"I've prepped everyone on your limits. If anyone crosses what you've agreed to, let me know immediately. Okay? Like, I mean, halt the filming. Raise your hand, say something, anything. Don't just go along with it. I want this to be a pleasant experience for you and for everyone involved, so we have rules that cannot be crossed, and your personal boundaries cannot be violated. I have a zero-forgiveness policy on crossing boundaries for my female talent." He falls silent and smirks with a grimace. "I generally don't have issues with this, the other way around. I will kick a dude out the front door in a heartbeat, nude and with a hardon, I don't care." He chuckles. "I'm not kidding, and yes, I've done it. His cock was wagging in the air as he made his way toward his car, running like a chicken. My staff brought out his things, and I never had him back again. This is not a place I want trauma born from. This is an establishment celebrating sexuality, empowerment, and the freedom to be sexual. That especially applies to goddesses like you and every female that crosses this threshold, and the beauty and essence of the incredible thing that is human sexual energy, and a place of pleasure and worship. Kinks are all allowed, as is extreme fetish, but it must always be with enthusiastic consent, or it doesn't happen. I don't waver on any of this. Do you have any questions?" He winks. "We men are here as tools, and just to get off in the glow of all the wonderful women we get the honor of being in the presence of." He heckles. "We dudes are just the props and the backdrop, and every man knows it."

"Wow!" Mallory says, blinking.

"That's my speech," he grins.

A knock comes at the door.

Jax looks up. "Come in."

The door opens, and a big-bodied woman walks in. She has long dark hair and very voluptuous curves, wide thighs, and a beautiful smile upon her lipstick-red lips. She is in a skimpy red, blue, and yellow superhero costume with a cape, very low cut on her gargantuan boobs. "Hey, Jax, sorry to bother you while you're in a meeting."

"Delilah, how fantastic to see you," Jax pronounces happily. He glances at Mallory. "Delilah is one of our fastest-growing stars."

"Awesome! Nice to meet you," Mallory retorts. She thinks she's seen this woman on social media. And if it's who she thinks it is, she's got over a million followers.

"Hey, love," Delilah says to Mallory. "You must be Mallory. I've heard a lot about you. You are even more stunning in person." She gives Mallory a flirty gaze.

Mallory melts. To receive a compliment from such a woman sends beams of sunshine through her.

"You like women?" Delilah asks with a gleam in her eye. "We should do a film together if you do. I'd absolutely love it."

Mallory's jaw drops, and her brain stalls on the invitation. This day just keeps getting better and better.

"Now that I would love to see," Jax says with a juicy eruption of lust across his face. "Let's book it."

And just like that, Mallory has another collab lined up with one of the biggest BBWs in the industry. "I'm totally all in."

"Great! I'm excited! Let's get our calendars together." She shakes her head. "I saw stars when I walked in and totally got sidetracked on why I came," she laughs. "Damn, ADHD. I swear I see something that catches my eye, and I completely lose my train of thought. I might as well say 'squirrel.' And tattoo it on my forehead!" She laughs with her whole body jiggling. "I was just stopping in to say hello and thanks for the gift you just sent me. Wanted to catch you before I head out to the forest for the filming." She spins. "Plus, I wanted you to see me in this." She flips her cape up as she spins. Her sparkly personality radiates from her as if she's glowing. "It proves I have superpowers."

"You do have superpowers, Delilah." Jax looks very pleased.

"It's all those years as a mom, I saved up all those superhero saving kids from disasters moves, and now I have a giant stockpile in my psyche. It's second nature." She moves her hands in the air like she's casting spells. "I've changed more diapers than the whole state of Vermont," she jokes. She leans over with her hand at the edge of her mouth. "And that's no lie because their father was a fucking deadbeat piece of shit permanently affixed to the couch when he was home. He never even got a close up whiff. And I also did daycare for a few years."

Mallory's eyes widen. "Wow, that sounds like a lot. How many kids do you have?"

"Six. All boys. They are all over eighteen now. Living their own lives."

Mallory jerks her head back in shock. "Really? You look too young for that."

"Aww. Made my day. Yeah, I had two sets of twins, and I started way too early." Her expression is dazed, then she makes a goofy face, then falls into a happy one. "No lies. Well, let me stop interrupting you. I'm about to get railed against at least fifteen trees by various superheroes with their cocks out. At least that's what the whiteboard out there says." She gives a wave of her hand, then zooms out the door, her cape flying up with the wind of her movement.

"Two sets of twins!" Mallory exclaims.

Jax gives a sharp nod. "The Italian Stallion of women," he slurs. "That woman is white hot right now. People love her down-to-earth honesty. Plus, they love her size and that she's unapologetic about her body. Then there's the fact that she is a mom, too." Jax looks proud. "I found her and pulled her into my production company immediately. Best decision of my life."

Mallory stares at him in amazement but remains silent. She's often wondered if she should sign on with someone, but she really likes being her own boss.

"You look surprised," Jax says with a chuckle. "She's the epitome of a popular fetish, and I mean mega popular." He rises and moves toward his desk. "Let me make a note about scheduling you two to film before I forget." He stops and glances at her sharply. "That was a 'yes' from you, right?"

Mallory nods before she finds her voice. "I'm still stunned about two sets of twins!" She laughs. "And, yes, absolutely. I'd be honored. I'm definitely in."

Jax drops his eyes to the paper as he nods. "She's an amazing woman. This is going to be a huge hit. I can already predict it. I'm thinking a double film day so we can get you also fucked side by side by some big cocks."

Mallory can't stop feeling jarred. The whole day has been full of shockers, all good ones so far.

Her reverie is interrupted by a hard knock on the door. It opens, and a short bald black man enters. There are so many people working at the house that it's blowing her mind.

"We're ready," he says while ogling Mallory. "You look divine. You're very photogenic, my dear. I've seen all your films. Big fan. I'm super honored to get to film you. It's nice to meet you. I'm Edgar, one of the directors here, of which there are several." He grins. "But I'm the best."

She giggles. "Oh, I love to meet fans. I met my first one in person at a sex toy store." She sounds inexperienced, but she couldn't care less. It was an exciting day.

Jax roars in a tirade of guffaws. "You've only met one with your giant success? Oh, you need to fire your manager. You should be attending cons and meeting so many fans you can't see straight."

"Oh, I don't have one. I do it all myself." Mallory shrinks, feeling rinky-dink.

"Well, all you have to do is sign up and fly there. It's easy. Let me send you the name and location of the next one. Last I heard, they aren't full yet. This one will be local too, in Vegas."

Mallory gets a text from Jax. "Okay, I'll be sure to sign up. Thanks. Appreciate it."

Edgar gives her a pointed look. "Okay, I'll be out there waiting. Just come out when you're done talking with the big man."

Jax beams a hefty grin. "I am a big man." He hoots as he leans back in his high-back leather desk chair, resting his hands on the armrests. "Why don't you fill it out now? I'd hate to see you keep missing out on this kind of opportunity."

"Now?" Mallory is aghast. With Edgar saying he's ready for her, Jax wants her to take the time to fill out a form?

He rises and walks to his bar. "I'll mix you a drink. You start. It won't take long."

"Um, okay. Are you sure? I can do it after filming. I don't want to piss everyone off."

"Baby, no one questions me. They start filming when I say they start." He turns his back to her, then looks back over his shoulder. "Everyone who works for me is pretty chill. It's one of the criteria I have at the top of my screening list. They must be go-with-the-flow kind of people. And go with my flow." He grins widely.

He begins to mix a drink. "You like anything specific?"

"Anything you're making would be good, just nothing with straight alcohol." She makes a face even though his back is to her. She doesn't want to get drunk.

"You got it. I'll surprise you, and keep it light."

Mallory taps the link. It's called *Hot Erotics Con*. She finishes filling out the name and address fields as Jax returns. He sets the drink on the little table beside her chair.

"Pomegranate martini, heavy on the juice. Most of my female talent say that's the drink I make the best." He plops into the chair beside her. "If you ever decide you want to sign rather than be independent, you come see me. I'll sign you in a heartbeat, okay?"

Mallory's eyes flare again as she raises her gaze to meet his. Now this! How could the day even get better?

He cackles. "You aren't good at a poker face, are you? You are the most innocent-looking thing," he mutters. "Truly, you don't seem to understand how much of a splash you've made." He shakes his head. "I like a humble woman, though."

She'd never thought of herself as humble before. She blinks as she stares. "Well, I know how much money I'm making and how many of my fans are devoted to me, so I guess I kind of know."

"What you've achieved, on your own, is what most women in this business dream of. It doesn't happen for everyone as it has for you. And this is a very female-dominated field. Women owning their bodies for business as they desire, making their decisions, and the pay. It's the only field where women get paid more than men. I say more power to the women. And I'm more than happy to pay them for their work."

Huh. She hadn't realized all that, and she's liking Jax more every second. A fog of realization lifts as she realizes how likely he is to be right. "Wow. I really didn't know all that."

"Yup. I personally think it's also why all the rich dudes get pissed and try to squash the industry and shame the women, holding false pretenses like they're on some moral high ground, because they aren't controlling it. The women in the industry hold all the power. Women like you, Mallory."

"But what about the big studios, aren't they owned by rich dudes?"

"Some are, yes, but women like you, you own your own piece of the market, being independent. They get jealous. With the rise of the internet and the platforms, you all can take the reins and achieve huge success without them. So, they get pissed." He laughs heartily. "You all have successfully cut them out, for the most part."

"Is that why the big crisis happened with the payments recently?"

Jax nods slowly. "Yup. They were trying to squash the women's success and gain control. They failed for once. They faced such a huge backlash from fans that they had to put it all back together in a rush. They would have lost all the revenue, so they had to put it back to the status quo. I myself had even considered building a new site to replace it. Once they heard of all the developers ready to swoop in and take advantage of their idiot move, they backtracked with their tail between their legs. Right next to their small dicks!" He laughs with extreme hilarity, like he told the funniest joke of his life. "Fuckers couldn't do it. They had no idea what they were messing with." He raises his eyebrows. "I prefer to work with the flow of feminine energy. You are the real bosses. You collaborate differently from men."

Mallory shakes her head as she tries to process. She realizes she has stopped filling out the form as she fixates on what he's saying. "I had no idea."

"You're powerful, hon. Hey. How's that drink?"

She looks at the cup. She hasn't even tasted it. She takes a sip. "Oh, this is very good. They were right. It's incredible." She smiles at Jax.

"If you weren't attached," he says, shaking his head, "I'd be asking you out."

She blushes. And she never blushes. "Oh, wow. That's a wonderful compliment."

"It's all good. I know you're in a throuple. Rich white man and Derek, from your videos. Right?"

Mallory's brain is moving so slowly, she's dumbfounded and scrambling to keep up. She'd date Jax in a heartbeat, and she is poly. But considering that right now is making her brain even muddier. How would Max and Derek respond if she went on a date with Jax? She's free to do so. But that's too big to contemplate.

"You fill out the form, and I'll stop yapping at you."

She drops her eyes to her phone and tries to focus so she can fill out the form. She feels she should indicate to him that she's interested, but it feels awkward to say. The words are boiling inside her trying to get out.

True to his word, Jax remains silent. Within ten minutes, she's submitted the form.

"Well, it accepted it. Looks like it went through. It didn't reject me, anyway."

"Perfect. I think they'd make room somehow to add you anyhow, even if they were full." He stands up. "Let me know if you don't get in. I know a guy."

Mallory takes the last sip of her martini and sets down the empty glass. "That was really good. Thank you."

"Thank you. Wow. We got a lot accomplished, huh? Now let's go get you fucked and spent like a true goddess."

She stands up and releases a curt laugh. "Oh, I'm ready."

Chapter 13

Mallory follows Jax out the door of the office. He leads her to the studio room across the hall. Inside, there are way more people than she's used to while filming.

She takes a step back as she scans all the people. There are her five male co-stars, who are all dressed to the nines in nice suits, several makeup people at the ready with various colored totes in their hands, likely filled with multiple kinds of makeup, several people who look like they have no purpose, and one dude standing at a whiteboard writing on the surface in a green marker. Mallory sees her name, and beneath it are things she likes, her absolute yes acts, her no's are starred and underlined. There's a tentative schedule, marked as such. The men's names are listed, but no kinks; only her name has elaboration. She reads the names she expected to see: Billy, Jayvaughn, Hector, Pirate, and Lonesome, the last of which is the name she's most curious about. She saw him online in some pretty rough sex videos. She's not going to kink shame. But how did he get that name?

The director, Edgar, approaches her. "Hi again. We have a general outline, but we go off script as the actors find what is working in each moment, and what is not. You are all professional performers; I have no doubts it will go smoothly. I know you've spoken with Jax. Being spontaneous is not only okay, but welcomed. That keeps things more genuine. The men will love it, whatever you do. I guarantee it, though it's not about them, mind you," he whispers the last part in her ear with a knowing sparkle in his eyes, then leans back from her. "Good luck, hon, and have fun with it."

Mallory looks beyond him at each of the other performers and gazes into each of their eyes. She knows each of them, and their reputation precedes them, and she researched them all. Thoroughly. She knows this is about sex, but it's also not about sex. They are all here to perform, as is she. They are to put on a show to entertain, but that doesn't mean they as actors won't also get off. She's got the ability to separate sex and pleasure from love, which is a necessity in her line of work, and something not many people can do. Falling into one's body so readily and on demand is not a skill many seem to have, but it allows actors to be able to do what they do.

Edgar gazes around at everyone, looking like he's about to give a speech. "And again, I'm Edgar, and I'll be the director on set today. It's nice to meet you all. Let's get started. Mallory, and everyone, be sure to check out the whiteboard. Study it for a moment. It's a skeleton plan. You and the boys can mix it up as you find yourselves going with the flow of the scene. We'll take breaks as needed. You are all top-notch professionals, and usually filming goes well with caliber talent such as yourselves." He guides Mallory all the way to the whiteboard with the light touch of his hand on her back. Edgar isn't tall, but he's got a commanding presence.

She's still wondering who all the extra people are, but she likes an audience as a kink, so she's not going to protest. It's both flattering and surprising that he's singling her out. Is it because she's new, or because she's the woman? She's not sure, but she's not annoyed by it.

"Mallory, we use a whiteboard so we can easily and quickly change things," Edgar explains motioning toward it. "Do you have any questions before we start?"

Mallory shakes her head. "Nope. I'm good."

This is such a different type of filming experience than she's ever done. Having so many people involved rattles her brain and splits it in too many directions for comfort, but the drinks have helped calm her nerves. She's feeling steady and collected. She glances at Jax, and he raises his chin up in a sharp jab upward, his arms crossed over his chest. This is his role, clearly, to observe, to silently oversee, and monitor, and to remain silent, unless he needs to speak up. It's oddly comforting to have him here, too.

Her mind is not behaving as it wanders to imagining what it would be like to fuck such a man as Jax. She'd welcome that in a heartbeat.

Her thoughts are interrupted as all the male talent approach her in a mini herd. They each have a drink in their hands, and one has two. The one with two gives Mallory a glass.

"Not alcohol," he says with assurance and a wink. "The only thing not real, here." His smile is very suggestive and flirty. He has dark hair with ebony-toned skin and a debonair, suave aura. He's dashing in his sleek black suit and shiny shoes.

"It's great to meet you all. I'm excited to get started." Mallory melts a little as her arousal is ramping up, thinking about this man's cock about to be inside her. What a lucky woman she is!

He gives a quick nod. "We have to apologize. Given Hector's schedule, we couldn't do our usual pre-filming meet-and-greet. We usually build that into the schedule, but with him about to fly to Europe later today, we had no choice but to skip it. We aren't happy about that, so we just want to take a few minutes now to introduce ourselves. I'm Billy, and it's an absolute pleasure to meet you." He smacks the shoulder of the man to his left. "And blame Hector. He's the one in a hurry."

"Oh, you gotta be all that?" Hector says, shaking his head. "You're just jealous. Hi, Mallory, I'm Hector, and I'm delighted to meet you. I was watching your content to prepare for today. You are killing it. Really nice work. Stellar." He whistles, then does a quick movement of his hands in a slicing motion, moving one over the other in quick succession. "Hot as hot can be. Bang-zoom!"

Mallory giggles at his display of interest. "Oh, thank you." Her brain stalls; she had not walked into this day expecting so much praise from all these people, but it's really fattening her up with desire from her praise kink, which is ideal to get her in the mood for lots of sex. These guys are so charming that she doesn't even feel she needs the longer meet-and-greet. They ooze charm.

"I'm Lonesome. Pleased to meet you." This guy is proper seeming. She'd figure he's likely a pearl-clutcher if she had met him anywhere else. He has a stern demeanor. He has the best hair that is taller on one side, then dives down with a shaved-to-the-scalp slope leading behind his ear. Her eyes just swoop down easily, getting her to scan his body. He's very sexy.

Mallory adores his work, too. And she's always craved running her finger down that bald strip of his, like finger skiing. It will be especially hot to do while he sucks her tits. She tries not laugh at the thought of her finger skiing along his head.

She's so honored to be about to work with all these men. Their work has been incredible. She's a bit starstruck and hopes she can maintain their level of professionalism and not melt into a blubbering puddle on the floor. Her pussy feels wet just being in their presence. All she needs to do is stay in her body and feel the sensations, and stay the fuck out of her head, as much as possible. But this can be a huge challenge to accomplish while performing, but if they can manage to flip back and forth, she will be in the mind frame she needs to think on her feet, but still really feel the sensations, so she can portray the scene as genuinely as possible.

"I'm Pirate. Name is accurate," he says with a strikingly wicked grin. "We want you screaming and full of real body jerking orgasms. I'm ruthless, and I'm brutal. And I won't back down until you're as floppy as a rag doll from pleasure." He rubs his hands together and shoots her a seductive look that also says 'wolf'.

She shivers with delight. He smirks at her, and she flushes slightly. They are all succeeding at making her feel prioritized. Real men do this for women, and everyone benefits.

"Jayvaughn," the most solemn-looking man states. He's the tallest. He says nothing more.

"Don't mind him, he's practically a mute," Hector teases. He looks as if he's very comfortable making fun wherever he goes.

"Shut it," Jayvaughn says without a speck of a grin forming. He rolls his eyes, then crosses his arms over his chest, looking more cross.

Edgar approaches them. "I hate to break up the party, but in order to stay on schedule, we need to get started. We're already behind." He taps his wrist. "Time is ticking away, and this is a shortened shoot to begin with."

Mallory has heard about their long filming days, and she's a bit nervous about whether she'll be able to hold up, even on this shortened day. And will her pussy hold up to five barraging cocks is the bigger question. In her own films, they keep the filming sessions short, and usually it's more about her enjoying herself than performing. They have fun and take what they get. She loves the amateur subgenre, as do her fans, because it feels so real, and most often, it is. Not that Jax's films aren't genuine, but they do tend to be more orchestrated, and it comes across to her that way. Nonetheless, she's excited to embark on this new filming adventure. Her studio in Max's house seems lame compared to this one, but this is a professional setting. They do things differently.

She takes a sip of her drink. It's sweet and tastes like a soda, the bubbles rising up the champagne glass.

The group of them stays close, as if they're conversing at a cocktail party. She wonders how much of their conversation is even being picked up by the camera, given how far away it is. Maybe the scene is going to just give the impression of a cocktail party. She shakes her head quickly; she needs to stop analyzing what's going on and just be present with these men. That's her job here, not to direct. She's literally being paid to react and perform, and that's it.

Mallory's heart beats wildly in a string of flurries as she gazes at each of them. They are all very strong-looking, capable of many physical feats, no doubt. Her impression is that the five of them range in age from their late twenties to their late forties. Her body is a livewire of adrenaline on the cusp of the erotic scene they all are about to embark on. She again observes each man in turn as they talk to each other.

Her plan is solid. She will do best during the sex scenes if she just focuses on what her own body is experiencing, but she also has to be ever mindful of maintaining optimal placement of her body for the video camera lens. This is the true challenge for her: to remain genuine and still allow herself the feelings of pleasure so she is believable. She is also still struggling with not imagining what she looks like in the lens of the camera. This used to freeze her up, but she's getting better at letting that go now that she's becoming more comfortable. Her fans want to see everything, including when she looks out of control, discombobulated, and raw, even if a bulging flesh roll pops as she moves or she gives a momentary ugly and unattractive expression. They want the real her.

This was shocking for her to realize that they didn't want her glamorous and perfect every speck of filming, they want to see her come undone, get messy, and look unsightly, uncollected. They eat that shit up and ask for more. It makes the film more real. They don't want AI, they want her as a real human being. And that's lovely.

Her journey to today has come from a shedding of shame, an embracing of pleasure, and a freeing of the restrictions common culture puts on both women and men about sex. She draws from that empowerment as she engages in small. She's indulging in the story they are spinning, flirting, and getting to know the sexy guys. It's clear their words don't matter; it's the vibe they're giving off for the camera from a distance that is important.

She catches the eye of Edgar for a split second. He seems happy, as does Jax. She refocuses her attention on the men before her, though. Knowing all the people in the room are watching is hot, but she can't focus on them too much, or she'll lose her connection with her co-stars. As a performer and as a human, she's learned that she can have sex just for the sex, but the connections they make talking and flirting create intimacy that's real, albeit new, which comes across nicely in films, if there's a spark.

Love *and* sex are not synonymous, but separate. Love *with* sex, as she enjoys with Max, Derek, Sam, and Maria, is full, juicy, and wonderfully consuming, almost gluttonously satisfying. Sex with these men will be a glimmer of that, but their performance together, their professionalism, and their honoring of her stated boundaries, well, that's all just gold and paves the way for her to be able to climax with them. This is all business, but it's also her pleasure, as it will also be theirs.

One of the things being in the lifestyle club has taught her is that she can be very fully in her body and be okay with that, and focusing on her own bodily pleasure is a learned skill, a valuable one. And she uses that mindset to perform for the camera, while not forsaking herself.

She's been lost in her thoughts, watching each man's lips move as they converse for too long. She studies them; their love of life is apparent, except for Lonesome, who seems to be a bit closed off. But now it's time for her to be present and get out of her own thoughts.

Billy gazes at her, then smiles brightly, his face lighting up. "I'm betting you might like something to light up that body into pleasure, am I right?" Billy asks with a twinkle in his eyes. "We might know a thing or two about how to pleasure women."

"You're the experts," Mallory coos as real excitement floods her body. "That's one thing I've learned about porn stars, sex, and giving and receiving pleasure, those are our superpowers." The word reminds her of Delilah, and she grins deeper. That woman left an impression on her that isn't lessening.

"Emotions, skin, sounds, kinks," Billy whispers in a sexy voice. How is everything he says seductive? "Shushing of a woman during sex, he ain't no man if he does that. Am I right?" he asks much louder.

All the actors chuckle along. They get it. She's instantly even more thrilled she got this job.

She grins back at him, loving the shame-shedding nature of his words. Mature content can contain education and good guidance. It's not just fucking when made right. And this point is one that many need to learn, especially some men she's encountered. There are many men out there who have a lot to learn.

"Absolutely, I love making sounds," she says with a sigh that relaxes her whole body. She already feels accepted by these guys.

"Certain men," Lonesome snickers, coming out of his stoic shell a bit. "Be thinking they are all that, but if they're shushing their woman during sex..." He doesn't finish, but cracks up while shaking his head, and waves his hands. "I won't go there. But I'm guessing you might know where I was going."

Indeed, she does. That's toxic masculinity, and no sane woman wants a man like that! Unless it's a kink, and temporary play, that is. She glances down at Lonesome's crotch, and his meat is pressing out his pants at an alarming size. She startles and blinks.

Someone touches her arm, and she turns in the direction of the touch.

"May I have this dance?" Billy says smoothly. "The music is my body on yours."

Awwwww. How wonderful. She nods and bites her lip. These men have been seducing her without her even noticing. That's talent.

He pulls her close, and they blend like magnets. She follows his lead as he moves her smoothly around the floor, without effort. The other men are at a greater distance as they dance.

"I'd like to make your insides dance, too," he pulls Mallory close. "Make that lovely female organ send vibrations of pleasure all over your body. Ever been with men like us? But mind you, this is about you, not us. We are blessed to be with you." His curiosity is not shielded, but blaringly evident in his eyes.

"No, not like this, but I've always wanted to." Her heart pitter-patters as his tone carries with it an assurance that she doesn't doubt for a second. They mean her the best.

"It will be an experience like no other. I can promise you that."

This is the latch that will hook her into the meat of the film. She's already buying into their angle. She's getting reeled in. They remain still for a few seconds longer than would be expected as he stares intently at her. His eyes are wanton and determined. He's commanding and caretaking at once. It's intimidating, but seductive as fuck.

She has learned this trick in her own films; the exaggerated stillness, the pregnant silence carries power, then the sudden launch into movement serves a dual purpose because it gives those who like to fast forward to the action a clear marker for when to start watching. Some horny people don't want the story part, they just want to get right to the penis inside fucking.

He twirls her, like a princess at a ball, and when he reels her back in, he makes his move to kiss her. The kiss starts slow and sensual with lots of curling and plucking lip action, then the dive of his tongue into her mouth is deliberate and almost in slow motion, like he's savoring. He's hungry for her, and it sends her arousal zinging through her body like lightning.

Oh, this move has got her under his spell. She swoons in his arms. He's a damn good kisser. Fuck, she's gonna get so lost in the reverie of this, it will be like she's on another plane of consciousness; she can feel it coming on. The anticipation loads her arousal.

Her lust swirls even more as he cups her ass and presses her lower body to his. With this movement, they fall smoothly into private touching. It feels natural, and she adores it. He's moving with her so sensually that his dancing itself is the charm of his seductive move. And it's working. She falls right in line with his carrying her body as if it's effortless. It's not true heartfelt intimacy, but in a way, it is intimacy, two bodies pressed together, eye to eye. The only way to get closer would be for him to be inside her. She's falling in line with the enchanting swells of his moves. His attention is full and comprehensive, and she's taking his brand of sexual magic like it's the very air entering her mouth.

They kiss, and the world around her becomes liquefied.

"May we join in?" Hector says in her ear.

Shit. She hadn't even noticed all the men coming in around her and Billy. She nods with exaggeration, so no one misses it, including the camera, which is now close and seems zoomed in on her.

Like sexual voodoo, they surround her.

Bodies press to her on all sides. Multiple hands are on her. These men aren't afraid of each other, nor are they threatened. They are confident, working together to lather her up into a sexual frenzy, and their confidence and collaboration are sexy as hell. Their touches are for her, not for them.

One is kissing her neck, another is playing gently with her hair, and yet another is fondling her breasts.

Her eyes fall closed as all their hands on her make her feel as if she could be weightless. They are hungry, dominant, and grabbing at her, but they're skilled and careful rather than gruff and violent as things escalate.

The elegance and collective focus on her bring her dreamily along into the notion that a group fuck is about to unravel.

Lips and kisses befall her flesh, some suckling and nibbling with teeth bared. She jerks from the quick nip, and an exclamation befalls her lips.

There's a low rumble of a chuckle against her flesh as he releases her from his teeth. She glances down; it's Lonesome giving her a sassy look.

Billy drops to his knees and places his lips on her, loading her belly with kisses. Hector moves in to kiss her on the mouth. He tastes like the soda pop. He's a more forceful kisser, and her body bends backward slightly from his press.

Jayvaughn whispers in her ear, "That butt." He grinds his hard cock against her bottom and grunts while gripping her hips strongly from behind.

"You're so hot. You're a sex goddess," one of them whispers, but she can't figure out who said it.

Her clit twitches, sending a noticeable twinge through her womanly parts. She's kind of amazed she's still dressed with all this action from all five men. They are taking their time, and the slow burn buildup is working wonders on her. In any other situation, but this controlled one, her fears would be ablaze, but here she feels safe, especially under Jax's watchful eyes. She groans. She's getting to the point where she might beg for more.

"Between these luscious thighs," Billy says against the skin of her bare thigh. He pushes her dress up until most of her leg is uncovered. "Mmmm," he hums as he kisses his way up to her pussy. "Ripe and no panties. Perfect." He nuzzles his nose into her labia folds, and she crumples forward with a moan. "Mmm, the scent of you drives me wild."

"Oh, fuck," she mutters as he dives into her more aggressively.

He tickles his fingers along her labia lips, making her hips undulate instinctively.

The men are pressed to her body, all moving in tune with her gyrations. Their hands roam her, cup her, squeeze, and caress. She leans her head back against Pirate, who is now the one behind her. His cock feels huge and sits just above her ass at her lower back. She shifts her hips in response to all the sensations.

"You are gonna take some good black cock, sweets," Pirate slurs into her ear before he pushes her hair off and nibbles. "Mmmm," he says with a grunt. He rotates his pelvis against her, then presses on her upper back, bending her slightly over.

She's not a short woman, but these men tower over her. She feels petite next to them, but being their sole focus, she feels bigger than life itself.

Billy begins to insert his fingers into her from beneath as Pirate drags his firm cock head along the curve of her ass cheek.

Her eyes keep partially closing, making it even more difficult to keep track of which man is touching her and who is where.

Billy's fingers are constantly moving, out then inside her as he ramps up his finger fucking of her. The sloshing sounds of his fingers against her cunt drive her desire for cock in her even higher.

"Please," she pleads, meaning it for them all.

Someone pulls her dress down, and her breasts swing out. Her nipples are tight.

The men react with appreciative groans, and she smiles. She loves it when men worship her body. It's one of her greatest kinks.

"Yes," she coos as someone takes her right nipple into his mouth.

Another is fondling her other nipple, pinching it and tugging it slightly as if milking it.

"Yeah," Billy says.

"Mmmm," she moans.

At that command, which is a weak one, Pirate presses his cockhead at her slit and presses himself in. The penetration is swift and fast.

He groans as she does as well, and the fucking has begun.

The hands on her, the mouths kissing her flesh, do not cease as Pirate slides his cock in and out of her. The grip of his large palms on her hips has her pinned in place. He uses her hole as Billy still rubs her clit. Their touches and rubs bring her to a place of bliss.

Her peak is charging at her full force as Pirate's cock slides along her G spot, and Billy stimulates her clit. Her sounds amplify, and it makes the men work harder and faster.

With all of their hands on her, she needs very little effort to stand, which is a blessing because the overwhelm into her full blast of pleasure is going to be an easier launch that way.

Her sounds increase as they take care of her, and with harder slams, Pirate and Billy successfully push her into her climax. Her body curls forward, and Billy increases the speed of his rubbing of her clit, and she explodes into her orgasm with ease. The sensitivity magnifies, and she whimpers; it's almost too much.

She flounders, reaching to grab onto arms, bodies, anything around her. Her body chugs through the strong vibrations her lovely female sexual organ complex gifts her. She yells out in response. This is the kind of strong orgasm that usually has her ripping the toy off, but she is cloistered inside the group of men, so she must just endure the intensity.

She screeches as she's flung right into another orgasm. As her body shudders through the contractions, clenching on Pirate's cock inside her, he pulls himself out and spills his jizz across her bottom. She suspects that normally he would have waited, but the shortened filming day warrants his early indulgence.

Another man quickly scoops her up and carries her to the couch. They lay her down on her back, and Jayvaughn pulls her dress from her waist down her legs, making her fully nude. All the men are still dressed, but Billy strips off his jacket and shirt, like he means business. He's toned and built like a brick house. Mmmm, eye candy for her.

Hector positions himself to enter her pussy missionary. She turns her head to the side and runs into Billy's balls. She licks at them, grasping at his cock with her hand like she's desperate for it.

He chuckles and strokes her hair, then urges her so her mouth aligns with his cock head.

She opens her mouth to invite him in, and he enters quickly, filling her mouth with the large head of his cock. He mouth fucks her gently as Hector pounds into her pussy relentlessly. All she can see is Billy's skin as hands maul her breasts, touching her everywhere in a frenzy of lust. Her body flops like a rag doll between them. Her lust is their clay, and she's accepting their brilliance.

She gags on Billy's cock as he goes in deeper, making her torso lurch upward.

He groans as her throat closes in on him.

She struggles and coughs.

"Fuck," he says before yanking himself from her mouth.

She smiles up at him, and he smiles back, with a generous twinkle in his eyes. She's just thankful he's out of her mouth.

The rotation at her pussy switches to Lonesome. He pumps into her a few times, then pulls out. He steps back and motions with his hand for her to flip.

"I wanna ride that ass." He gives her bottom a harsh slap, and she cries out. He chuckles, then fingers her slit.

He drags the head of his cock between her wet lips and quickly slides inside. He takes her hard and fast, making her body flop and her mouth fall open. He's big, and his girth takes her higher in her arousal. She's going to lose it again soon.

Both her tits are being pinched, and the rocking movement of him fucking her from behind makes their grips on her more of a tugging than just a simple pinch.

She grunts as he works himself in and out of her. She reaches back for her clit, but a hand beats her to it and rubs.

"Allow me," Jayvaughn says.

She's tipped over the edge in a flash and falls into another luxurious body quaking orgasm.

"Take that cock," Lonesome says as he drives into her so roughly, she might split in two.

He backs away with a guffaw. "Shit," he mutters.

Cock after cock rides her doggy, then they flip her sideways and use her hole that way, each taking a turn, no one losing hardness as they fuck her back and forth across the gradient of ecstasy. If she looks used, it's really more that she's being ridden to shades of glory.

If time is passing rapidly, it didn't seem possible because her bliss was so full. Her concept of time has fallen away. Most of them hadn't come yet, but most of them could control it, so edging is in their toolbox.

Chapter 14

Back at it after a quick break, Mallory sucks Billy's cock as he cradles her cheek. She's grateful to have had the refreshing drink of water and very happy to be giving her pussy a chance to not be filled for a moment. She isn't sore yet, but if this goes all afternoon into the evening, she will end up quite sore.

She will do her best to endure for the sake of the film's final product. With her head bobbing on his dick and the camera up close, she abandons all attempts at trying to look good. She has no control over it anyway, and this is survival mode. Saliva is oozing out of her mouth, and some drops ooze down to her tits. When Billy grips her head over her ears and pumps harshly up into her, making her gag violently, her body jerks from it.

This is the kind of crap she doesn't like, but she said she'd do a hardcore mouth fucking scene exactly once today, and Billy is apparently the lucky winner. He pulls her off him, then drags her up his body to kiss her on the lips.

Good. He listened. She had wanted it to be short.

"That was beautiful," he says as he presses on her back so their bodies become flush.

She remains silent as they kiss deeply.

"Cut," Hector announces. "That was great. Fabulous job, Mallory." He turns and shouts, "Jasmine, erase the mouth fuck from the board. It's a one-and-done deal."

Mallory is grateful. She did not want to repeat that. She slides off Billy to the couch with a sigh. She laughs. "That's not my thing, but I made it."

"You did incredible," Billy says with a grin.

"I've seen you do much rougher than that," she says, shooting him an accusing look unapologetically.

"I'm equal opportunity," he says, squeezing her body close to his.

He's legit cuddling with her, and it's exactly what she needs.

"We're going to break for lunch, then come back and do another group scene, and incorporate some spanking. Lonesome will do that with you." He looks directly into her eyes. "Are you doing okay?"

She nods. "I'm doing great. All the orgasms they gave me have made it a wonderful experience."

Hector grins. "Good. I think we captured some great filming already. The camera really likes you, hon."

She nods. This isn't the first time she's heard this, and it's likely why she's been so successful. "Thank you."

"Everyone, grab some lunch, and we'll reconvene in an hour. Food is in the kitchen."

She takes the robe offered to her by a small brunette woman. "Do you need anything special?" she asks Mallory.

"Nope. I'll go peruse the food and get a light lunch. I don't want too much."

She wanders out of the studio and waves at Jax. He's deep in conversation, but stops and motions to her, before calling out, "Mallory, can we sit and have lunch together?"

His interest in her tickles her. "Yes, for sure. Just going to make a quick phone call and I'll be right back." She snatches her phone from the wicker basket by the door.

He nods and goes back to his conversation with Hector.

She walks down the hallway and sits on a loveseat. She opens her phone and finds a text from Derek.

Derek: I'm staying here at the hospital another night. Then I'm going to the house to pack up stuff. Give me a list of what you need. Contemplating staying in town to pack. And get fucked by Sam, if he can manage it. Might be a while for that, though. But Maria is filling in, and I'm seeing Faye later. Good pussy here. It's really good to be back, really, really good. Are we sure we want to move? Love you, bye.

She slumps into the couch. Well, that's a fucking loaded text! The last thing she needs right now is to travel there and pack. And do "we want to move"? At least he used "we" but is he fucking serious? Stress fills her as her stomach begins to churn. Shit. How will she eat with this load of news swirling in her gut? She should have left her phone in the basket.

She calls Max to bounce her worries off him. He always makes her feel better. Unfortunately, he doesn't answer.

If she and Derek marry, would it be weird to live in different states? She frowns. Well, she guesses it's possible. But then, why sell the house? Why not keep it to give Derek a place to live while he's back there if he wants to be there so much? This all isn't making sense to her, but there's no sign of answers to alleviate her concerns. She has to carry on.

She stands up and makes her way back to the studio.

Jax is still talking. He holds up his hand and catches her attention. "I'll be right with you, Mallory."

She nods and grabs a bottle of water. After plopping on the couch, she got royally fucked a few mere minutes ago, and she downs half the bottle of water. Her brain drifts to Derek. She loves him. She wants to marry him. He's settling into his own with accepting his sexuality, and apparently, his impact play kinks, but he's unsettled with her. And they've always been so in sync that this is a touch-and-go situation.

He's her home. Max is her home. How can she and Derek live in different states? This will be tough. How will she live with her boyfriend, and not her husband? She's used to being unconventional, but she never imagined living long-term separately from Derek.

She pushes the thoughts from her head as Jax approaches her.

"Let's grab a plate, and we can eat out on my private patio."

She nods and follows him.

After taking more food than she intended, cause it all looked so incredible, she follows Jax through the studio, across the hall, and through his office. The sun is shining through the big glass doors, and as Jax opens them, he moves his arm outward in a gallant gesture.

"You first," he grins down at her.

"Thank you." She walks out into the sunshine, and it feels blissful. The sun's rays are warm, and it's pleasant out.

"This is our ideal time of year. Things are blooming, it's not too hot."

"Yeah, it's beautiful," she says, gazing at all the flowers around his patio. "I'm getting used to the weather."

"I try to spend as much time outside this time of year as I can."

He sets his plate down on the table. "Let me get you another water."

"Oh, well, that would be nice. Thank you, Jax." She had almost finished her bottle and neglected to grab another when they got food. With all the water she's consuming, she's going to have to pee something fierce before they start up filming again.

"My pleasure." He disappears back inside.

She sits down at the table and finishes the last swallow of her water, impressed that he noticed she's almost out.

He returns and hands her the bottle.

"I guess all that fucking made me quite thirsty." She smirks.

"Oh, yeah, sure. I can imagine so." He gives her a wanton look. "That was really sexy, I have to say. You were incredible. Knocked my socks off." He grins widely.

"Oh," she says with surprise. "It felt pretty normal to me. I don't think I did anything special."

"Not true. You really are humble, or perhaps you can't see yourself as others see you. You're a true star, it's obvious, Mallory. A natural. You come off so honest and genuine. Believable, if you are acting. You're hypnotic to watch." He gazes at her after his gushing. His eyes twinkle with charm. "I thoroughly enjoyed that."

Well, if she can impress this man, she's doing great! She plays with the hem of her robe above her right breast. "Well, gosh. Thanks! I was just reacting to them all. Being myself."

He sits down and looks intensely into her eyes. "I can't resist. Mallory, would it be too bold of me to ask you on a date? As you know, I'm clearly dominant, and I know you already have one. But we could play, if you're interested, and if he's okay with it."

She tries not to look shocked, but clearly it doesn't work because she can't mask it.

His face softens as he holds up his hands. "I don't know your setup, so if you don't do this kind of thing, just tell me, and I'll shut the hell up." He chuckles, and it travels his body. "I get it. One of the few times I'll accept someone telling me to shut the hell up." He raises his hands again with a sincere look in his eyes. "I mean no disrespect to you, your situation, or your Dom."

"We are poly." She stares at him, assessing with astonishment how this very rich, jovial, good-natured man is interested in her when he could likely have any woman and have her how he wants her.

"Ah, I admit, I had heard that, so that is also why I decided to ask. Are you looking for another relationship?" He smiles suggestively. "With a big black man?"

She smiles easily and allows it to reach her eyes. "Yes. I'd love to go on a date with you and, yes, I'm interested."

He visibly relaxes. "I am very pleased to hear that." He ticks his finger in the air. "Now, mind you, this isn't just about fucking, though I want to fuck you, very much so." He scoffs then launches into laughter. "But I want more than just sex. I'd seek a relationship with you, however much you want or can handle. I'm good with it. We'd take it slow."

She stares at her food. Try as she might, she can't stop the small smile that grows. She's attracted to him, and she likes him and his worldviews, and his take on sex. So why not? She's not sure how Max and Derek will react to her adding him in, but poly is poly, and she doesn't need their permission, just her honesty. "I'd love to pursue a relationship, and sex, of course, with you, too." She gives him a gaze full of wanton abandon, showing him her full desire.

"Well, shit. With a look like that, I'm tempted to cancel the rest of the day and spend it with you." He beams back at her with utter delight. "Whew, doggie! That's..." He shakes his head.

She laughs. "I love your interest and your enthusiasm."

"Oh, I've had the interest for a long time, since I first saw you, but I wasn't sure how our in-person chemistry would be, so I wanted to wait until we met."

"I feel it," she says with excitement growing.

"We will need to discuss everything, but just to appease my yearning, do you like to be tied up? Handcuffed? Dommed? Spanked? Controlled?"

"Yes," she says with zero trepidation.

"Orgasm control?"

She nods aggressively. "Very much so. But I haven't done a lot of rope play, yet. I'm inexperienced but interested."

"Praise the Lord, and I thought so." His eyes go even hungrier. "This will be a slow buildup. I do enjoy BDSM with a submissive, especially one who is new to things. This is like Christmas." He nods as he takes a deep breath, then releases it. "But you know how I feel about things, so your enthusiasm means everything to me."

"I do, and that really has impacted my desire to say 'yes.'" She wrinkles her nose, then smiles, shimmies her shoulders, making the robe fall more open along her cleavage.

"Oh, I like that. Please do it again." He's very deliberate and appreciative in his tone. "Lawd have mercy, baby! Getting me going."

She shakes her shoulders, and her robe falls all the way open to expose her full breasts. Her nipples harden with the exposure to the air.

"I can't focus worth shit no more. Geez. You have the most incredible breasts. And I have to tell you, I'm very much looking forward to the day when you are across my lap, and I'm paddling that priceless looking little princess bottom." He chuckles as he stabs his fork into his salad. "And I've done spankings for films, severe acts for the camera, but I want the real thing, you know, not just an act, but true meaning and feelings behind it. Reinforcing my dominance over my submissive with a good, solid paddling."

She tilts her head at him while narrowing her eyes. "You don't strike me as someone who likes to share."

"Oh, I'm over that bravado. In my younger days, I couldn't have handled it. But I've matured." He slaps his thigh. "I want you pleasured and happy, and how you are with me has nothing to do with how you are with another. I'm poly as well, and I have my bitches. I won't stop all that. I'll tell you stories if you want someday. Some are hardcore into severe bondage and impact play, so I get those kinks filled when I see them. Being poly works out well, we can each get our kinks met without having to try to convince each other to do kinks that aren't ours. There is no coercing."

Mallory shivers, and not from any cold wind. He's right. The thought of him tying her up, using her, controlling her, and spanking her, then fucking her, sends her lust on high alert. "I'm imagining some of it."

"Aw, shit. That look," he says with a big grin. "Getting me all excited over here. I'm seriously tempted to halt filming." He sighs and shakes his head. "We have a golden day, though. I tried for months to get you all aligned, so we will have our own day soon. And I can't wait."

"Same," she says. The whole idea of taking on another lover is titillating. Her whole body is alive with electricity at the notion.

"But I have to say I'm a very slow burn. I can jump right in and fuck, like any guy. But when I want a relationship with someone, there's zero rushing. I believe building trust takes a long time, and I'm not going to go too far because you can't go back after overstepping. It doesn't work. So, we will take it very slowly on every aspect. I won't expect you to trust me with anything until you're truly ready. I will often wait for you to bring things up. But this will come after we chat more and learn more about each other. But if you want a quick pop-in, bump-and-grind, tell me, and I can certainly accommodate. I want to meet your needs, but not until we have had several full discussions. The nice part is, I already know a lot about you from your forms for the shoot. But you do not have the same bandwidth of knowledge about me."

"So, you're going to make me wait for your cock." It's a statement. She accepts this. Sort of. She shoots him a sassy look, silently daring him to change his mind.

"We're going to have lots of fun together. It's nice we are so close in location, but I'd fly to see you." He strokes his chin. "I like to travel quite a bit. Maybe you could come on a trip with me in the future. Do you like to travel?"

"Yes," she says as she fixates on her good luck. Finding a man like Jax seems like a rarity. He's truly a gem. Her legs tingle. She's antsy to work again, but loving her time with Jax. "I'm getting horny from all this talk."

"I'll never not want to hear you say that sentence." His eyes indicate it's not a lie.

Their lunch goes on pleasantly with small talk, and she eats with her robe wide open. He can't keep his eyes off her chest, and she's growing as randy as a wildfire, wishing she could hop and land on him. But alas, she is here to film, and he's right, it was hard enough getting all of them together, so they need to finish what they started.

Chapter 15

The drive home has Mallory suffering.

She's sore, but sexually satisfied, and excited for not only the film to come out, but the collaborations she started while at the mansion, and most of all, the thoughts of entering into something with Jax. She's nervous to tell Max and Derek, though; she doesn't want them to assume this means they aren't enough for her. But time will tell.

Her pussy pounds from all the sex she endured, and she's throbbing all over. It was a long fucking day, and she was tempted to stay the night, as Jax had offered. But she's in a tizzy about the move, and if she needs to fly out, she'd rather make the drive now. Duty sucks.

Her body is deliciously worn out, and she's been fucked and used to within an inch of her life, so downing her second energy drink just to make it back home is a necessity. Max texted that he is waiting and has a nice homemade pizza and crisp salad waiting.

Her mind drifts again to Jax. Max and Derek are okay with her fucking all the talent in the other videos, so how is Jax any different? He's not. It's the same thing. Seeing him for dates will be no different from what she just did in going to film at his place. And if they become a thing, she's likely going to be going there to film anyway, so that's where they'd spend time, and when they'd fuck.

Though she might have to tell him she can't handle such long days of sex for filming if she's also going to be fucking him, too. One will have to give. Today was long enough, she can't imagine how she will feel after the length of their normal filming days.

The drive is filled with her emotions zinging, rising, dipping, peaking with elation, and then taking a nosedive. Talk about mood swings, geesh! But by the time she pulls into the driveway, her mood is up again.

She's lucky, and she knows it. Her numbers on her socials and memberships keep rising for both followers and subscribers, and if she's branching out to Jax's audience, this will expose her to more new people. It's exciting to be in demand and basically a wild dream she never even imagined would come true.

She really is sitting in the best possible scenario she could imagine, short of her situation with Derek.

Maybe Derek could come with her to the filming sometime and be in a film himself. There's nothing stopping him from pursuing that. She sets her mind to asking him, and then he could meet Jax. She doesn't know if Jax has any bisexual tendencies, but she's positive Derek would get fucked and get spanked by him, in a heartbeat.

Derek's got a soft spot for dominant males. That's something to explore. Max, on the other hand, hmmm, he may or may not like it. He seems to really like to be in charge, so maybe he stays home when she goes to Jax's and just directs the filming at his house. That might be for the better. She's started calling it a house because there's no logic in calling the massive place a cabin. Please. Five cabins would fit inside!

She drives to the end of the driveway and parks. Even her muscles are screaming at her as she exits the car. She had to hold so many awkward poses and stay bent over for hours on end. She might need a massage, a bath, and a bed after dinner.

"Oof," she says as she's moving slowly.

Max barrels out the door in a rush. He holds his hands up and takes her bags. "Babe, it's so good to see you. You look sore and tired. It's hard to move?" Concern fills his eyes.

She nods as she creeps along. "Yes. And I am exhausted. I feel like I legit ran a marathon. I will need some recovery time for a few days, but there are so many things I need to do with the house and moving. I'm freaking out." Her troubles come barreling out at the sight of him. She doesn't want him to be her dumping ground. He doesn't deserve that. She grimaces as she takes the steps. "Shit, I feel like I worked out for way too long."

"You kind of did," he says jokingly. "But I'm dying to know how it went. Did you enjoy it?"

She nods. "I did. So much has happened. I have so much to say." She limps along. "Shit. I can't believe my body!"

He helps her into the house. "You get in the recliner, and I'll get the dinner, then you can tell me all about it."

She purses her lips, then sighs as she slowly lowers into the big, puffy chair. She leans back and pops out the footrest. "Ah, I needed this. I almost spent the night, but with all the stuff going on with Derek and Sam, I might need to fly tomorrow."

"Tomorrow?" he asks, pausing his leave.

Her emotions rumble again, and panic seizes her.

"What's happened?" he asks with concern. He moves over to her. "Tell me."

Her emotions flare raw again, and tears spring from her eyes. The whole damn thing is a new panic. "Oh fuck! Max! How am I going to do all this? And we've already started the ball rolling on the event, too. This is awful timing." She shakes her hands before wiping away her tears.

"Hey, hey, hey. Honey, there's no need to stress. I know you are new to this way of life and not used to help, but there's nothing to worry about. This is why I have a team. They can pack up everything and move it all here for you. You don't need to do a thing." He sits on the arm of the big chair and wraps her up in a hug, pulling her arms tight in the cocoon of his encircled arms. "I can even have them unpack it here if you want. You don't have to do a dang thing. This move literally doesn't have to impact you at all." He kisses the top of her head. "There's going to be no stress for you with this. Let me take care of it." He kisses the top of her head.

She sighs as she dips her head against his chest. This is exactly what she needs to hear, but the whole thing is not just about moving. "Okay. But I still have to go there and sign the papers, don't I?" The overwhelm is real. She gasps as a sob overtakes her again in her spiral downward.

"Things can be done digitally these days. I'll get my admin on it. She can contact them and see if it can be done from here. I'm almost positive we can do it from here. So, no, I don't think you have to go there."

"I could see Sam, though. And Maria." Her voice is small, defeated, cryptic. How can she also talk with him about proposing to Derek? How can she also bring up her new plans with Jax? Everything has become a lot more complicated and messy.

"True. That's up to you. I'm just saying it's possible to do it from afar if you don't want to travel there right now." He pets her hair. "You seem quite stressed. I want to help."

"It was just a really long day." She sighs. "Okay. I'll sleep on it." Her nervous system calms as he holds her and keeps petting her hair. "It would be good to see Sam is okay with my own two eyes, though." She blows out another big breath. "But the thought of travel sounds rough right now, especially with how sore I feel. It sounds like torture to sit on a plane tomorrow or even the next day."

"Yeah. Slow down. Just think about it overnight. See how you feel in the morning. You need to take care of yourself. Your body is literally your career."

She smirks, and her eyes fall into slits. "Hmpf. You're right. I hadn't thought of things that way."

"It's true. Well, it's kind of true for everyone, but even more so for you." He stands up. "Let me pamper you. Get a good night's sleep. Then we can reassess in the morning. Together."

She nods slowly, and instantly she is feeling better. "You are so good for me. Putting things in perspective and helping me through this."

"It's what I live for. Anything you." He pats her thigh. "I'll be right back. Sit tight."

She stares at the ceiling as her eyelids feel heavy. They droop as Max returns. Her eyes pop open as he sets her plate on a TV tray beside her chair.

"That smells really good."

"A nice big slice of homemade pizza, a salad, and a glass of wine. Plus, water. Gotta get mine. Be right back."

"You're waiting on me, again." She gives him a grateful look. "You take the best care of me, Max. Like no one else."

"You deserve it. And I love it. As your Dom, I take care of all of you. And I take great pleasure in it." He smiles big. "It makes me feel good to hear you say that."

"I know. And you're the best at it." She smirks. "It might be the one time tonight that I'd say 'no' to sex, though."

"Oh, I'm not even considering bringing up sex now. You need to rest your body, especially your pussy, after today."

She nods, super happy he understands. "It was a lot of cocks in me and nonstop. It's so foreign for me to not want sex, but I had a lot of sex today!" she says with a laugh, then a scoff. "It was really incredible, though. Five sexy black men who really, really, and I mean really know how to fuck. Their skills at getting me to climax were top-notch. I was so woozy and floppy after coming so much. It was unreal." She holds back a mention of Jax at first, but then slips in a sliver about him. "The owner, Jax, really took good care of me." She hesitates to say more about Jax, now doesn't seem like the right time to talk about her dating him.

"Ah, I love to hear you got so much pleasure and good care. That's exactly what I want for you as your dominant. You pleasured so much that it's mind-blowing, that's what I seek. I love it when you come undone." He points at her plate. "Try it."

She grabs the pizza and takes a bite. Chewing, she groans. "Oh, this is so damn good, Max. I so need this." Her body melts with the relief of a soft chair, and food in her mouth, plus the presence of Max.

"Sit tight. I'll be back in a flash."

True to his word, he's beside her in no time with his own food and wine.

"So, tell me more."

After she finishes chewing her bite of pizza, she says, "Well, I met this woman. She was incredible. We are going to do a collab on a female-female film. She's big time. Really big time. Delilah. Heard of her?"

"I think I may have." He looks interested.

"She's amazing." She pauses, wondering if she has the energy to bring up her dating Jax. She decides she doesn't. That will be a discussion for another day.

She eats in silence as Max taps on some music from his phone. Then she's ready to talk again. "Oh, I'm so glad I drove home. It's really good to be here with you."

"It's really good to have you home." He tilts his head as a tender look takes over. "I missed you."

Her phone buzzes with a text. She considers not looking at it. She doesn't need more drama at the moment.

She flips her phone and taps into it with a sigh.

Derek has texted: Things are going well. Sam is doing much better. I'm with Faye. Just wanted to touch base with you while I had a free moment. How did your big filming day go?

She texts back: It went well. I'm exhausted. Got my brains fucked out, then some.

Derek: You coming here tomorrow?

Mallory: I don't know yet.

Derek: Okay. I understand.

She scowls. Does he?

Mallory: Max is going to see if I can do things from here. I'm just fried, Derek. Today took a lot out of me.

Derek: Yeah. I can imagine. Have fun, though?

Mallory: Yes. Very much so.

Derek: Good. I gotta go. Faye is back. Love you.

Mallory: Love you. Goodnight.

Derek: Goodnight.

She glances up at Max.

"Derek?"

"Yup. He asked if I'm coming there."

"And?"

"Said I don't know."

After dinner, she can feel it in her bones that she will fall asleep. So, she rises. "I'm not going to make it much longer. And if I stay here, I'm going to fall asleep. Thank you so much for the amazing dinner, the incredible support, and I wish I had the energy to offer to help clean up." She stumbles in her first few steps.

"I've got it. Don't worry about it one bit. I want to do it. Now. Give me a hug and a kiss, and get that precious body of yours between the sheets." He stands up and wraps her in an embrace. "Sleep good, babe. I'll see you in the morning. Love you."

They kiss on the lips.

"Love you. And thank you. You're the absolute best."

Then she goes to bed at 9 p.m. The bed is heaven as she settles in.

THE MORNING SUNSHINE highlights the window. Good. She's slept in enough for it to be full daylight. She was afraid she'd wake in the dark having gone to bed so early. She glances at the clock. It's 10 a.m. Wow. She hasn't slept this long since the last time she was too sick to walk around. She craves a lazy start and closes her eyes again, savoring the comfort of the bed. Max has gotten up already, so the bed is all hers.

Her body is still sore, but it's better. Well, that might be false. She hasn't gotten up yet, so things might change in a heartbeat once she leaves the bed. She likely might need to be wheeled around today. Too bad she has no wheelchair. Fucked so much that she's too sore to walk. Is that a thing? She's never had sex for that many hours in a day before. Clearly, she's an amateur compared to the talent Jax employs. She's not entirely sure she will be able to handle a full, long day, but she desperately wants to meet other professionals at their standards.

She grabs her phone. She's gotten a text from Jax.

Jax: Good morning, beautiful. How are you feeling today? I woke up thinking about you.

She smiles, and a ping of excitement rushes through her. She texts back.

Mallory: Good morning, sexy. I'm feeling good. I got lots of sleep, but damn, I'm sorry. Your boys fucked me into some big day-after pain. She adds a pained face emoji.

She smirks. Then texts again.

Mallory: But I truly loved the whole day. But this kitty needs a bit of a break.

Jax: Not uncommon. That was a lot of hungry, big cock riding you. And we got the excellent footage to prove it. You were a superstar. Thanks again.

Mallory smiles. Her heart swells.

Jax: Don't forget you are welcome to return and hang out with me at any time it strikes your heart. Just call or text me to make sure I'm home. I'd love to have you over. Make you some good food. I can cook, even though I have a live-in chef.

Wow. A live-in chef. She can't even fathom. Another rich man in her life. This is becoming an absurd theme. Except Derek, who's dirt poor, she's got two men who have more money than they know what to do with. She knows some good charities!

It's time to donate. She grins. Something to work on for them to do. Donation through rich dudes. Would this make her a sugar baby? A sugar little? Maybe she's coining some new terms. It should be a thing. Sugar daddies who donate. Get your sugar daddy to donate big! It sounds like an ad. Maybe it's a kinky film. Fuck the sugar daddy, and pick the charity he donates to. She likes it! She laughs. "Fucking for charity," she whispers. Might be a good goal for a collab film. She bets the fans would love it! They could vote on the charity she's getting fucked for! She likes it.

Jax: Have a wonderful day. Call me when you can. I'd love to hear your voice.

Mallory: I will. You have a wonderful day too.

She stretches as she smiles. He likes her voice. That was so nice to read.

But now, it's time to try to get up.

She swings her legs over the edge of the bed. It hurts to move. She stumbles toward the shower; each step is an effort. "I need to work out more, so I have better muscles to tolerate Jax's filming days."

She turns on the hot water and waits for it to heat up, holding her hand in the stream while she hums. Once it's hot, she moves in. The hot water is a gift. She soaks up all the comfort of it and slowly washes her body. Maybe she needs a bath, too. Just to soak her aching muscles.

Her heart is wanton this morning. The desire to get engaged to Derek is tugging at her. Maybe it's with the new addition of Jax that's getting her to want to solidify her marriage plans with Derek; she's not sure, but the urge to ask him to marry her is a huge green flag that's smothering her. She needs to act. Instead of going on a flight, she should really be going ring shopping for Derek. It hurts that he's never brought up his proposal, but with all he's been going through, she can't blame him.

Once she gets out of the shower, she sees a texted image on her tiny phone display. She goes into it, and it's a picture of Derek's very red ass. The text reads, "Faye's on board with giving me what I'm due. Spanked, fucked, pegged, drained. Happy."

She smirks. That man of hers. The man who was terrified and hesitant to dive into the pile of sex orgy at that first time they went to the lifestyle club party is now getting his ass beat and fucked by an older woman, and getting spankings regularly by an older man, willingly. He's come so far in shedding his shame and leaning into his kinks. She's proud of him. She assumes the spanking has something to do with him processing the shame, renaming it. More power to him if he can navigate his way out that way, and to a better, healthier place. He certainly doesn't deny himself like he used to. That's progress.

She enters the kitchen holding up her phone with the picture of Derek's ass displayed. "Good morning, and Derek found a substitute teacher for his discipline."

Max scans her with a smirk, then gazes toward her phone, squinting. "Good morning, and let me see."

She hands him the phone.

His expressions go from surprised to amused to proud. "He sure did. Looks like she did a good job of it, too. Faye? Maria?"

"Faye."

He doesn't look upset at all; he looks whimsical. "And how's your body feeling?"

"Beat up. It was rough getting out of bed, but the shower helped. Might take a bath later to help further things along."

"Good idea. There's the hot tub, too. That would help." He peers at her over his reading glasses. "I've made serious progress on your issues. My admin has arranged for you to sign from here; she's worked her magic. Plus, we have a moving company that will pack up the entire house and move everything here. All your stuff, and Derek's. Derek doesn't even have to be there, but it just needs to be coordinated so they get a key from him. I have fully validated this company with her, and we've completed all the checks. They are reliable and have a great track record for honesty, swiftness, and no broken things."

She brightens. "Perfect. That's unbelievable. And whew, that lifts off so much stress." She smiles as she moves toward him. Wrapping her arms around him, she holds his face. "How are you so wonderful?"

"I say that to you every day," he smiles back.

"This is huge. And I don't mean huge, I mean huge! And also, I'm wondering, where the fuck are we going to put it all?"

"I have a team that will figure all of this out. They will have questions, but honestly, we have no rush on this. It's not like you two need much other than personal items and clothes. The rest can be slowly gone through. If we need space, I'll build a storage building."

She laughs exuberantly. "Now that's insane."

He grins. "Never can have too much storage space. A storage shed will be a great selling point when I move, if I ever do."

She shakes her head. "A storage shed for a mansion? I can't even imagine being about to say that." She presses her lips to the right in a firm line as doubts arise. But come to think of it, with Max footing the bill for literally everything in her life, her paychecks are really mounting into a nice stockpile. Her finances are completely shifting.

"I'm going ring shopping today," she blurts.

"Oh?" he asks, curiosity twisting his face. "When do you plan to ask him?"

She's so grateful he doesn't look mad or jealous.

"I don't know, but I've got something in me that's itching to make our engagement a solid thing. But he's been so erratic, and he hasn't even brought up marriage again since he proposed." She shrugs. "Maybe I'm fearing he's changing his mind, and I need validation? I don't know, but I need it to be the right timing. The perfect timing. We've had enough botched debacles around our potential engagement, I don't need to add to it."

"I'll come with. You need a man's opinion."

She laughs. "Do you realize how crazy that sounds?"

He nods. "Yup. And my kids would send me to the loony bin."

"Speaking of, when do I get to meet them?"

"Funny you should ask, Marianna was just texting me that she, Davis, and the kids might be in town next month."

"I'd really like to meet them. How would you introduce me? As your girlfriend?" she gives him a saucy look. "The one who makes you come." She laughs. "I'm kidding."

"Yeah, I need to figure out how to proceed. But she's pretty open-minded."

"Just tell her you're my sugar daddy and I'm your whore." She wiggles in a dance as she settles into her chair. She smirks, reaching for a croissant as she flicks her eyes to meet his.

"I don't think that's a wrong assessment," he says with a jovial glint in his eyes. "But..."

"And I'm happily so." She again wonders when she should bring up Jax with Max. While shopping for an engagement ring for her nesting couple, man? The whole scenario is wild.

"When do you plan to shop? I have a break in an hour."

"Perfect. That works." She stares at her croissant, contemplating taking a bite.

"I'm buying, by the way."

"Lunch while out?" She takes a bite of the cream cheese-smothered croissant. The sunshine highlights all the flakes of the pastry as if they were art.

"The ring."

Her eyes go wide. "What? No. No way. I'm buying it. I'm the one proposing." Protests rage up in her.

"Nope."

"Max, you can't be serious. And I have money now. I want to buy it." Just...no.

"Don't make me put you over my knee, too," he scolds, his brows knitting in a stern expression. "I might like that a little too much, though." He heckles.

"My life gets weirder by the day."

"Plus, Lacey's Secret is having a sale on panties. And I want to pick some out for you." He taps his phone. "I got a notification they have a sale going on, and I want to buy you some skimpy ones."

"Panties and a wedding ring. That sounds like a kinky book title."

"Skimpy panties and a wedding ring," he corrects with amusement. "And don't argue, or I'll spank you in the dressing room with a pair on, fully pulled up your crack."

She lights up with a bursting laugh. "You wouldn't."

"Try me." He shrugs. "I'm not joking." He looks serious, and it sends a chill through her.

"I'm not Derek." She has to admit that the scenario does turn her on, however.

"No, but I'm still your Dom, as much as I'm his." He swats the air as playful arrogance floats across his expression.

She hadn't thought about it much in that way, but it's very true. He had truly become Derek's Dom as well. Sam was still dominant, but Derek was having much more interaction these days with Max than with Sam.

"Faye pegged him, too," she blurts.

"Good. He got his then, in full. Next time I beat his butt, I might tell him to go open his cheeks for some ass fucking aftercare with you in a strap on."

"And no doubt he'd love it."

"It's a plan. Let me get to my meeting, then we can head out to shop. Make sure you're commando."

"Oh, I am already." She is going to fight him on this ring buying plan. There's no way she's letting him pay for the wedding ring she's giving to another man! That's ludicrous.

Chapter 16

Mallory and Max walk through the mall toward the jewelry store, holding hands. Their little polycule is shifting with Max at the helm as they proceed with their plans to pick out a wedding ring for Derek. Mallory has considered doing their own informal ceremony to marry the three of them, but she needs to wait to bring this up with Derek first.

He needs to be in a good place with all the chaos in and out of his brain, and they need to then be engaged and solid before she brings up the idea about adding Max in a more formal way. It's a glowing, powerful nugget of truth in her that's goading her to talk to Max about it, but she's holding off. It's not the right timing. Derek needs to come first. Then if he's on board, they do it. Of course, it will just be a union in theory and mutual commitment only since they can't really marry as a threesome, not legally anyway.

But she loves the idea of it. Their rules, their way, and very curated their needs and wants. She's wondered if this participation and offer to pay for the ring is Max's way of being involved integrally in the proposal and engagement, and that is a sweet thing in and of itself that he desires that. She's suspecting it's not really even about the money at all, it's more about him being involved, and in being their mutual Dom. He wants to provide for them. So, she's considering letting him foot the bill, perhaps after he makes good on his promise to wrangle her into submission with a spanking in the lingerie dressing room, in a hot skimpy wedgie of panties. That idea sounds hot. She's ready to roleplay that, with the full intent of allowing him to pay anyway. She's ready to play the brat full stop. But that doesn't mean she's not putting up a fight to cover it herself! The whole thing is juicy as fuck, and a bit twisted and kinky, which is literally perfect.

In the store, Max pulls her to the most expensive section and points to a ring with five medium baguette diamonds embedded along its full circumference.

"I don't know, that's a lot." Even though she has enough to cover it, largely thanks to not having to pay any bills lately.

"I'm not concerned with how much I'll be spending; this is about finding something nice Derek will like."

"How can I help you?" asks the man who appears behind the counter. "Shopping for a ring today?" He has short brown hair and a neat goatee. His eyes are warm and welcoming.

"Yep," Max states as he points at another one with even more diamonds.

"Helping your daughter find the right ring?" the man asks.

"Oh, she's my girlfriend," Max states proudly.

The man's head recoils as she shifts his gaze from Mallory to Max, then back again. The look of disbelief is priceless. "Okay, then, a ring for yourself. I get it." He smiles, the awkwardness now shifting from his face.

"No, it's for her boyfriend. She hasn't asked him yet, though. That's why we are here." Max tries to mask his chuckle, but fails.

Mallory giggles along, enjoying the man's confusion a little too much. "Yeah, we want to find a ring that will suit him."

"Wow, that's one I haven't heard. Um...okay," the man says, clearly trying to process what they've said. He recovers quickly like a pro. "We have many to choose from, and I'm confident we can find one that will be ideal."

"Yes," Mallory says soothingly. "I want to surprise him."

"Can we see this one up closer?" Max asks, pointing into the display case. "Yeah, that one, right there."

The man pulls out the ring on the velvet stand and places it on the countertop.

Max picks it up and slides it on his finger.

"Your fingers are bigger than his," Mallory spits.

"Yes. But I can put it on partway. See, you can see what it looks like on skin."

"I suppose," Mallory says coolly. "I do like that one." She sneaks a glance at the salesclerk, and he's watching them with widened eyes, a look of amazement on his face.

"Derek's not really that flashy, though, for so many diamonds." Mallory peers into the case at the plain rings.

"It should be flashy, it's a wedding ring," Max retorts.

"It should match his style," Mallory protests.

"You are just picking the cheaper ones. Don't do that. I'm paying," Max says through clenched teeth.

"No, you're not. I'm buying my husband-to-be's ring. And that's final." Mallory catches the clerk's astonishment, and his face shows his confusion in his skewed expression. She stifles a laugh. His face is so comical, she wishes she could film his reactions.

"Stop being a brat," Max says sternly.

"I am a brat, and you like it," she throws back at him in accusation. She throws her arms down to her sides, her hands balled into fists.

"Here's my card," Max says, handing the man his credit card.

"Hey, that's not fair," Mallory protests while digging out her card.

"Too late. I'm faster," Max states with a haughty expression. "Charge that card only," Max instructs the man.

The clerk's jaw drops open, and he's flat-out staring at them without blinking.

Finally, he blinks.

"You are not to charge my wedding ring to his card," Mallory tells the clerk loudly.

"It's not your wedding ring, it's Derek's." He grunts. "That's it. We'll be right back," Max tells the clerk.

He grabs Mallory's arm and drags her toward the door.

"Sir, your card," the clerk calls.

Max turns back to him. "We'll be right back after her spanking."

Mallory guffaws. "Holy shit! You just yelled that across a store!"

"I just yelled that," Max confirms as he continues to pull her along. "Across a store," he repeats with gumption.

Him taking charge is a turn on. He makes a straight shot to the lingerie store, his hand wrapped around hers.

"I'm buying it, and no spanking will stop me," Mallory whispers in a strained voice. Being quiet is hard.

"Yes, it will." Max grabs a handful of panties off the table display as they walk past.

He's rushing her along through the store so quickly that her hair flies up.

"Max, slow down. We're catching stares." Mallory's humiliation kink is blooming, and her clit lurches.

"Can we get a changing room?" Max asks the woman behind the counter. He sounds irritated and rushed. He waves his handful of panties in the air toward the changing rooms.

The woman jumps quickly and practically runs to the first changing room to open the door. Without a word, she sweeps her arm to the inside. She looks nervous and forgets to maintain her polite expression. She stays mute even as they enter. Together.

"Do not disturb us," Max says with firm authority as he pulls the door shut.

She nods through the crack in the door before it fully shuts. She looks terrified.

Mallory wonders if she will call security on Max for his bullying moves.

Max plucks one pair of panties from his fist, making a slew of them fall to the floor.

Mallory resists the urge to pick them up and stares at the lace panties he's presenting.

He brings them to her eye level.

"I hate lace panties. They hurt." She crosses her arms over her bosom.

"The spanking will hurt. Now get nude and get these on before I have to help." He looks legit angry, his words hitting her like a warning. "I won't be gentle if I help."

She kind of wants that. It stirs her arousal, which she also knows only could happen because of how Max treats her, coddles her, pampers her, and makes all her wishes and wants his top priority.

She tugs her pants down and slides them off before stepping out of them. Slipping her right foot in, then left into the panties, she pulls them all the way up, then crosses her arms, giving him a challenging glare.

"That's not nude," Max blurts, raising an eyebrow over his stern face. "Off with your shirt and bra. I want your tits out."

"I'm not nude if I have panties on," she says in a spicy tone.

"Don't sass me or it will be harder on you," he warns.

"Well, it's true." She smiles at him and bites her lower lip as she slowly pulls her top off, then dances as she undoes her bra. She tosses it to the seat in the corner, it hits, then slides right off to the floor. She leaves it, even though it bugs her.

Max grabs the seat and drags it to the center of the dressing room. "Over my knee." He slaps his thighs. "Now."

She doesn't move a muscle, but taps her right foot against the carpet.

"Now," he seethes in an angrier tone. "Don't tempt me or I'll use something stronger than my hand."

She's seen this side of him with Derek, but he's never pulled out this side of his kinky persona with her. He's gotten close, but today this deepens their level of domination. She's also curious about what he'd use other than his hand. She spies a hanger on the rack, wondering if maybe that's what he was referring to. That would hurt in a spanking.

"Come on, I want to see those tits hanging down. I want to see them swing like they do when I fuck you from behind, only this time it's gonna hurt, not give you pleasure."

Shivers travel her whole body. She wants this and doesn't at the same time. The domination is lush and seductive, but her body is still a bit sore from the filming ordeal. Her mind reels. Is she willingly submitting to a rough spanking despite her bodily aches?

She carefully lies across his lap, which makes her labia lips plump up with arousal, causing her to feel as if her slit is flaring. She loves this sensation, and when a partner incites it in her, she usually has fantastic sex. Only this time, she laments there will be no sex. It will be a waste of a clit boner. She hates that idea already. Trepidation and excitement grow in her as a shudder overcomes her.

Max presses on her upper back to pin her in place, and lays the first slap on her already tender ass cheeks. He tugs the lace panties right up her butt crack in a swift, firm wedgie.

She cries out louder than she had expected to.

He slaps her bottom five times in a row, hard.

She manages to stay silent for the first two blows, then loses her control. "Ow, ow, ow," she protests, kind of regretting all this with her soreness. Maybe today wasn't such a good day to be a brat on purpose.

He leans back and pulls something from his pants.

Her curiosity piques. What could that be?

He keeps going. His hits are firm and well placed, sending shockwaves through her pelvis, arousing her.

"I will pay for the ring. This is my part to play, and I'm not stepping back from it." He spanks her three more times, hard.

It hurts, and she instinctively yells. It's involuntary, and she can't stop herself despite being in public.

He does it once more, then drags something across her tender flesh. He whips it down against her.

She's assuming it's a rope flogger.

He thrashes her a few more times with it.

"Do you accept the terms of this union?"

She's astonished he's walked around with a flogger hidden in his pants. She looks up and can see in the mirror that his hand is poised over her ass at the ready, the black rope toy in his fist. Seeing herself over his lap with a pained face is affirming. She's never considered herself much of a masochist before, nor Max as a bit of a sadist, but it's staring her in the face. She's his submissive, and there's zero question of his dominance. This is further than they've ever gone with this kink. She wonders how it will impact their dynamic going forward.

"No."

He hits her again, and she winces, then cries out.

"Submit," Max demands.

She wants to submit. This game is dangerously seductive, especially in public. They are risking a shit ton of drama from mall cops to befall them, and that's making it even hotter. She'd get great pleasure explaining all of this to a few sweaty mall security guards.

She shakes her head, feeling like she can't tolerate another hit to her sore butt.

But Max strikes her again. "I'm your Dom. I'm Derek's, at the moment, both of you. And I'm providing for you both. You will accept my help." He whacks her once more.

She yells, then falls limp as he rests his spanking hand at his side.

"What do you say?" Max implores.

"I'm sorry, Daddy. And I'll accept your help in buying Derek's ring."

"And?"

"I'll be sure Derek knows you not only bought it but helped me pick it out."

"And?"

"And that you had to spank me in a dressing room to get me to comply with your plan." She droops her head, wishing with all her heart that Max would fuck her next.

But she knows he won't.

"Get up. Get dressed. And don't forget to get a good look at your flaming red butt in the mirror before you do."

He roughly lifts his thighs upward to get her to rise.

She stands up, a sheepish grin creeping across her face.

He points at her lower half. "Wear the wedgie while we buy the ring to finish it. Don't loosen it. I want it shoved all the way up exactly where I placed it for the duration," he demands as he takes a few pics of her reddened bottom with his phone. "I loved watching your tits swing as I hit you." He grins devilishly. "These pics are getting posted."

Her hopes are crushed. "Will you please fuck me?" she asks quietly, dropping her eyes to the pile of panties on the ground.

"No. Now get dressed." The hint of a smile creeps into the crinkles of the corners of his eyes. But she can tell he won't be changing his mind.

She glances at her red butt in the mirror, and her lust is raging. "I really want to come. Please, I'm so turned on, Max."

"No." He grabs all the panties off the floor in his fist. "I'm going to pay. I'll meet you out there."

She watches him go, leaving her alone with her burning desire left high and dry.

He pulls the door shut.

Damn. This sucks.

She bends over and rests her body on her arm propped up on the chair, and begins to rub her clit. She's so aroused that her rise to climax is deliciously near. There's no question about it, she's making herself come. She spanks her clit, causing her body to lurch in response. She moves her hand quickly over her aroused bean, her body twitches, and she launches right over the edge of her climax with very little effort. Her internal walls contract aggressively on repeat, sending waves of heavenly pleasure through her body. After the intensity lessens, she gets dressed.

The pleasure helps alleviate the pain of her beaten flesh, and she grins.

Out in the main part of the store, there are very few patrons shopping, but no one looks her way with concern. They must not have heard, however, the woman behind the cash register counter stares downward at whatever she's doing, a look of worry on her face. There's no greeting or even a glance up from her as Mallory zooms by. Mallory feels bad for her, so she tries to catch her attention with a wave.

She doesn't look up, so Mallory says in a pleasant voice, "Thanks! We appreciate your help."

The woman looks up, and her relief is evident. All she does is a single nod.

Mallory's flesh burns as she moves, but she's super glad she took a moment to alleviate the clerk's concerns.

Max is standing at the entrance of the store with a bag stuffed full. She hadn't thought she was in the dressing room alone long enough for him to shop for that much lingerie. He grins and says, "Good girl. Now let's go get that ring."

She slips her arm through his and smiles up at him. "Yes, Daddy, sir."

"Got your rocks off well enough?" He darts his eyes downward to meet hers as they stroll along.

"Yes. I'd have taken more. And I wanted your cock."

"You'll have more, later, at home, if you're up for it. You're supposed to be resting."

She scoffs. "You call what you just did to me resting?" She laughs. "That's a funny definition of resting. And, yes, I will be up for 'it' later." She rests her head on his bicep for a second.

"How are you feeling?"

"Sore. Ass beat."

He snickers. "From yesterday or from me?"

"Both." She keeps her tone steady, even as the gasp lives in her throat. "I liked it, in case you were wondering."

"Good, I did, too."

Back in the jewelry store, the same man watches them saunter in, still arm in arm.

"Attitude adjustment is complete," Max says in a boast. As they stop at the counter, he reaches behind her and slips his fingers under her waistband, then tugs the panties up, securing her wedgie even more firmly. He gives it another rough tug.

Mallory flinches in response, then blushes, which is a rare thing. Max smiles at her.

The clerk looks aghast. "Okay," he says as if he has no idea what else to say.

Mallory leans over the counter, and Max gives her butt a big swat. She gasps loudly and hollers as the spank boosts her forward. She barely catches herself from falling face-first onto the counter as her hands smack the glass. Damn. That one hurt badly.

"Ow! Hey, what was that for? We've already figured things out," she blurts as she pouts. She reaches back and rubs her bottom.

"It's a reminder." Max meets her gaze with a twinkle in his eyes, then shifts his eyes to the man.

"I don't need reminders. I have all the reminders I need from my red, painful ass."

The man behind the counter scoffs and fidgets with the calculator on the counter before him. "Uh. What can you get out for you two to look at?" he asks in an awkward rush. "And you want to see closer? I'll get them all out." He speaks way too fast, and Mallory bites her lip to try to keep from laughing. Poor awkward dude!

She points downward. "Can I see that one, this one, and the one closest to you, please?"

"Sure thing." He pulls them all out and spreads them across the glass.

Max comes in behind Mallory and hugs her from behind. She grimaces as he presses himself against her sore butt. "Must you?" she complains.

He chuckles in her ear. "I like that one. What do you think?"

"Yeah, I do, too. And this one. If Derek had already said 'yes', I could be texting him pictures right now."

"That defeats the purpose of your surprise proposal," Max points out.

"Yeah. I just want to get it right, you know?" She taps her index finger on her lips.

"Do you have a back room we could visit?" Max asks the man. "If we need it."

"Umm, for what?" he asks, seeming a bit nervous.

"In case I need to give her another attitude adjustment."

Wow. He is really laying it on thick. She can't keep her eyes from flaring wide.

The clerk smiles as the awkwardness shrouding his eyes gives way to lewd appreciation. "You'd spank her here?"

Max exclaims, "Ah, yes. I would, if need be."

They are clearly in the company of another kinkster.

Mallory's cheeks flush again, and she loves that Max is rubbing his discipline of her in her face in front of him.

"Yeah, right now I'm the only one here, so I could allow that. But I'd have to be back there to ensure things."

Max laughs. "So, you like this?" He looks skeptical.

"Yes," he says as he sheds even more of his awkwardness.

"I'll take this one," Mallory says quickly, trying to interrupt their connection, though she's not sure why, because she always likes watchers. But her ass couldn't take more hits.

"Care to see what I did to her?" Max asks, suggestion loaded into his tone.

"Seriously? Oh, I'd love to." He leans forward.

Max opens his phone and shows the man her spanked bottom. "Nice and red."

"Whoa," the man says in a low whisper, intrigue laden heavily in his words.

"I'll be posting them on her account."

"Account?" he asks with piqued interest.

"Yeah, she's a content creator. Getting pretty big. I sponsor her work."

Mallory smiles big. "Yeah. Check me out at Mallory's pleasure spot dot com. All one word."

"Oh, I will. I definitely will. Without question." The excitement of lust swells in his eyes as he looks from Max's phone to Mallory's face and back again.

It's so satisfying.

"She's getting famous," Max says with pride laced into his sentence.

"Oh, stop, not really," she coos as she fingers the ring. "Do you have a nice velvet box for this so I can present it to my boyfriend when I ask him to marry me?"

"You are getting famous. Seriously, you should check her out. She makes films, too."

His eyes pop. "Oh, now I'm really intrigued." Stars form in his hungry stare at Mallory. "Like porn?" he asks, shifting his eyes back and forth, as if he's not supposed to say the word, but loves to.

"Yes," she says proudly. "I'm a very sexually open person."

He seems floored, but interested. "Like, I can see you naked?"

She laughs. "Yes, that's generally how it works. And you just already saw my bare ass." She shrugs.

He scans her body as his professional decorum literally melts away. He repeats, "Yeah. 'Mallory's pleasure spot dot com'. I'd really like to see that spot."

"Oh, you can, and way more. Check me out." The idea of him jerking off to her is super hot.

He scoots around the counter in a flash. "Can I get a selfie with you in that case? I'll post it and tag you."

She smiles happily. "Yes, I'd love that. More fans, that's exactly what I want."

"I might just join," he says as if having to prove that he's more than ready.

"I'd love to have you be a part of my sexuality journey," she coos and raises her arms up for a hug. "I like hugs!"

He hugs her back, crushing her body firmly to his, crossing regular social norms in his close contact.

She senses the growth of his arousal just as she separates from him.

"You are truly amazing," he says with awe. "I can't wait."

"She is," Max says. "There's no one like her. She's totally a unique woman."

"So, we will take this ring with a nice velvet presentation box, please," she says, bringing things to a head.

"You have my card already," Max states with a nod.

"Yes, I'll get everything in order."

Mallory turns her attention to Max. "You know, you really should send another donation to the dog shelter and the local food shelf."

"Oh?" Max says as he gazes down at her affectionately.

"Yeah," she says, wrapping her arms around Max's middle. "A donation to match the cost of the ring...times ten." She laughs with exuberance.

"Oh, you think so?" He smiles down at her, matching her energy.

"Yes," she coos as she goes up on her tiptoes to give him a kiss on the lips.

"You have me wrapped around your little finger," he says with pride.

"And other parts," she says suggestively. "What can I say? I'm a slut for the greater good."

"You get me donating way more than I ever did before," he says, his shoulders relaxing. "And I'm way happier than I've ever been in my life."

"I'm your golden glove," she says as she pops her pelvis in a single gyration.

"Indeed, I love to be in your glove." He cracks up jovially as he sways her. "You have dramatically improved my life by more than I imagined possible. I'm so happy."

"As am I," she says, giving her best happy face.

"Here's your ring. All the paperwork, box, and receipt." The salesclerk holds up the credit card. "And card."

"Thank you, my man. And don't forget to subscribe, she's got the best content out there!"

"I will," he says. "I can't wait to check it out, honestly."

They wave to him as they head out into the main mall.

"That was a shopping trip for the books," he says.

"It was a wild ride!"

"You should write the story of it to go along with the pictures," he suggests.

"You know, that's a really good idea."

"I didn't go too far, did I?" he asks with a genuineness.

"No. But you rode the edge."

He nods. "Thought so. Good to know."

The walk out into the sunshine, a wedding ring richer.

Chapter 17

"You've really come a long way," Mallory says as they enter the house.

"How so?"

"Your generation is more rooted in the people pleasers' realm, and you just shed that."

"I'm entering my pleasing you, realm." He ushers her into the kitchen.

"You've been into pleasing me for a long while. I mean, how you were with the salesclerk. Like you didn't seem to care if he was judging us. Your generation was the one that forced behaviors, like hugging, even when someone was uncomfortable. Just to be polite."

"True. It was kind of more about keeping up appearances than the other person back then. Things have certainly shifted. Consent has come a long way." He sets down the bag of lingerie and begins to pull it all out.

"You practically bought the store." She grins as she picks up a sheer red nightie.

"You can never have too much lingerie." He pulls out a handful of panties and begins to sort them.

"I think I might need more space. Especially with all my things coming from the house." She's dutifully worn the wedgie all this time, but now plucks it out from being crammed up her butt cheeks. "Whew, I needed that out."

He chuckles with appreciation. "Nice." He gives her a knowing look. "No worries on that. I will renovate to make room for all your lingerie. Happily so! And a sex toy cabinet for the bedroom closet, too." He chuckles once more. "A man can only be so lucky to need to make more room for lingerie for his lover."

"True." She wants to sit, but her flesh is screaming at her just standing still. "I'm brainstorming ideas for the proposal. But I still believe that Derek isn't quite ready. He's close, but he's still working on something, I can tell. I wish he'd share more with me."

"Well, it's likely about you."

She nods. "Yeah. I'm guessing it is. But then he should be talking to me about it."

"But if he's not at peace with it, it's not time to discuss it with you yet."

She sighs and drops the wad of panties in her hands. "I'm trying to give him space. But I'm so ready. I want to ask him. He's asked me already, for fuck's sake. And now I have a ring."

"Yeah. I see a shift in him, too. I think he's making progress. He's also accepting more help from me, like the flight. He didn't protest when I bought it, and I sent money with him, too."

"Ah, you did. Okay." She slowly nods. "That's a good sign."

"Have a seat," he says, patting the stool beside him, a devilish twinkle in his eyes.

She huffs up her chest, then releases a puff of air. "I'll stand, thank you very much."

He looks tickled.

She curves her shoulders as she's filled with humiliation. This kink seems to be ballooning for her, and she's not intending to suppress it one bit. "So, about the event. I've reached out to most of the talent and the vendors, and about three-fourths are confirmed. We should perhaps choose the venue. I'd like Derek to be back, but last time I talked to him, he wasn't sure when he'd return." She moves over to the cupboard and pulls out a mug. "Tea?" she asks.

"Sure."

She pulls out another mug and fills both with water. "I'm thinking we should tour them, right? Have you been to them?"

"No. Well, one I have. Yeah. I'll have my admin set up times for us to tour. Maybe in a few days, and perhaps Derek will be back by then."

"Sounds good."

THREE DAYS LATER, DEREK strolls into the house. He hadn't even texted that he was coming back.

She squeals and runs to him, falling into his embrace.

He looks bright and happy, complete with a huge grin. The way he always was before.

"You look good," she says.

"As do you," he replies, then kisses her.

"My car died," he says plainly with a shrug.

"What? Oh no. Seriously?"

"Yup. I left it on the side of the road."

"How did you get here then?" she asks with concern in her voice as she steps back.

"I called Max. He sent a car." He shrugs. "My car was old. I'm sure it needs another repair."

Normally, in the past, this would have sent the two of them into a panic because they never had savings for car repairs and would just have been forced to add it to another credit card. It had been so stressful. She had paid all the cards off now. Every last credit card was sitting at zero. It felt damn good. She had lots of credit history, and it was all good now because she'd paid off all of the debt with her own earnings.

There is such a wonderful, powerful feeling in being able to do such a thing. It erased their past struggles. It was like she overcame them in one fell swoop. The freedom is worth every bit of hard work she'd done. But she also knows that this is only possible because Max literally paid for everything else for her, and now Derek's subsistence.

"Okay. Now what?" she asks, crossing her arms. "We can afford a nicer car this time. Maybe it's time for a new car with a warranty." The words coming from her mouth are a delight.

"Max and I are going car shopping. He's going to just buy me a car." He smirks. "I never in my life thought I'd be so lucky."

She blinks. This is quite the change. Now he's flat-out accepting a whole paid-for car from Max?

"I know. I know," he says, shaking his head. "I'm moving into being okay with how things are." He gives her a little smile. "And I'm grateful for it."

This sends a zing of hope through her. Maybe it's getting closer to the time when she could propose to him. Butterflies burst in her gut. This is the most exciting news ever!

"I'm very happy about that. And I texted you about the venues. We've visited two in the last few days. Would you like to come to the one tomorrow with us?"

He nods. "Yeah, for sure. Hey, right now I need a shower. Max has a break in meetings, so we are going to go car shopping in fifteen."

"I'm so proud of you," she coos. "You and Max. You're getting to such a good place together."

"We are. And I honestly didn't see it coming." He doesn't look one bit upset.

He makes his way down the hallway.

She has a date with Jax in an hour. She's regretting that she downplayed her intentions with him to Derek, so she hurries after him.

"Derek, can I talk to you while you shower? I have something I need to share with you."

"Sure," he states with a shrug like he's all good with it, no big deal. He strips his clothes off with a grin. "If I had time, I'd love a quickie, but Max is ready in ten minutes now, so that's not quite enough time."

"We can do it later. Plenty of time for that now that you are back."

He turns on the water and sticks his hand into the stream. His ass has red streaks across it.

"I told you about Jax, the man who owns the studio I just did the filming at. We have a date today."

"Okay." He gives her a grin, then steps into the water stream. "Have fun," he says through the shower door.

"He's coming here. So, you can probably meet him at some point if you two are back from shopping in time." Thoughts of seeing Jax again thrill her. Texting him on overload the past few days has her ready to jump his bones, but he's still dragging his feet on the sex front. He still purports that he wants to "do this right" with her. She's used to just diving right in with fucking, not this slow dance. His gallant approach is charming, but she simply desires to get down to fuck. The slow approach is painful!

"I am intrigued by the idea of working with him, too. So, he's serious about that?" Derek asks in a muffled voice as he scrubs his face with his hands.

She leans against the bathroom counter and watches him wash. "Yeah. He is. His place is incredible, Derek. I'm not kidding. It's so professional and elaborate. Like he has a salon in his house and a whole complement of staff. I've never imagined anything like the setup he has. It's a dream studio. But it's also his house, which is truly a mansion, bigger than our house. Bigger than this house, I mean." It still feels foreign to call it that. But she's getting more and more used to it.

"I'm so happy for Max setting up the moving crew. I had imagined I'd be there for the next month, packing up our stuff by myself." He steps out of the shower and rubs the fluffy towel all over his body, very gingerly over his ass.

"Aw, you'd have packed up my stuff, too?" Her heart melts.

"Well, of course. You have your commitments, and mine are just to help you, so I had assumed I'd be doing it for the two of us. Maria would have helped, and Sam, if he'd have been able."

"How is Sam doing?" she asks quickly, feeling bad she hadn't asked until now.

"He's really good, Mal. Like really good. He's getting around well. Maria is treating him like a king. He's set to make a full recovery." He looks pleased. "He'll live to fuck again," he says jovially. "I gave him enough head and lap dances to choke a letch, so I'm sure that helped." He laughs. "I really like that I just said that." He cracks up.

"So, who gave you all the marks?" She refrains from revealing her worries to him, even though his skin looks bad. If he's reaching a stable point, she's not going to rip the rug from beneath him.

"Who didn't? Maria, Faye, and Sam." He grins wickedly as he turns to show her his full monty.

"Oh, I've seen. And Sam did, too?" She wonders when he will have his fill of this act, but since he seems so well adjusted and happy, she's not too concerned.

"Yeah, he was only too happy to do it. It wasn't an effort for him at all. I made it convenient for him." He walks out of the bathroom and heads to the walk-in closet. He chooses a pair of athletic pants and a T-shirt. "Jeans are too rough at the moment."

"I can imagine." Her own skin has been healing well.

"I liked your shopping dressing room story." He smooths his shirt down his taut belly. "Sounded really hot."

"It was." She's itching to spill the beans about how it was while ring shopping, but that little nugget of info needs to stay under wraps until she pops the question. She's bursting to say but restrains herself.

"Well, I'm going to check on Max. If he's not ready yet, let's fuck. I'm horny, and we haven't been together for days." He shoots her a brilliant grin.

"I'm in." She follows him out of the bedroom and down the hall toward Max's office.

Max pops out of his office just as they approach. "Ah, you are ready, my boy. Excellent. I'm good to go right now. I have a window of time, so let's get on the road." He turns to Mallory. "Care to join us?"

"No. Remember, I have a date with Jax." She clasps her hands as she gazes back at Max. Her love for him has grown. He had taken the news of her dating Jax much better than she'd expected, which meant he's confident in their relationship. That was a total turn on for her and made her feel loved. He knows he's her main Dom and Jax is a date, who happens to also be a dominant. And Derek had simply texted, "okay".

"Ah, yes. Well, have fun. We may be gone for a while, if no fires emerge that I need to extinguish, that is." He presses his hand on Derek's upper back. "Let's get on move on when the gettings good."

They leave, and Mallory bolts for her closet to slip into the sexy dress she picked out to wear on her date. Even though they aren't going out, it's going to be an incredible date, and she's dressing up for it. He's bringing an entire meal, some wine, and some surprises. She hopes the surprises are sex paraphernalia. But she also knows they may not have sex yet. She's resigned to that and is okay with it. She doesn't have much choice if he's not ready. If need be, they will wait. It's highly unlikely that they will never have sex.

She tugs the dress over her breasts for optimal cleavage exposure. She intends to tempt him into dipping his cock into her one way or another, if she has anything to say about it. It can be a game of seduction if that's what he wants. She's not too proud to beg for cock while he's treating her like a queen.

She slips into her heels and walks into the kitchen. Her mind drifts to Jax quite easily, and she smiles. She puts on some music and then dances around the living room. The excitement of a new connection has her on cloud nine. Jax isn't just any man; he's her ideal man. If it weren't for her career, she'd never have met him.

He should be arriving any minute. She jots down a few notes in her notebook about the event. Taking a seat at the island, she adds more items to Derek's to-do list. She glances at her phone, noticing she missed a text where Jax said he's running late.

SHE PEERS AT JAX ACROSS the table, their plates emptied, wine glasses drained, and she's feeling cozy, rosy, and warm.

"That was delicious. Incredible. You were right. They really know Italian food." She sighs. "I'm very full. Too full to fuck."

He laughs. "Is that a thing?" he asks with a growing chuckle. "The owner is an Italian chef. Grew up in Italy and came here as a teen. I know him personally. Best damn chef I've ever encountered, and I've traveled a lot."

"Nah. I could still fuck," she gives him a seductive grin. "I just wanted to bring up fucking."

"You don't need a reason," he assures.

"I know."

"I love your dress. Very sexy on you."

"Thanks." She raises an eyebrow. "Again. I'll take every compliment."

"Praise kink, too?"

She nods. "For sure."

"We are a match there because I do like to praise, where it's deemed worthy." He leans forward on his forearms, the candle glow highlighting his eyes. "This is quite the house. Tell me more about your situation. I don't want to step on your Dom's toes."

"You aren't. He's totally fine with me being poly." She raises both hands. "And doing films. With anyone."

"Okay. And Derek?"

"Yeah, him, too. He's poly, too. Max was poly, but mainly within our club, but he's decided he no longer wishes to be with anyone but me."

"Ah, okay. Interesting." He nods with a knowing growing on his face. "I'm poly, as you know, and have been for a long time."

"Yes," she says. "Puts us all on a different standard, doesn't it? We have to keep earning the rights to be together. No being lame or shitty."

"That's the truth. There's no getting lazy, or your partner just moves on." He knits his fingers behind his head and leans back. "It's the way it should be. No obligation, only genuine true intentions and real choosing."

"Agree. My parents are great together, but they choose monogamy mutually; many of my friends' parents were basically stuck together, forced into monogamy, and very unhappy. I never wanted to end up like that. Being trapped is not sexy or fun, and it sounds miserable. So, when Derek and I met, he was in the same situation. Our goals were the same. His parents were miserable in monogamy, still are; they are still married and making each other unhappy every day."

"Sounds like the worst plan on the planet."

"Yeah." She shrugs. "I mean, it does work for my parents and my sister. But not everyone is that lucky. Could my parents be happier if they turned poly, or at least were swingers? Probably. But they won't. They're trapped in the limiting cycle of religion." She grimaces. "Notice I said 'religion', not faith."

"Yup. I got you."

"I've read anthropologists and other experts who believe monogamy is not our natural state."

"I have read that, too. It's interesting how society has shifted from that."

"Yeah, and many condemn those who live how they want."

"Yep. But we just ignore them, right?" He snickers. "So, tell me more about this event. I'd love to be a part of it. I mentioned it to a few of my people, and they are interested as well. And I was also wondering if I can throw some money at it as a sponsor? I'm always looking for more advertising opportunities."

"Yes, absolutely. I'll mark you down. Whatever amount you want to do, or whatever you want to do, I'm good with. Max has money, but I'd never turn down more. We can make it even better. Plus," she says, grinning, "now I'll feel like I did some fundraising and earned some money for it."

"I always aim to make you feel accomplished." He stands up. "I'll clean up. It won't take long."

"Oh, I'll help." He shakes his head. "Nah. I'm pampering you. Fill up that glass and go sit by the fire. I'll join you soon."

She does as she's told. Watching him move about the kitchen is sexy. He's a big and tall man with large hands. Hands she'd love all over her body, if she can entice him to do so.

From the living room, she hears sounds from the kitchen. It doesn't take long, and he appears with his own full wine glass.

He takes a seat next to her. Pats her hand and looks into her eyes. "We need to have that talk."

She nods. "I'm game." It means they are closer to sex, so she's way in.

"I am very big on enthusiastic consent. I'm going to fire questions at you and answer honestly, please. Be brutally honest. You can say 'I don't know', or maybe. I'll file away your answers. I also like to re-do this exercise periodically because our sexuality changes over time."

She appreciates that he recognizes this. "Yeah, mine does change, based on how I'm feeling and what I've been exposed to. And how much energy I have for the day."

"Same. But I have my hard no's, as everyone does. I know a few of yours since we just talked on the filing day, and from your consent form, so I don't need to re-ask those. Unless they've changed?"

She nods. "I understand. And no, they haven't changed."

"Do you like to be tied up?"

"I haven't done much yet, but I'd try more of it."

"Suspension?" He raises an eyebrow at her. "I'm experienced at it. And I love to fuck a woman in suspension."

"I like the power exchange and the vulnerability of it. The idea of being used is always hot to me, but only in the scene itself. And only with the right partner who has shown me I'm a priority. So, it's only roleplay, not real."

He nods. "Yup. Of course. And I'd never broach that act with you until we are very well established. I just like to know your interests. So, I can dream of the future."

"That's fair. And sexy."

"How far would you go with impact play?"

"Hands, of course. I've done the paddles, a crop, a flogger, and a belt. But nothing severe. I like a little pain, especially in domination, but if it's too severe, I'm turned off instantly." Images of Derek across Max's lap and his cries flood her brain. "I'm not a pain slut beyond a bit of red skin. Just barely. So, definitely pretty minor." She presses her lips together as she folds her feet under her. "No blood. No broken skin. No torture."

"Noted. I have one woman I date who goes pretty far with that. She's in LA and I only see her about once a year. I get my fill of it with her, so I'm good for a long while. She's developed a strong tolerance, so it takes a lot with her." He eyes her up intently. "I don't need much of that and can do without it..." He pauses. "Does knowing I do some of that turn you off to me? Be honest."

She shakes her head. "No. I'm confident in what I like. You do you and I do me."

"Good. If it did turn you off, I could refrain from telling you."

She startles and does a double take. "Oh, I don't need details."

"Noted."

"So, I'm guessing no knife play, no to weapons?"

"Right. I'd not be into that kind of stuff. But definitely yest to sex toys, sex furniture, paraphernalia." She watches his face as he processes her response.

"Again, I have done the harsher things, but I don't need them to get off. I have my outlets for that anyhow if I crave it." He shrugs. "I don't really feel like I need it, either."

"Okay," she says simply, and honestly, is alright with it.

"Breath play or choking?"

"Nope. I am claustrophobic, so you will kill my high if you do that to me..." She pauses. "But I'm okay with a little."

"That one gets me nervous, honestly. I don't want to cause brain damage accidentally, so while the domination turns me on, I don't generally go beyond a hand wrapped around with light pressure. Is that still too far for you?"

She shakes her head. "No, that's okay. I do like to be dominated."

"Both Derek and Max dominate you? Correct?"

"Yes. And sometimes I've dominated Derek, but it's only been for like a scene or something. I used to dominate Derek a lot more before we joined the club. I don't really need it; I mostly did it to fulfill his needs. Like I'm malleable that way, but I don't have the drive to be dominant. I can just play one."

"Yeah, a bit of a switch, but like your main persona is a sub?"

"Right. Exactly. Kind of like sometimes I like to eat fish, but I'd never eat fish every week."

"Kink compared to fish." He cracks up. He laughs with his whole body as he sways.

She joins him in laughter. "I guess so!"

As he calms, he faces her. "Humiliation?"

"A little bit, yes. Especially with a spanking. Recently, Max dommed me in public and semipublic, with a lot of humiliation and a wedgie. A salesclerk knew about it all."

"And?"

She blushes. "It did turn me on."

He nods with an intrigued look. "Mouth fucking?"

"A little. But I'm not a glutton with it being severe. You saw me at the filming."

"Yeah. I did. But, what about like head hanging off the edge of a bed, mouth fucking?"

"I've done a little of that with Derek. Again, the domination of it gets me going." She flushes. "But that is not a top kink, so I fade quickly. It has to be short if I do it or I'm out of the mood for sex entirely."

He nods. "That's a caution or no-go area for me then. Too close to your edge. And hitting beyond spanking?"

"I'm okay with titty spanking. But mainly I'm only wanting ass, tits, and pussy spanks."

"Noted. Public sex?"

"Oh, I'm very exhibitionistic. Which is why I love the content creation and filming."

"Stockade or other restraint structure?"

"Yes. Hey, come with me. I want to show you our studio."

"Oh, I'd love to see it." He looks eager.

She rises and leads him down the long hall. She likes that he's behind her, watching her walk.

Once inside the studio, he gazes around. "Whoa. This room is turning me on. Very, very nice. I could really get into this space. You have a bit of everything going on here."

"Yup. Max basically bought the catalog. And, hey, you can book some time in here to film during the event. We are hoping to provide the space for any out-of-towners to be able to do short filming collabs since we will all be here."

"Yeah, I'd like to do that, possibly. Maybe you can be with one of my people." He scans the room again. "I'd have to convince my crew to travel, which we have done on location before. We once did a shoot in Hawaii. Mostly because I just wanted to travel there and film, so it was to satisfy my whims more than anything else."

"I'd love to go, I've never been."

"Hawaii? I'll add it to the list." He crosses his arms across his chest. "You'd travel with me? I'd really love that. I don't have a partner who can do that easily. Most have kids or spouses who don't want that."

"Oh, I would love to. Max and Derek wouldn't care. If anything, they'd be jealous, but they'd be okay with it." However, she knows Max would want to travel with her, but they haven't yet.

"That's fantastic to know. And excites me."

She slides her fingers down his bicep. "You could take more advantage of this room right now, with me." She gives me strong fuck-me eyes.

"Whew! That look. We'd better go back to the living room before I lose it." He leaves the room quickly.

What? Seriously? She must be losing her touch. She follows his leave and can't even catch up with him, for how quickly he strides down the hallway with his long legs.

She's feeling sheepish. She overstepped when perhaps she should have let him take the lead.

He is already seated on the couch when she arrives in the living room.

"Now don't give me that face. I'm not done asking you things." He is stern and stoic.

"Okay." Her hopes are dashed, but she gets how serious he is about all this, so she tries hard not to be offended.

"Safe words." He raises both hands. "I like the stoplight method. Because it gives me a warning and helps me gauge how you are feeling. Do you prefer a safe word or stating a color, like green, yellow, or red?"

"I'm good with saying the colors."

"Okay. Hand signals?"

"Yeah, I do the single hand clap."

"Ball gag?"

"No."

"Harness?"

"Yes."

"Sex swing?"

"Yes. You saw one in the studio."

He nods. "Toys?"

"Big yes! All, but not a fan of anal toys."

"Restrained to a bed or other structure? Handcuffs?"

"Yes, and yes."

"Blow job."

She scoffs. "Of course."

"Rough sex?"

"Somewhat yes. But again, not too far."

"Any positions off limits?"

"No."

"Lap sitting?"

"Yes."

He motions. "Come on over. I'd love to have you on my lap."

She hurries over and settles in. Looking deep into his eyes, she likes what she sees.

He wraps her up, and she nestles in.

"Making out?" he asks with hope.

"For sure."

"Good."

She slides her hands along his chest and biceps, feeling his body up close for the first time.

"Shit," he says with a big grin. "I'm going to lose this holding out game, aren't I?"

"Maybe." She gives him a seductive look while pressing her lower body flush with his as she places her hands on his shoulders. "All this talk has me hotter than a feckless nun."

He laughs. "Feckless, huh? You say some crazy shit, mama."

"I do. Get used to it." She threads her hands along his scalp as she settles in close for a kiss.

His erection is a full rod against her. He peers into her eyes. "I don't need to tell you, you turn me on immensely."

She dives into a kiss with him aggressively, grinding herself against his firm cock.

"Hot damn, I'm a goner." He runs his hands up her back. "You feel incredible. I've been dreaming of this."

"Same," she coos. Getting him this far, she's not holding back. "I want your big fat cock in me, riding my G spot, finding my depths, touching me where no man ever has. I'm guessing that's your skill."

He chuckles lightly. "It is. One of them." His grin is telling.

She rolls her pelvis against his hardness relentlessly. She can feel it; he's telling the truth.

"Fuck you're good at that, baby doll." His hands slide all over her back, then cup her ass firmly. He squeezes her.

She squeals.

"Oh, I like that." He dives into a deep kiss, riding his tongue along hers with an appreciative groan. He breaks their kiss. "I'm caving like a wall of water," he whispers in her ear.

"I like that." She rubs her cleavage on his goatee.

"Mmm, mm, mmph."

"We could just, you know, get off together," she coos as she rubs herself on him. "It would be so easy."

He chuckles deeply. "You are persistent, aren't you? But I like that. A woman who knows what she wants and goes after it. Shows your strength and determination." His voice is full of pride, not chastising.

This boosts her will. She wants him.

"And I want you inside me. Your big, fat, swollen rod of a cock. Touch me where no one else can, Jax. Please. I want you." Her begging tone is in full force, and she's not dampening it one bit.

"I'll hold you down, giving you orgasms until you beg me to stop and fuck you. Then I'll slide in and ride you hard, so you come on my cock like a good fuck hungry whore. That's how I'll touch you that deep."

"I love it. Tell me more."

He nuzzles into her neck for a kiss, then pulls back, whispering into her flesh, "I'll drop to between your legs, licking and sucking like you're my very breath. Tugging on your sweet, peaked nipples as I suck your clit. Not letting up. Not stopping until you're screaming and squeezing my head between your thighs, but I won't move. I'm not done. I want your body rocking as you can barely breathe, gasping, vying for breath. I'll spank your clit. Then I'll fuck your tits and cum on them. Paint you with my cum. Lick it off. Then I'll still be hard, so I'll bend you over this couch and fuck you doggy until you can barely stand. I'll rail you, missionary, looking into your eyes, commanding you to come on my will. What I wanna do to you, mmm, fuck, dominate you, claim you as mine. Strip you of all control and play you like the beautiful sex instrument you are. And submit to me, admitting you're my whore as I make your cunt ripple with contractions that make you forget your own damn name. You'll be a blubbering mess of spent orgasms, so much so that you'll never forget my name. It will remain on the tip of your mind every time you fuck someone else." He pauses for a split second. "Bliss isn't even the right word; there isn't one. I'll drive you to heights no one has. Work your pussy hard as I fuck you into submission. You'll beg me to enter you. I'll feel the want electrified in your veins, your eyes tell me it all, babe. This is only the beginning. Let's fuck."

Her lust rages; his dirty story of pleasure has her salivating, huffing in desire, ready to burst into wild abandon, but held in the power of his asserted domination. She'll snap when he directs it, until then she lives in the fire of her own enraged passion, a well waiting to be tapped by a man who knows how to handle a pure sexual fury like hers.

He kisses her, manhandling her roughly as if he's giving in to his desires, despite his wanting to wait for their relationship to mature.

It's not happening.

They will fuck.

He pulls down her dress to reveal her breasts and devours each nipple, gruffly feeding on her. He moves his hips beneath her, and she jostles, but his hold on her back has her secured on his lap.

His sounds of slurping on her breasts fill her ears, and she floats in the lull of his suckling. His mouthing of her nipples sends poking jolts through her chest, and she slightly cringes. His suction is strong, and a whimper sits on the edge of her throat, readying to spill.

He stands up, while still holding her, and pulls her legs around his middle. She clamps her legs tight around him, and his hands firmly hold beneath her thighs.

They kiss again. She bounces slightly in his arms. Hungry kissing sounds and their impatient grunts fill the room, egging her on for more.

He's aggressive in his groping, and it turns her on. It means he wants her, and that's a wildly wicked turn on.

"Yes," she says, finally finding her voice. "I want all of that. All of you in and on me. Take me like you want, Jax. Don't hold back. Fill me. Ride me. Fuck me like I'm yours."

He growls and spins them as a unit, then charges the wall like a bull, slamming her back against it, sandwiching her body between him and the wall. Her head bounces backward, hitting with a little smack, and she gasps. He sets her down and hefts one of her legs over his shoulder before diving face-first at her pussy.

He inhales her womanly scent in a loud sniff, his nose inches from her lower lips. Groaning in satisfaction, he goes at her ravenously, eating up her loose flesh, pressing her clit with his tongue, soaking her slit with his spit. He licks her over and over again, then smashes his open mouth on her clit with such a force that she throws her head back against the wall, her mouth open upward as she moans. She clenches his scalp as he works her over.

He moves back, his breath on her flesh. "You're coming for me like a good, horny slut. I'm not stopping until you're folded in half, throbbing with so much pleasure you're dizzy and cum drunk."

He continues to eat her out as her arousal skyrockets. When he focuses on her clit, she launches. Gasping and whimpering, struggling to grip his head, she gives in to the sensations and orgasms, her body dancing through the ecstasy.

He doesn't stop, true to his word. She's so sensitive she screams, bats at his head, squirming to get away, but he keeps going. She easily erupts into another rise and peak. He pulls her to the ground and goes at her pussy again.

She arches her back, her tits rising up.

He's fucking relentless.

He grasps at her tits and plays with them while he sucks.

She shifts her hips in tune with the waves of pleasure wafting through her body. The edge of her climax threatening to toss her off the cliff. They kiss. His groans melt into her mouth as she adds hers, too. He goes after her clit again, rubbing with his fingers. Their pleasure in each other is a symphony of the sweetest raging, riding the undulations of delicious edging until a flood seeps from her as she comes with great force. He goes at her even harder with his finger fucking, her wetness squelching. She comes again violently, her sounds enhancing her ecstasy, magnifying her passion as he welcomes her into another rise to the edge.

He abruptly stands up, snatches her from the ground, and throws her over his shoulder, caveman style. He tosses her onto the couch, her head and limbs flopping. Gripping her hips, he spins her and shoves her head into the crack of the couch.

"Head down, ass up," he commands.

He knocks his cock against her clit several times, then lines up to penetrate her. He slides in with ease and immediately thrusts into her like he's trying to touch her cervix. He damn near reaches it.

She cries out at the size of him inside her, but her body accepts him better as she relaxes. His fingertips press into her flesh as he pounds, and she's pinned, desperate and wanting more of him even though he's already in her depths.

"Yes, fuck me so deep," she whispers, barely getting the words out.

He grunts and swivels her whole body away from the couch, so she's hunched forward. With nothing to grab onto, she flounders, arms shaking haplessly in the air. He grips a fistful of hair for control, her arms flopping as he rams himself into her. He's brutal, and it sends her searing toward another peak.

Jax tugs on her mane, entwined in his hands, and her face is forced further upright. She closes her eyes as he roughly humps her backside but pops them open when she hears a gasp come from across the room.

Max and Derek are standing motionless in the living room, side by side. They both look shocked. No one speaks, but Jax stops hammering himself into her. They've been exposed, on display in mid fuck.

"Wow," Max says in a low voice, amazement full in his words.

"I need a spanking," Derek blurts in a loud, firm voice.

"Alright, let's go," Max says, authoritatively taking his hand.

Jax's cock is still deep inside her, and he begins sliding in and out of her again, but very slowly, as the men walk out, but then he stops altogether. "So, your boyfriend is spanking your boyfriend?" The surprise in his voice is comical, especially given that his cock is still deep inside her.

She laughs in a burst of sound. The absurdness of what just happened fills her up. "Yeah. That happens. Frequently."

"Then they fuck?" Jax asks with intrigue as he slowly fucks her. "I know, I'm being nosy."

"No, they are asexual Dom/sub partners."

"Shit. Seriously?" Jax asks aghast, stopping his movements.

"Yeah, sometimes he and I fuck after the spanking, though. Max is straight." Her chin is jutting out as they converse. They are frozen in the middle of a fucking stance, like a conjoined statue, and it's honestly funny to her. She smiles, a laugh almost percolating out.

"I know it's a thing, but I never actually met anyone who did the no sex thing like that."

"Yeah, it's wild. I'm still not used to it." She wonders if they found a car and if that's why Derek needed the discipline, or if it's because they walked in on her and Jax. Both of them have seen her fucking enough people for her to think that's not the reason.

"You're wild. My wild bitch in heat," he retorts quickly with great satisfaction dripping from his voice as he retightens his grip on her hair. His shock has worn off, and he's ready to finish the fuck.

He yanks on her strands, and she yelps. Grunting in a deep snarl, he slams his body against her, making her ass bobble from his mighty pelvic blows. "I'd want the sex after. I'd fuck you to within an inch of your life, then hold you until you pushed me away."

She agrees and loves his rendition of it, but can't seem to muster the strength to respond. She hears the very faint sounds of the spanking happening from across the house, or she thinks she does. Whatever. It doesn't matter. The thoughts ramp up her arousal, and she moans loudly, her whimpers escalating.

Jax responds with an aggressive clit rub, and she launches into an intense orgasm; the contractions rocking through her pelvic region are so good, so strong, so intense, she shudders. Her muscles clench on him inside her on repeat. She loses count of how many times in her blissful reverie.

He growls, grunts, and grips her hips with both hands before driving himself into her so fast and hard she falls forward. He doesn't stop.

Her hands hit carpet, and he lifts her back end up slightly, so her feet leave the ground as he obliterates her with powerful thrusts.

She cries out as another orgasm ripples through her.

Damn! She gasps and sputters.

He yells out his approach to climaxing as he shouts, "Gonna."

"Yes, please do," she slurs sleepily.

He pulls out of her and squirts his jizz on her left butt cheek. Then he smacks his hand down on the cum. "Nailed ya."

"Wow," she whispers, crumpling to the floor as he releases her. She lies in a slump, her ass still the highest part of her body. "Mmmm. Shit. That was wild, really hot."

"Whew!" he shouts loudly. "Fucking excellent! Yeah! Fuck yeah!"

She pulls herself up slowly, a giant grin on her face.

They both plop on the couch, cheeks flustered, sweaty, and her hair askew.

"Always a sign of a good fuck when ya end up this like this." He grins back at her. "You got me good. I couldn't resist you."

"That was the plan. You cooperated."

"Woe is the man who refuses a woman cock when she tries that hard." He rubs her hip. "I've got my plans, but yours won. Yours will always be the most important."

She beams a smile even brighter. "I like to win."

He chuckles as he pulls her close to snuggle. "That's how I like it."

Chapter 18

Mallory and Jax are seated at the island in the kitchen when Max and Derek reappear. Both of them look refreshed and satisfied.

"Hi," Mallory says. "Derek, you need anything?"

He shakes his head. "No, I'm good. Got it all covered."

She wonders what that means, but in light of Jax being there, she lets it go. "Max, Derek, meet Jax. Jax, meet my boyfriends Max and Derek."

"Hello, it's nice to finally meet you both," Jax says. His friendly expression is genuine and pleasant.

"Likewise. It's great to meet you," Max asserts with a kind look.

"Hello, Jax. Great to meet you." Derek chuckles. "We've heard about you, but that was one hell of a meeting."

Everyone laughs heartily.

"No shit, you're not kidding. That was crazy." Mallory examines Derek with narrowed eyes. "You sure you're good?"

"I'm good. And Max bought me a BMW. Felt like I needed to do a bit more to earn it."

"Ah, I see," Mallory states. "What happens if he buys you a plane?"

Derek laughs exuberantly as he shoves his hands in his pockets. "I'm not sure I want to find out," he jokes.

Max smirks and laughs, too.

"Got him pretty good that time," Max says proudly.

"I asked for it," Derek agrees. He raises his hands with a cock of his head.

"Absolutely fascinating," Jax says with his hands folded on the island. "You three are quite the case study. For someone like me who studies sexuality for fun."

"Sounds like a great past time," Derek states.

"Oh, it is, especially owning a studio; my passion has become my work."

"Same," Mallory says proudly.

"True," says Jax. "We are similar creatures, aren't we?"

"Indeed, we are." She smiles at him before turning her attention to Derek. "So, tell me about this car. And I can't wait to see it. Did you drive it home?"

Derek glances at Max, then leans toward him. "We did. I mean, I did. It's a four-door, and it has more bells and whistles than I thought possible. It's incredible, and I'm incredibly grateful. Max flat-out bought it for me. No payments."

Mallory's jaw drops as she twists slightly in her chair. Everything is making sense now. Plus, this is without a doubt evidence that Derek is getting to a healthier place because he accepted this giant gift from Max. Well, with a spanking. "That's wonderful! I mean, think of it as a company car, being CEO and all."

Jax smirks with a tick of his head. "Nice."

She glances at them all in turn, then blinks. "Wait. We are all CEO's at this table. How insane is that?"

Max laughs. "Well, babe, you're right. We are. And we will do great things as our individual companies converge on projects."

"Jax is going to sign up for studio time. Have we figured out a schedule yet? He is the first one ready to sign up. Others have given a confirmation but have not signed up. Once we have that, Derek, I'll get all the email addresses to you to set that up."

"Perfect." He stands. "I need a beer. Anyone else?"

"Sure," Jax states, leaning back. "It's been a full day, but I'd love one."

"You don't have to drive back; you can have more than one and just sleep here. Max has an abundance of guest bedrooms." Mallory tilts her head as she intently stares at Max. "He shares."

"I do. You're welcome to stay. Any time." Max raises his hands, then drops them to his chest. "I suppose you two have eaten already? Maybe I'll make something for Derek and me."

"Yeah, Jax brought food. We ate a while ago. It was incredible."

Once Derek returns from the basement bar with a bin full of beer, he offers it to Jax. "Take your pick. Max keeps it stocked like a liquor store around here."

"Thanks," Jax picks an IPA and opens it immediately.

"Derek, what would you like to eat? We have leftover smoked chicken, pork chops, or I can make a grilled cheese or quesadilla."

"Oh, any of that sounds good. You are so good to me." He smiles at Max.

Mallory never thought she'd see this day, but her two boyfriends are not only tolerating each other but also gelling in their own relationship.

Derek's expression is one of bliss, and Max looks happy as well. If this isn't the best setup for a marriage proposal, she doesn't know what is. They are all happy, Derek has a new car, and they saw her and Jax together without getting pissed. Perhaps tomorrow she can pop the question if the stars seem aligned. Then, in addition to planning the event, they can start planning a wedding. Her thoughts are she'd like to do their wedding at the house, so that way, only family who are really devoted to them will make the trip. This will be the way to trim off those not interested, those who don't care, and maybe all of Derek's family, if they are lucky enough. His obsessing about who will come and what they will find out about his current life might shove him backward in his progress.

Shit. She can't risk that. Maybe she should wait a month before asking him. Let him coast on the good waves of his current high progress toward stable, good, free-flowing mental health. Yeah. He needs time to sparkle and savor before she rocks the boat. But this is also kind of dumb. Would a proposal really upset his smooth sailing? She's not ready to find out.

She watches Derek as he talks with Jax about the awesome features of his new car, about the industry, and the possibility of Derek shooting a film for him. Life has drifted into such a good place that she hardly recognizes it. This also makes her nervous because when things seem perfect, that's when tragedy hits.

Yup. The proposal will have to wait. Now isn't the time.

Max busies himself making up a plate of food for himself and Derek while they all chat. It's something of an enigma to be surrounded by bliss, and to want only more of what she already has. This is new ground in life.

Max places the plate before Derek, then takes his own seat. The evening is full of good sounds, enjoyable conversations, and growing friendships.

"I THINK WE'RE GETTING closer," Mallory says over the breakfast table two mornings later. Her mind is focused, being that it's the beginning of the day. She taps her finger on the wood.

"I think so, too," Derek states before biting into his piece of toast. After he's done chewing, he says, "Five slots are left for the studio time. They filled up that quickly. We have a tentative map for the hall. And the banquet menu is being worked on."

"I can't believe we let Max talk us into a banquet," she says in a huff. "We have enough going on without adding that in."

"True, but this sets us all up for time to network and socialize, without fan interference. I think it's a good addition."

"Okay. I can buy into that, but I'm overwhelmed with what we are doing already."

He raises his right hand. "I'm the CEO here, let me worry about that. You brought me on to relieve some of the organizing stress off yourself; let me do my job."

She slumps her shoulders. "You're right. I'm trying to do everything when I've already handed stuff off to you." She rubs her forehead with her palms. "I need to stop feeling so damn responsible. I had the idea, but it doesn't mean I have to manage everything. I'm not used to this, but I promise, I'll get better at it."

"So, smile then," he says as he beams her a bright one.

Max walks into the kitchen. "That's not a good look, babe."

She sighs. "I'm not very good at letting things go. But I'm going to get better. I just need to focus on my brand, advertising, stirring up interest, and let Derek do his job." She grimaces. "I just suck at this." She throws her arms upward.

"Hey, you'll get there. Just remember, you're the star, not the CEO of the event. Derek and I are more than capable. What we can't do, I'll delegate to my staff. So, you have nothing to stress over."

She sighs and slumps in her chair. "Yeah, I'm a bad team player, I guess."

"I give great attitude adjustments!" Max declares.

She snickers. "I'm good."

"Just sayin'," Max blurts with a wink.

"How are the sales from your latest video release doing?" Derek asks as he gives Max a silly look.

She hushes her giggle. "Fantastic. It's the best one so far to date." She shakes her head. "I never dreamt this, and it's become a reality. I'm blown away." Tugging at her hair she decides it's okay to let her excitement build.

"That's great! And how are plans coming along for your filming during the event?" Max asks.

"Terrible. I haven't even started mapping it out." She shudders. "See, I'm way behind."

"If you step back from all the other stuff, I bet you will find you have the time." Derek taps his finger on the counter at a slow pace.

"You're busy, too, though. When do you go to Jax's to film?" She glances at her phone as a text from Jax comes through. "Talk about timing." She lifts her phone and reads the text.

Jax: Are you coming with Derek tomorrow?

"Tomorrow," she states with a purse of her lips.

"Tomorrow?" Max asks with a quick raise and drop of his eyebrows.

"Jax." She waves her phone at Derek. "He's asking if I'm coming along."

"You should," Derek says. "You can cheer me on from the sidelines. It'll be the first film I'm in where you aren't the star." He looks proud.

"Derek, just think. If you keep going, you could be a content creator, too. Make a name for yourself." She would love it if he did that. He'd be good at it. "But remember, once you're out there, you can't take it back."

He scoffs. "I'm already out there from your content. Too late."

She nods slowly. "That's true. You are. Switching careers will be quite limited for us both."

"Good thing we have a big cushion to land on," Derek says as he looks directly at Max.

"Hey, who are you calling a big cushion?" Max asks jokingly as he rubs his round belly.

"You." Derek grins at him with a raised eyebrow, while leaning back slightly. "A very wonderful and caring cushion."

"I guess that sounds better," Max says with mock anger paired with a bit of indignation. "Come bounce off this cushion any time you two want!"

"I only get one way, though, it seems unfair," Derek teases.

"Well, that's the lay of the land, my dear," Max chides. "Your bum is bouncing on me only one way." He flaps his hand in the air.

Derek pretends to pout but can't stop his smile.

"Well, I have lots of options for that!" Mallory muses.

"You do," Max agrees. "So, babe, are you going with Derek? It doesn't matter, I'll just pack my day if you two are both going to be gone."

"Yeah, maybe I will. It will be a good little break from all this chaos, plus, I'll get to spend some time with Jax."

"You mean getting a massive cock?" Derek twirls his fingers in the air, then wrinkles his nose. "I'm just jealous."

"What? You'll be getting good cock yourself." She leans forward on her arms. "You are with a male talent, right?"

"It's a threesome, a male and a female. Jeffers and Mallizza."

"Oh! I love them! I didn't know you were filming with them! Well, now I have to go, I must meet them!"

"Yup. I'm both taking and giving cock, and I get pussy, too. It's my ideal." He looks proud.

"We don't have time for this, but I'm glad it's happening. What time do we leave?"

"Tomorrow at 6 a.m., no later."

"Shit! That's early!"

"Just don't stay up too late fucking Max, and you'll be good," Derek teases. "I'm off the board. Saving myself for the filming."

"Yeah. It's best to rest," Mallory says. "I find it's nice for arousal, too. But I guess it's different being a woman with multiples and all." She shimmies her shoulders. "Ah, it's so good to be a woman."

"True. You women are lucky," Derek says. "But I don't do too bad."

"Yup. You are a bit of a never-ending tape. Which really is an ideal way to be for films. See, you are a natural fit."

"Yep." He stretches. "Well, I'm going to work out. Dinner at 6?"

Max nods, dropping his arms at his sides. "Yes, 6. I'm grilling pork chops and making funeral potatoes."

"Yes! I love that meal!" Derek rises. "Off to burn off some calories so I can eat a shit ton of your cheesy potatoes and meat."

Derek leaves, and Max grabs a seat at the table. He reaches across for Mallory's hand.

"So, are you going to do it?"

"I don't know. I think so?" She purses her lips. "Every time I think I'm going to do it, I melt down and come up with a reason why I should wait."

"Well, look at it this way. Whether you just keep dating, are engaged for fifteen years before you marry, or get married right away, it doesn't really change anything because you are still together."

"It will change everything. Plus, we'd have to invite all the family for the wedding, and hide our throuple-hood from Derek's side." She frowns, her eyebrows knitting together hard.

"Why would they have to know? We don't have to advertise it." He takes both of her hands in his. "I think this is adding to your stress level, and Derek has no clue. I say just ask him, and that way you can shed the stress hanging over your head. You will have your answer and can relax." He eyes her up intently. "Babe, he's going to say 'yes', you know it."

"But what if he doesn't? What if that's why he hasn't brought up that he proposed to me, because he's changed his mind about marrying me?" She can't stop her sad puppy dog eyes from drooping.

"Oh, that's what's adding stress, too, yup, I can see that. He wants to marry you, honey. I can guarantee it."

"Then why hasn't he brought it up? He's not said a peep, not even one acknowledgment of it, since he asked me." She drops her chin to her chest.

"He's been in turmoil."

"And now he's not, but he's still silent." She meets his gaze again.

"I understand, but I'm telling you, he loves you. He wants to be with you." Max rubs her fingers with his. "You need to trust this. Ask him. I think you should just do it. You'll feel much better."

"We don't need to be planning a wedding while we plan this event."

He gives her a stern look. "Now that's reaching for excuses. You can be engaged for as long as you want; there's literally zero rush to plan them both at once."

She shrugs and gives a weak attempt at a smile. "You're right. As usual."

He laughs and the corners of his eyes wrinkle. "Don't sound so sad about that!"

"You're right a lot. I admit it."

"Age is wisdom, unless you're a fool."

"Makes perfect sense." She pulls her hands back and lightly slaps them down.

"Why don't you suck my cock?" he blurts. "I need to get off before my big meeting." He rubs his chest. "I need a stress reliever. There's some wisdom for you." His eyes are lit with a tease.

"Sure, Daddy," she coos, slithering off the chair and crawling toward him.

"In the living room, I need to sit. My back is all knotted up. I need to nut down your throat."

She swivels and follows him, crawling behind him like a puppy dog. She loves moving under his direction.

"I wish I had the leash on you," he says, looking back at her affectionately.

"You don't need it. I'll follow you anywhere."

"Aw, you're the best pet." He drops into the easy chair and leans back, shoving his hands into his hair. "Fuck. I have so much going on. Tell me again why I haven't retired yet?"

"Lay back and let me take care of you." She unzips his pants and digs out his semi-hard cock.

"I am telling you. This day is brutal. You're a lifesaver, babe."

"Always." She puts her mouth on his cock head as she strokes his shaft.

He starts to harden immediately.

"What are you forgetting, darling?" His eyes are expectant.

"Oh," she glances down. "Yeah. Tits out."

"Tits out when you suck my cock. That's right." He closes his eyes, then reopens them. "Good girl."

She pulls her top off, then her bra, and her breasts bob as she moves.

"Nice. Fuck I love your tits, babe. Never tire of watching them."

She pounces on his cock and sucks hard while stroking. Then she fondles his balls aggressively, with a force that says she's making him come, and come hard. She goes after his orgasm like a fiend, sucking and rotating her tongue around him, and giving extra strokes of her tongue along his frenulum.

He groans and grips her head, helping her bob faster on his cock. He grunts, groans, then his back arches as he comes with a force inside her mouth.

She gags slightly but manages to also swallow it all, then falls off him with wild gasping. "Damn, that was a lot."

He laughs. "Yeah, I felt it. Whew! Fuck I needed that. That made a huge difference. Thank you, babe. You have multiple orgasms coming your way later." He shakes his head. "I feel like a million bucks."

"Early, it will have to be early. Because I need to go to bed at a decent time, apparently, since we are leaving at the butt crack of dawn in the morning for the shoot." She leans back on her arms, and his eyes fall and rest on her chest.

"I wish I had time to make you come. If you're horny, go get your toys. But I'll make sure you come on repeat later, until you're begging me to stop."

"I love that, you know I do." She watches him rise and stuff his deflated cock back into his pants.

"Off to the grind. And it's a painful grind today. But you helped make it better. Thank you."

"My pleasure."

She watches him walk down the hall back to his office. She has some shopping to do for the proposal date. Max is right. She should just do it. But first, she needs to ask Derek about the date. Then she needs the courage to follow through with her plan. This seems unlikely. But, then again, maybe Max's urging will help her get it done. She needs to simply do it and stop obsessing over everything. Their plan has always been to marry, and despite all the changes in their lives, she feels strongly that she still wants that.

The question remains, does Derek?

Chapter 19

Mallory wakes early to her alarm clock. She slept so damn good after Max gave her so many orgasms that she simply fell asleep, like falling into puffy, luxurious cloud. Max doesn't stir as she rises. The alarm didn't even wake him. He was so exhausted, but he was true to his word in his promise to pleasure her. She's not filming today, so there was no reason not to let him indulge her last night.

She showers and meets Derek in the kitchen. He looks rested and bright-eyed as she approaches.

"You look ready," she says, kissing him on the lips.

"I'm ready. Very ready. And horny as fuck."

"Perfect set up for filming."

"I am excited to see Jax's setup. His studio sounds awesome, but the rest of the house, too."

"Yeah, house. Use that term very loosely. It's like a damn complex. And he tells me I haven't even been to the back lot."

Derek raises both eyebrows. "He has a 'back lot'?"

"Apparently."

"How have we landed with such elite rich people?"

"I don't know. But I suck cock and give Max sexual favors for donating constantly. He lets me twist his arm. It's become a kinky game. I'm all for rich old men like him."

Derek nods with a chortle. "You do this with Max?" He looks at her aghast. "How did I not know this? You're a genius."

"I know," she says. "I got him to donate half a mill last week alone."

"Wow. Fucking for donations. Sucking for charity." His face brightens. "I just got the best idea ever! Why not make this a thing in your account? Fans ask you to do sexual things, and then they have to donate. If you reach a certain level of donation, you do the sex act live."

She squeals, "Derek! That's brilliant, and I love it!" She dances in place. "We must do this!"

"Yes! And I just got another idea. What if one of the donation categories is to sponsor a new content creator to fly to the event?"

"Whoa! That's utterly genius! I could have new content creators apply and then somehow choose one. That will be the hard part." Doubt fills her as she pinches the bridge of her nose.

"Not if you just draw one randomly, vetting them all first, mind you." He shifts his shoulders upward, then drops them.

"This will be a great promotion and help a newbie at the same time." She slides her arms down her sides. "Brilliant! And it will be fun as fuck. I like the being coerced kink, as you know. Like I owe them and I have to do it." She releases a big sigh. "Shit. This is turning me on."

"Me too. But we'd better get on the road. We can talk more about this in the car."

They dash out of the house. The whole drive, they dream up ideas for the new charity effort, and Mallory writes furiously in her notebook.

As they drive down Jax's driveway, Derek releases a low whistle. "You weren't kidding. Holy fucking shit!" He continues to drive slowly as he scans his head from side to side. "This place is incredible. How do people live like this?"

"Derek. We live like this."

"Not like this, we don't."

"Very close to what we do, though."

"Yeah."

Derek parks the vehicle next to several nice cars. "These people make money."

She shoots him a look laden with disbelief. "Derek, you are driving a BMW."

"Oh! You're right! But I don't make money." He laughs. "My Dom does."

"Yeah, so for all you know, there's lots of sugar daddies and mamas buying their candy asses cars." She clears her throat. "And Max hired you for six figures to be a CEO, so you need to change your worldview. You are exactly who you are talking about now!"

"I'm a candy ass? I think that's you. I'm certainly not a candy ass. But true, I am a CEO."

"What do you think a candy ass is?" she asks wildly.

Jax pops out the front door and strides toward them. "Hello, Mallory and Derek, welcome!"

He embraces Mallory and gives her a lingering kiss. Reaching for Derek's hand, he boldly nods.

"Hey," Derek says. "Amazing place you have here."

"Wait until you see inside," Mallory says as she leans into Jax's side.

Jax wraps her up in his arms. "Oh, it's so good to see you. And welcome, Derek."

"Same," she says, her heart fluttering with excitement. Seeing Jax brings on all her glittery feelings. She loves this part of a relationship and wishes she still had these stirrings with Derek and Max.

On occasion, she does, but there's also something to be said for comfort and feeling at home, which is exactly what she feels with the two of them. Jax is exciting but too new to be that level of trust and comfort, yet. But she's not telling him that, especially since they just had sex, too early for Jax's liking. Her bad, but she's not apologizing for that!

Jax guides her in, and Derek walks beside them. Her heart sinks. Is she distancing herself from Derek? Her fears diminish as they enter the house, and Jax removes his arm from around her. She leans toward Derek and whispers, "Wait until you see the salon and the dressing room. And his staff, they are incredible! You will love them!"

"I guess I'm getting makeup, aren't I?" He makes a silly face. "Never had my face done up before!"

She giggles. "Yeah, they will be doing that." She grabs his hand as they walk down the hallway.

"I'm a bit giddy," Derek admits with a joyful expression, making him look even more handsome.

"My staff will treat you like a king." Jax ticks his head in a quick nod.

As they approach the salon, Jax waves his arm toward the room. "Enter and have a seat. Spencer will be in shortly. Then it's makeup time. Then you will move down the hall to the wardrobe room, then, lastly, visit me in my office, the last door. After we chat, you will enter the studio across from my office. Just make your way down. You can't miss it."

"Okay, got it, boss. I'm in. I'm excited. I'm horny and ready to go!" Derek says with exuberance.

"Oh, and how's your ass? Can I see? I just want to know what we're working with for colors." Jax clasps his hands behind his back.

Derek pulls his pants down and turns his back toward Jax. He has some redness and a few streak marks from possibly a switch. But he's much more healed than Mallory's previous viewings of his bottom.

"Oh, Lawd have mercy! It's a man butt!" Spencer hoots as he skates into the room. "I love this job!" He does a little perky jig.

"Walking into my salon and seeing a man's ass is about the best day of work I can ever get! And I didn't even have to go to the studio for the sight." He pretends to faint as Derek pulls his pants back up. "Heavens, I need the fan on now." He walks across the room and switches it on to high. He stands in front of it while waving his hand in front of his face. "Now that's an ass on you, my dear. Whew!"

Everyone laughs, Derek the hardest, though he looks utterly delighted.

"Okay, Spencer, we'll leave him in your hands. Do your magic!" Jax insists with a waggle of his finger.

"Oy, damn, don't I wish!" Then he mumbles something, but all Mallory makes out is a repeat of "...I wish." His flustered expression takes over.

Derek looks very interested and intrigued, and humored.

Mallory gives him a questioning look. She loves him getting pampered with compliments like this. It's a major confidence booster. Maybe Derek has just scored a new potential play partner. Heck, she'd be happy for him if he does.

Ever since she took up with Jax, she's had a nagging guilty feeling. Perhaps this is what is forcing her to harbor hesitation with the proposal. She hadn't considered that being at the core of it. Mostly, she's been fucking confused as fuck. One day, she's ready to dash to Derek and drop to her knees, ring box in hand, and other days, she wants to forget she bought the dang ring.

"Now that I've met your ass, I need to meet the man. Derek, right?" Spencer says in a cooing voice.

"Yes, I'm Derek. It's nice to meet you." He leans back with a bright face and a sigh.

"Not as nice as it is for me to meet you after that introduction." Spencer looks hot and bothered.

She smiles at Derek, and he grins back.

"Have fun," she says with a wave toward him.

Jax grabs her hand. "We get some time along while they fix him up. Let's go to my office and talk." He gives her a suggestive look. "And by talk, I mean talk, so don't get any ideas with that hungry goddess pussy of yours looking to gobble me up again." He chuckles. "I'm a sucker for yours, so I'd cave in a heartbeat."

"Ah, good to know I have such fabulous leverage," she says with a devilish grin. "If we didn't have the impending filming, I'd take that as a challenge to tackle!" She gives him a dashing smile. "I'd win, too."

He nods, his eyes twinkling. "Darn right."

They walk down the hall and enter Jax's office. It looks pretty much the same as last time, but he's added a sex chair next to the middle of the sitting chairs.

"Well, walking in and finding that doesn't exactly quell my lusty hell fires any!" She laughs. "Consider me spurred on instead!"

He cracks up. "I know, right?"

"You used that recently?" she asks because being nosy about anything sex with Jax is a turn on.

"Yeah. I used it with Delilah earlier today. We've started playing. I love me a good, round, curvy woman now and then. Love so much to hold on to with doggy." He grunts while making gripping motions with his hands.

"Nice. I'd love to do a film with her. I'll have to reach out."

"Please do. I'd be in heaven while y'all are filming that together." He ushers her to a chair and sits next to her. "Today will be fun to watch. I'm excited to see Derek take and give cock. A male switch who is into impact play is not a place I've often gone for films, if ever." He grins widely. "New ground. I love new ground."

"Will there be BDSM acts in the filming today, then?" Mallory asks, realizing she didn't question Derek about what he was going to be doing.

"I believe some, yes. Derek and the other two talents have agreed to it, so we will see what comes out of their union. I'm not going to push anything. I'm letting them guide their interaction for how far they will go. Let them revel in their natural inclinations. You know my style. My goal is to just get hot spontaneous footage, no matter the kinks they engage in." He taps his temple. "Branding of it will come after. I like the genuineness of such a fluid environment."

A knock comes.

"Come in," Jax says, glancing at the door.

A sexy, tall, nicely built, dark-skinned gentleman walks in. He has the body of someone who has worked out extensively and is perhaps a bit obsessed with it.

Mallory recognizes him in an instant as Fort Knox. "Oh, I know you," she says with a squeal.

"And I know you," he says, smiling, giving her a suggestive, interested, yet playful leer.

"I'm guessing there's a problem." Jax looks concerned, his brow furrowing.

"Yeah. Bellis is throwing a fit. Wants to talk to you." He rubs his hands together. "Always something with Bellis."

"Shit. Yeah. That's the truth." He stands up. "Alright. So much for catching up, hon. I have to go and take care of this. Fort, keep her company till I return?" He looks at Mallory with an apology in his eyes. "I'll be back as soon as I can. Sorry."

"Oh, no worries. We will still have time." She gives him a smile, so he won't worry.

He leaves, and Fort takes his seat. "I'm excited to meet you. You're making quite the splash for a newbie." He licks his lower lip. "I really am loving your content."

She flushes. "I am still kind of new, aren't I?"

"New isn't bad. It's fresh. And you are smoking hot and fresh." He leans forward. "I am a subscriber."

"You are? Oh, wow. Yeah, thanks," she says, blushing further in delight.

"So, you and the big man hitting it off, I hear?" He raises an eyebrow as he places his right ankle over his left knee while leaning back. "We're good friends," he says, nodding toward the door Jax just left. "I'm up on what he's doing."

"Ah, I see. Yeah. We've started dating, I guess you could say that." She rubs both of her thighs with her palms. "I'm poly."

"Yeah. I am, too. A swinger in the lifestyle is how I got started in this biz. But for now, I'm just fucking. Performing. Making a stockpile of videos to live off the sales for years to come." He smirks and scoffs. "Too hard to have a relationship right now while I'm filming so much. I'll seek that in a few years when I move into the director role."

"Ah, that's your plan. I see." The opposite of what she's doing, cultivating three close relationships, and faraway ones with Maria and Sam. She's definitely not just performing; she's in the thick of maintaining relationships while performing.

"Yeah, I'll film for a few years. Get some more content created. Enough 'til I think it's enough. Then I can earn on it for the rest of my life, you know? Like a cash cow that keeps making milk, right?" He snaps his head quickly. "Make the content while I'm young and fit, then coast the ride of the sales off into the sunset." He smooths one hand over the other, then raises it in the air.

"True. Once it's created, you have it." She flutters her feet up and down. "Put it everywhere to earn." She hasn't thought that far ahead.

"Yeah, exactly. It's a no-brainer plan. I know a retired performer. He was creating films back when they were put on DVD's, when they were making little stories with it, more back then, like erotic romance."

As he pauses for a second, her mind fixates on how wonderfully sensually he said "romance."

"My man. He's still making money on that content. It's gold. Now it's digital and on DVD. And the crazy thing is, people out there be giving away entire sites full of content for peanuts now. Today's the time to make content, though, because who knows what the future will hold, but, yeah, once you have the films, they're yours for life. Sell, baby, sell." He snorts and swipes his chin with his fingers. "As long as you can find a place to sell them. There will always be places. No matter how hard they try to censor it. People want it. People want our stuff. It won't be a business that dies."

"They do, yeah. Sex won't ever go away. The more they censor it, in fact, the more people fight for it. Look at the prohibition. Pot. This is the same thing. Old crusty white rich guys who watch our stuff in hiding and try to control everything out in the world, but they can't. Not when we're craftier."

He cracks up. "Got that right. Crusty old white rich guys. Plus, they need to watch us cause none of 'em can pleasure a woman to save their damn life!" He keeps laughing like it's the funniest joke.

It's her turn to crack up, and she roars with laughter as he does. "True, you're not wrong." Max floats into her mind. He is a "crusty old white rich guy" stereotype, but he knows how to pleasure her very well, and he pays for her to make content. But likely, he's the exception, so there's no need to bring him up. Fort might not even believe her.

He shakes his head. "They gotta learn somehow. It's hard for them, being so entitled and all." Sarcasm heavily drips from his words. He purses his lips as a knowing look takes over. "Sex skills aren't intuitive, especially for entitled dudes."

"That's the truth," she agrees. She's heard enough stories to know she's a lucky woman with all the eager, sexually competent men in her life. But that's nowhere near the typical situation. It's only because she met Derek and she joined the club, where sexual competence is more the norm than in the general population. Heterosexual women orgasm the least of all the groups. It's alarming! She knows this from reading and from past friends reporting personal experiences. Being bisexual has kept her out of that category, and now, as she's living in sexual bliss as a creator, even less so. She comes on repeat multiple times a day, usually in the double digits.

"I'm all about the woman I'm with, whether it's on set or on my personal time. I know I'll come, that's easy. I want her pleasured to the absolute max." He stretches his hands outward, then curls them inward. "One bite of pie tastes the same as the rest, but I'm greedy. I want the whole damn thing."

"I love your take on it." A warm feeling grows in her belly. She meets the best people in her new life.

"So, you're with Derek, too?" He glances toward the hall as a loud ruckus breaks out.

"Yeah. We've been together for a long time." He's clearly been filled in by Jax.

The sounds don't stop but get louder.

Fort stands up and walks toward the door. Mallory follows.

"What the hell is going on over there?" Fort yanks the door open to find two dudes raising fists at each other.

"Bellis! What the fuck are you doing? Back off." Fort inserts himself between the men.

The other man is much smaller than Bellis.

"He's crazy," the other man says, stepping back. He's a smaller white man with a shock of red hair and enough freckles to almost hide his pale upper cheeks.

"He's fucking Janie!" Bellis shouts, his face reddening.

"You don't own Janie. For fuck's sake, you dumbass, you broke up with her six months ago. She's a free agent." The red-haired dude sticks his chin in the air as he looks up at Bellis.

Bellis charges at the pale carrot top dude, but Fort wraps him up in a chokehold in an instant.

"Cool it. Where's Jax anyway?" Fort is cool as a cucumber.

"I don't know. I'm not his keeper." He pretend spits.

POWER PLAYS

"Watch it," Fort warns.

Jax comes barreling down the hallway toward the group at lightning speed. "Bellis! Quit running from me. We need to talk. My office. Now!"

He snatches Bellis by the ear and drags him into his office, with Fort still restraining him.

"Yikes," Mallory whispers as Derek appears near her. "That seems a bit crazy."

"Very."

The thin man skedaddles away quickly without a word, his eyes still blazingly irate.

"You look amazing," Mallory states. "I'd fuck you."

"That's not saying much, Mal." He snickers. "You always fuck me."

"Maybe not saying much, but you look very sexy." She caresses his arm. "You ready?"

"I am. Was just stepping down to have the conversation with Jax, but I see that's not happening."

"Yeah, seems like he has a tough one to deal with."

Shouting comes from Jax's office, Jax's voice coming through the walls the loudest.

"He's got some pipes," Derek says with a chuckle.

"That he does. Everything about him is big. Super size!" Mallory says with humor, expanding her arms apart in the air.

"That's not hard to imagine," Derek says with an amused grin.

"Well, do you need anything? I can get you water or whatever you need. I'll be your assistant in waiting." Mallory smiles pleasantly.

"This is a switch." He puffs up his chest with a breath, then releases it, looking very much exhilarated.

The door opens, and Bellis stumbles out, looking pissed off. He brushes past them in a rush, giving them an annoyed glance.

Fort comes out and points at Derek. "Your turn. But don't worry, big bad Jax has now left the building."

"See around, Mal." Fort waves.

"Yeah. It was great to meet you. Hey, have you heard about our event? Maybe you want to join."

"Yeah, Jax was telling me about it. I'm in. Just let him know anything I need to know, and I'll be there."

"Awesome! That's great!"

Jax waves his hand. "Mal, you can go into the studio. I'll be right there after I have a quick chat with Derek, here."

She nods and heads into the studio.

Chapter 20

M allory scans the room. A few of the same players are on the edges, at the ready to do their roles. She smiles and nods at a few of them, including the director, Edgar, who waves. She settles against the wall in an open spot. It's odd not to place herself in the center of the room. She's the one usually doing the scene, and so this is a total rarity. She's happy to be present to cheer Derek on.

Her mind drifts to thoughts of the proposal. She's committed to doing it, and soon. The urge is welling up in her to solidify their dreams of marriage. What they are as a dedicated couple has been wonderful, but she craves something more solid. A union of marriage will act as a statement both to their own hearts and to the world.

Despite her career and now Derek's budding one in the adult industry, they are committed to each other. So many people assume that adult performers can't sustain a relationship or be married, yet she's met countless couples who pull it off seamlessly, and both are incredibly happy, well-adjusted people.

It's the nosy people who think they need to police everyone that cause the problems, not the people in highly communicative and mutually respectful relationships who want to be with each other. If both are honest and up front with each other, why do so many outside the relationship think they get to dictate acceptable boundaries for them? Why do people care what others do in a relationship anyway? There's not one way to be married, and they just can't seem to live with that. It's a them problem, so she doesn't care.

Her anger is flaring, and she realizes she's frowning, so she smiles on purpose to break her mood. She needs to get the fuck out of her head, and when Derek enters the room, it triggers her right to the present. And it makes her feel better to see him so eager and excited. She and Derek don't have to live by others' rules. They get to choose to live by their own.

She smiles and gives Derek a chin-up. She's proud of how far he's come in accepting and expressing his sexuality. It's been amazing to watch.

He mirrors her nod and smiles. He looks happy, confident, and the twinkle in his eye tells her all she needs to know.

He's ready.

This will be an epic day for him.

She will be his witness, his support, and his cheerleader for once.

He walks toward her, and they embrace. He kisses her on the lips.

"Thanks for being here, Mal. It means a lot to me." His eyes melt with vulnerability, and she notices his spark blooms. "I'm ready to do this, and having you on the sidelines, well, it's exactly what I hoped for and what I want."

"It's us together, living life how we want."

"Yes," he confirms.

She loves how she has no jealousy, only excitement for him. This day isn't about her; it's his day. Feeling genuine compersion is a blessing.

He takes both her hands in his and shakes them.

She giggles as she catches all the eyes in the room, which are glued to them.

"I think we are an anomaly."

"We are incredible."

"Indeed."

Derek follows her gaze and laughs, too.

"Wow, we definitely seem to be the attention getters of the room."

"Knock 'em dead, Derek. You're going to kill it." She nods and gives his hands a squeeze. "Go make the money." She chuckles. "And don't stop until you make them come."

"Wise advice," he says as she steps backward.

He joins the other two performers in the center of the room, where Jax and the director are migrating toward.

It's chatting strategy time, the mini pre-filming meeting.

That's always when her energy soars as her excitement peaks, too, when they are about to embark on the adventures of creating sexy content. It's freeing, and everything is yet unknown, like the greatness is on the edge about to burst free, but it's a time always loaded with ripe energy just busting at the seams to breathe life into the expressions of their combined sexualities. It's beautiful.

She smiles as she watches Derek talk. He needs this, and it's building him up in ways she could never do. It's a safe, controlled setting for him to be his true sexual self. Without judgment, without societal constraints, and in a space where sex is not only positive but delightfully shared as a human celebration of what the human body can do when all the conditions are right, or most are. Maybe not true intimacy, but the rest is idealized as much as possible.

All the discussions have been had, all the hard stops announced, the flexible "maybe" acts are known, the yeses and consents have been discussed, and all of that creates an environment where the performers can not only perhaps enjoy themselves, but perform in a way that celebrates the magnitude and range that is human sexuality. And then they get to sell it and make a living, using their own bodies to make money. That's empowerment.

And Derek is going to fly.

Jax has the final word, then the group breaks up. He strolls toward her with a giant smile. He loves his job, and it's apparent. It's a glorious thing to watch. In these walls, the prudish society can't frown upon them. They are in the safe zone, and it's evident on everyone's faces.

"Okay, let's do this," the director announces.

The three performers begin to talk to each other, making small talk as if they are friends who are getting ready to enjoy dinner together. The talk turns to sex after a few minutes. The conversation is genuine and not scripted, so their synergy flows like a natural interaction.

The other male talent is taller than Derek, and he pulls Derek close. They maintain eye contact as the man keeps his hand possessively on the back of Derek's neck.

The woman slides in right behind Derek, quickly pressing her body to his backside.

The man goes for the kiss, and Derek responds with enthusiasm as the woman presses her full chest to his back. Derek's the middle of a man and woman sandwich, which is exactly where she believes he desires to be.

They kiss, and their hands roam each other in their threesome embrace. The cameraman comes in close to get a tight view.

The heavy petting is quickly getting more aggressive, and the couple focuses intently on Derek. He sort of flops between their groping, their kisses landing on his mouth and neck.

The woman slips her hands up the inside of Derek's shirt, caressing his back, then slides quickly to his front. Her hands dance beneath his shirt as she plays with his nipples.

The man consumes Derek's mouth in another deep kiss. Their moans are escalating, and their growing passion is warming up the room. Electricity seems to crackle between the three. They have good chemistry, and it's coming through nicely in the scene.

The woman slides Derek's shirt off, breaking the kiss.

The man goes back at Derek even more hungrily, and Derek exudes a delightful, satisfied moan. He likes being desired, and his co-star isn't holding back his yearning for Derek one bit.

Neither is the woman. She quickly undoes Derek's pants and shoves them to the floor. Derek stands between the two in only his underwear.

The three sway in a dance of heightening mutual arousal, and it's hypnotic to watch. Mallory's own lust is thickening, and her desire to have sex grows. She might need to entice Jax into fucking in his office when they take a break in the filming. Glancing at Jax tells her his loins are stirring, too. She gives him a suggestive look, and he returns it, then pulls her in for a side hug, kissing the top of her head.

"Later," he says in a loud whisper. "Count on it."

She beams a smile up at him.

Derek is bent over sucking the man's cock, bobbing his head. His body is jerking in rhythm to the woman who is humping his backside. Somehow, like magic, she's holding a strapon with a medium pink dildo loaded in it. Some stealth move brought her that; Mallory had only looked away for an instant.

The woman backs up and removes her own shirt so she's bare-chested. Then she secures the strapon around her waist. Lining up the dildo at Derek's ass, she squirts lube generously on the pink toy and rubs it along Derek's pucker.

Derek keeps going at the man's cock, gagging slightly as the woman enters him from behind. Her slow penetration makes Derek's eyes roll. He struggles to keep sucking as she bottoms out inside him, a deep groan coming out from his lips. The man holds Derek's head to cradle it, and once he recovers from the fake cock entering him to the hilt, he continues sucking the man off.

The three of them bounce off each other until the woman backs up. She grabs Derek's hand, breaking the connection of the blow job.

Derek grabs the man's hand, and the three of them move in unison toward the couch. Her fake glistening cock bobs as she walks. Once they reach the couch, she strips off both the strapon and her pants, now she's naked. She's got a lovely curvy figure that Mallory wishes she could fondle.

The woman kisses Derek as the man grinds his cock against Derek's buns. Their hands move, their moans launch, and the juicy scene grows hotter.

Derek tosses the woman to the couch in a brusque move and spreads her thighs apart. He falls between her legs and darts toward her labia lips, his mouth wide open. He eats her out as she writhes on the couch, her legs moving, her hands pressing into his scalp. The other man provides nipple play for her. She arches her back and climaxes wildly within a minute of the dual stimulation.

Derek rises and enters her pussy while the man rides his cock into her mouth.

After a few minutes of missionary, Derek reaches for a crop, and the toy magically is on the couch. Someone is quite gifted in their moves to introduce props without being seen, either that, or Mallory is very distracted and is missing the hand off, which could be the case. She glances down at Jax's groin, and he's sporting a full load, which is generously pushing out his pants in a hefty lump.

She's tempted to caress it but decides to wait. She wants to see the full scene, and if she grabs his cock, they would likely be heading straight for his office.

Derek maneuvers the woman so she's ass up, head down, and begins to lay spanks across her ass cheeks with the crop. He has a new technique she's never seen him do before, and wonders if Sam schooled him on his recent trip back. Likely that's the case, though it could have also been Maria. She's got such skills, too.

Derek cracks it against her flesh, and she undulates and shouts with each thrashing. The man behind Derek undresses and then walks over to the toy shelf, his long cock wobbles up and down with his movements. Mallory can't take her eyes off him for a second.

He peruses the shelf with his backside to her, and while Derek is actively fucking the woman, she's finding watching him choose toys to be more interesting. He chooses a large wooden paddle, and Mallory cringes. Derek's ass is still not fully healed from Max's last spanking. He doesn't need more, but perhaps it's for the woman. Mallory can't wait to find out.

The man also grabs velvet-covered handcuffs, a ball gag, a string of chain, and nipple clamps.

Mallory rubs her hands together. "Now this is getting good," she whispers to Jax.

He raises an eyebrow with a look of approval.

An idea percolates, she opens her phone to her notes app to search through the recent passages she's written. Her desire to write spicy stuff has been swirling up in her, and she's spent some time writing little snippets of sexy phrases and scenes. She scrolls through and highlights one to send to Jax.

She pastes the passages into the text field. Peel me naked for things my skin yearns to feel, the grasp of your palm, the firm grip of your fingertips. Your fingers closing on my pink, eliciting shivers twisting across my body. We sink into our blast of lust, our legs now entwined. You've ripened me to crave the sweet pierce of your thick entrance. Want to smell us on me, the wet of our fuck, smear it as our skin slips across each other. Bind me with the passion of your grips as you melt back into my wet. I scream, "Mount me-ride me. I'm yours." I sigh. "Give me your rage." Gift me the squeeze of your lust as you bounce me to spike mine.

Then she texts: Wanna? We can do better than just watch.

As Jax reads the text, his face goes through a myriad of emotions from amusement to interest to flat-out lewd horniness. He grabs her hand while intently looking into her eyes. "Let's go," he says in a low, stern tone.

He practically runs out of the room with her in tow. No one says a thing because the filming is still going on. He tugs her through the hallway, and they fall into his office in a flash. He slams the door, probably the editors will need to edit that out of the film, and grabs her roughly.

They fall into an embrace, his eyes heated and ablaze as much as hers. He overtakes her in a strong kiss, his hungry grunts throwing her want for him into overdrive.

They maul each other as they make out. He's hungry and urgent in his movements, as is she, and they launch into a frenzied pre-fuck tangle.

"I want you," she slurs against his shirt, digging her fingers into the fabric. If she had the strength, she'd rip the damn thing off him.

"I want you," he copies while quickly stripping her of her shirt.

He dives in for another kiss as his fingers fumble at her bra's latch. He manages to unhook it and flings it away from her body. He consumes her right nipple, mowing down on her breast, taking as much of it into his mouth as he can. He plays with her other breast, tweaking and pulling her erect nipple.

She moans and throws her head back. She adores his bold devouring of her and lies limp in his arms as he feasts on her breasts. He pulls her into another kiss, and she grabs at his cock, stroking her hand up and down it through his pants.

He growls and spins her around, pushing her over his desk. He tugs her pants down to bare her ass and lays several spanks across her bottom.

She jumps with each hit, grunting.

He unzips his pants, and she spreads her legs, popping her ass up for his easy entrance.

He slaps his cock against her ass several times.

She imagines his precum flying off his tip.

His displays of dominance over her make her yearn more for him. "Please," she begs.

"I wanna fuck your wet pussy so bad, so hard, deep. Mmm...kay." He grunts as he lines up his cockhead at her slit. "You're mine. Bent over. Gonna pound you hard while you scream with every stroke," he says in a strained voice.

He slowly penetrates her and slides in easily.

She groans as he begins to thrust into her, balls deep.

"Our bodies gonna smack," he states breathlessly as he rides himself into her at an ever-faster rate.

"Fuckkkk!" she mutters as he hits her G spot in the right way. "Yes, fuck!"

He rams himself into her, rapidly making her body flop before him. Her tits rub the smooth wood of the desk.

He smashes into her particularly harder than she expects, and she throws her arm sideways, knocking things she can't see off the desk. They clatter to the floor, but he doesn't slow his pumping; he speeds up even more.

She lays her boobs on the desk for how roughly he's railing her, and then he stops.

She pants heavily on the desk, her cheek flush with it. She almost peaked, but it wasn't enough.

"Slow down and savor you," he mutters as he gently goes in and out of her. "Then I'll fuck you hard again until you cum for me, my hungry whore."

After thirty seconds of his slow ride, he launches into a beat down of his pelvis into her body. She's rocked harshly as he obliterates her with his thrusting.

"Clit," he commands in a controlled tone.

She reaches under and rubs herself. Within seconds, she's there, her body knows the drill, her back arches in response as her internal walls contract forcefully on his cock inside her.

She's coming with his cock deep inside her, and he groans.

He twitches against her body as he comes, his exuberant sounds further proving his climax. He lies still upon her, breathing heavily.

"Shit, that got me." He chuckles as he caresses her flesh. "Those passages. Shit. You write that?"

She nods against the desk with a growing smile. "I did. Thinking of you earlier today."

"Damn, that was so hot. I couldn't resist." He stands up and helps her rise. "I very rarely leave filming like that. But wow, you got me."

"Well, let's go back, then. We can always indulge more later."

"You really do get me. And yes, I'm planning on double digits and fucking you so much you can't walk straight."

She giggles. "And I know you could." She dresses, and they return to the studio where the fucking is still going on hot and heavy with Derek taking it in the ass from the man while fucking the woman beneath him.

Derek has the ball gag in, and the woman is handcuffed with nipple clamps on. The man clearly took the dominant role over both of them. The power plays continue with the promise in their actions that no one is slowing down one bit.

Chapter 21

The next day, Mallory wakes with the determination to propose to Derek, roaming around in her head. This is it. It's the day! She's not going to chicken out or let her fears guide her. She wants to be married to Derek and keep their throuple alive. With luck, Max will help her pull this off. He's going to take Derek shopping for car accessories. It's a stretch, but Max managed to convince Derek at dinner last night to go, and she's totally grateful.

Derek is so excited about the car, but he didn't want to take more money from Max. But after an impromptu spanking at the dinner table, Derek happily agreed to accept it. She could tell he had wanted to say "yes" from the beginning, but the discipline from Max made it okay to say.

She suspects that with healing, he may outgrow the desire to be spanked. But time will tell. The question is, how will Max respond if Derek decides he's done? They've become synergistic, almost like an organism where their domination and submission together are a living, breathing symbiotic creature. They will either adjust together through time or end their impact play dynamic. Her biggest question is if Derek no longer needs the act, will Max turn to her as a substitute?

And the crazy part is she has become a part of it, too, in being the main caregiver of his aftercare, though Max does some as well when he tells Derek to come. They are breaking all the typical rules others tend to follow, but their rules fit them, which is how she and

Derek, and Max, for that matter, have lived their relationships. Their rules are what matter, and that's it. Period. They aren't conforming to anyone else's standards, and she cherishes that.

She squirms in the bed as the door swings open.

Derek strides in nude, sporting a fat boner, which swings as he moves. Precum makes his tip shiny. He stops to pose with his hands on his hips, then purses his lips to smooch the air.

"Woke up with this. And it's for you," he grins widely.

Oh shit! She's hoping for post-proposal sex only. Now what?

She smiles and stretches. "Mmmm. That looks like a very tasty morning snack. Count me in." She hops out of bed. "I have to pee." She snags her phone and hurries to the bathroom. She needs Max's help to get out of having sex. She smirks. Has she ever had this thought in her life?

She texts Max: Help! Derek wants sex, and I have a big production planned for sex after I propose. I don't want to overshadow that.

Max texts back immediately: I'll be right there.

She pees and takes her time, hoping Max appears before she leaves the bathroom. She does not want to reject Derek's come on, especially since it was so cute, sexy, and playful. She'd love to have sex, but her plans are set, and she needs to adhere to them. It will be more special if they wait to make love until after the actual proposal.

She hears Max's voice in the room as she leaves the bathroom, so she's trying desperately to hide her tiny knowing smile.

"Derek, we have to go now. I have so many meetings later that we have to do this right away." Max has an urgent expression that pairs well with the impatience in his tone.

"Shit, are you serious? We were just gonna fuck." He looks so downtrodden that she almost changes her mind. He frames his cock between his hands with an open-mouthed stare.

"You can fuck her brains out later, but I've got to go now." He claps his hands. "Get dressed and let's go."

"We could shop another day," Derek suggests. "Just a quickie? Please, Max?"

"No. We've got the spanking on board that got you to agree. We are doing this now, or do I need to take you over my knee right here on this bed to remind you?" Max's dominance will work perfectly to get Derek to comply. Logic doesn't matter when your Dom wants something.

He sighs heavily and drops his hands. "Fine. Mallory, later I'll fuck you until you scream." His cock doesn't deflate one bit.

She almost laughs as she imagines him trying to stuff if fully erect into his pants. Poor man! As he turns to go, she notices his bottom is still red and tender looking.

"Good boy," Max states proudly. "I'll be in the car. We'll take yours in case we need it for whatever we get." Then he leaves in a huff.

"Ugh. I'm sorry. I didn't expect this," he says to Mallory as he goes to hug her. "We could have had a quickie, but he's being stubborn."

"It's okay. We have the rest of the day to play. I have a bunch of stuff to get done today, so how about a rain check? We can do dinner, just the two of us. Then we can fuck. Max has dinner with his buddies tonight, so it will be just you and me."

"Okay, sounds good. I can't wait."

"Have fun shopping!"

"Yeah, my brain is thanking my butt right about now. This is going to be fun, I just need to get this to calm down." He smacks his cock, snickers, then leaves.

She breathes a sigh of relief. Damn. That was a close one!

After Derek and Max leave, she dashes to the hall. She stashed all the decorations for her special date in the hall closet, behind several boxes, hoping Derek wouldn't see them.

She pulls out the strings of silver streamers and glittery pink hearts. Making a special wonderland for their at-home date is exactly what she adores about her proposal plan. She will make dinner, and they will eat it in the kitchen. Will he know something is different? Not as long as she keeps him out of the basement.

After dinner, she will take their champagne bottle and dessert and guide him to the basement, where it will be fully decorated. This might tip him off that something is up, but it won't matter, because she's proposing to him within minutes at that point anyhow. If her plan goes well, and he says 'yes', they will enjoy their champagne, dessert, and a good fuck as a newly engaged couple.

She smiles with excitement. How many couples can say they had two proposals, and a decorated wonderland to fuck in after? She's guessing not many.

She carts the decorations down the stairs, dropping some along the way. They will have to be picked up, but if she tries now, they will all spill upon the floor.

In the basement, she strings them all up, tapes the hearts everywhere, then pulls out strings of Christmas lights to align with the silver streamers. Once she's done, it looks like a festive, glittery wonderland, and she's very pleased. The trick will also be to make sure Derek doesn't go downstairs the rest of the day. But she's counting on Max to help that happen. Having him be Derek's leader is quite perfect because Derek now listens to what he says. It's like having a special magic sorcerer when she needs Derek to do something. She's not going to be manipulative, but in this case, it's to give her and Derek a memorable date and proposal experience, so it will be essential.

Once she's got everything set, she heads to the kitchen to make a marinade for the meat. Max is going to grill their chicken breasts before he heads out to meet his friends. The nice part about this is that Max is meeting up with friends he hasn't seen in a while, which he probably wouldn't have done if she weren't looking to be alone with Derek.

Then she sets up her laptop to work, so she looks too busy for sex once her men return. She might even leave if Derek looks like he's going to come on to her again. She's never run away from sex before, and it's such an odd feeling! It's not her norm!

SHE STIRS THE MAC AND cheese in the pot to get the aged Gouda to melt, but it's taking literally forever. As she turns, she spies Max at the grill outside. What man would happily make dinner for his girlfriend who is about to propose to her other boyfriend? Her life has gotten crazier than a batch of mindless bees whose hive is being poked. Yet she's so happy with everything, her heart is bursting.

Max is happy. Derek is happy. So, would a wedding throw a bad kink in all their happiness messing it all up? She's a bit worried this move will be disastrous. But with hopefully a wedding to plan, and the big adult performer event, she will be so busy she won't be able to see straight, just as long as this proposal doesn't fuck everything up. Life will only get better.

But that's also the fun of what she's about to embark on; the unknown can be exciting. A journey should be fun along the way, as much fun as living out the goal part.

Max enters the house with a steaming plate of chicken. "Thanks for marinating extras so I can try it tomorrow."

"Well, thanks for grilling. The marinade was easy." She scans his face. She can't resist it; she must ask the question that has been rolling around in her head lately. "Max, why are you okay with Derek and me marrying? And not wanting me to marry you?"

He leans back and puts his hands on his belly. "Babe, that's a really good question. And I have only one answer for you. Kids. You and Derek want kids. I've already had my kids. I don't want to take that away from either of you. I'm just so grateful you two want me in your life, too."

Ah. This makes sense. "I've been wondering. And I wasn't sure if you were just going along with it since Derek and I've been together longer."

"I'd absolutely love, love love, I mean love to marry you. And I would in a heartbeat. If I had my way, we'd already be married right now. But you both are still young. You can have kids together. And if you keep me around, I can help raise them, too. If you'll have me."

Kids. Wow. She's always wanted kids, but somehow, being a content creator as a career seems like a hard mesh with motherhood.

As if he's reading her skeptical look, he says, "And you've literally got years and years yet to have kids. Heck, many women have kids into their forties."

She scoffs. "Well, I'm not waiting that long." It's been a damn long time since she's thought about having kids. "I guess your reason makes some sense." She doesn't like to think about the fact that Max is so much older because it makes her think of his death coming closer. Geez. What the fuck? Why is this awful doom invading her brain?

"You look upset. Have I upset you?" Max rushes over to her and places his hand on her back.

She shakes her head. "No. It's just that I haven't thought about all that for a really long time. I'm so wrapped up in what I'm doing."

"Hey, honey, don't worry. You have so much time. There's nothing to fret about." He pulls her into a hug and kisses the top of her head. "You're so young, honey."

She bites back tears and hates that they were about to spill. "Yeah. You're right." Having a baby while filming sex scenes sounds so incompatible. But maybe by then she will retire from it? Or maybe just take a break. She has no clue, and deciding all this now is adding stress. Her brain muddies, and everything seems difficult all of a sudden, right when she needs to be clear-headed.

"Let me pour you a glass of wine before I go. To help you relax."

She nods as she tries to shift her thinking. Not exactly what she thought she'd be thinking about right now. Hell, she's not even engaged yet. Not that she believes she'd have to be to have a baby, but still, that's all too far in the future to darken today, so she needs to shove off all her fears. Today is about the proposal, and her and Derek.

She stirs the mac and cheese. "Damn. This aged cheese is so hard, it's taken so long to melt."

"It will. Just keep stirring. Trust me, it will be worth it once you taste it." He pauses. "Did you grate it or chop it? Next time grate it. It melts way faster."

"Oh. I chopped it. Thanks," she says, taking the glass of wine. She takes a generous sip.

"Where did you send Derek off to anyway?"

"To meet with Maggie and Goldie. They are finalizing the contracts for the event. Super boring shit," he laughs. "Perfect for keeping him there long enough for you to be ready, though."

"Yeah, I bet." She snorts. "That's the kind of snore job I despise."

"Derek seems to be okay with handling it, so let him. You have enough to do." He hugs her from behind as she stirs. "I have to leave in five minutes. Is there anything else you need help with before I go?"

"No, but please know you are wonderful." She stops stirring and spins to hug him, but holds his face between her hands instead. "Please know that both Derek and I, well, we want you in our lives. Just because we will be the married ones doesn't mean you are any less important to our throuple."

He kisses her on the lips through his smile, then pulls her into a hug. "I know, honey. I know."

"You'd better stir. The cheese can burn."

She releases him and turns back. The cheese is bubbling, and she quickly stirs it. "Whew, made it just in time! Sensitive stuff."

"Yeah, it is. It's a pain to make, but it's oh so good." He leans in and whispers in her ear. "Hey, you're going to do great. This is going to work, and you both will be so happy. We'll all be happy. Have faith, okay?"

She nods while crushing her desire to burst into tears again. "I didn't expect to be so stressed out before asking him."

"Yeah, I can see you are. I wish I could give you a massage. But I've got to go, and Derek is due home any time, so we'd better not."

"Yeah, plus I'm a slave to this mac and cheese dish, apparently," she jokes. She manages to give him a weak smile.

"He won't say no. I guarantee it, babe. He won't. There's no way." He caresses her cheek, then kisses her again on the lips. "I love you. I'll be back around nine."

"Okay. Have fun. I'm glad you get to do something fun. Having you here but not with us for our date would have been weird."

"Yeah. Especially when you're proposing, it would have been awkward." He raises his arms. "Okay. Here we go, to the rest of our lives."

"Here we go," she repeats and smiles back.

He turns and leaves the kitchen, leaving her to stir the cheese and try to keep from freaking the fuck out.

Chapter 22

Derek enters the house, and she freezes. It's go time. There's no turning back. She puffs up her chest and rushes to hug him.

"Well, that's a lovely welcome. What did I do to deserve that?"

"I missed you. And I'm bummed we didn't get to have sex this morning. But as soon as we eat, let's get to it," she says in a seductive tone. Turning on the sex appeal is calming her nerves considerably.

"It smells incredible in here. Is it ready now? I'm starved." He removes his jacket and hangs it on the coat rack.

"It's ready. We can sit down. I have our wine glasses poured and water on the table already." She had thought about appetizers first, but prolonging the time to when she's going to propose sounded too tough to suffer through, and made her stomach churn.

He follows her into the kitchen and through to the dining room. "Oh, we're actually using the dining room. Unheard of." He smiles at her with a twinkle in his eyes. "It looks amazing. You know how to make me feel special, Mal. You always have. Thanks for this."

He gives her a quick hug, then rounds the table. "You weren't kidding. The food is already on the table."

She's so anxious, the only way she could get by while waiting for him was to keep busy and keep getting ready. "Yeah, I had the time, so I just did it all."

"Well, I'm hungry, so I'm definitely not complaining."

They sit down, and she tries like hell not to let her nervousness show on her face. She needs to be careful not to clue him in on her plan and spoil the surprise. She quickly sips her wine and then hands him the bowl with the mac and cheese. "Wait until you try this. It's a recipe Max said he used to make all the time, but hasn't made it for us. It's to die for."

"Max is the best chef I know, but you're pretty damn good yourself. Never had something you made that wasn't good." He smiles brightly.

"Yeah, maybe. But you're right. Max has a certain flair for cooking. He grilled the chicken, I made the marinade and the rest."

"Oh, he's not eating with us?" He looks around the table as if he's just now realizing only two places are set. "I figured he was still just working or something."

"No, remember he's going out with some buddies he hasn't seen in a long time. But he said he'll have some as leftovers tomorrow." She's jittery, but raises her wine glass. "To us, and Max. May we keep making good food, good memories, and hot spicy videos together."

"Agreed," Derek says, clicking his glass to hers.

They eat and talk about Derek's updates from his meeting. She tries like hell to act normal, and the wine and food help. But as they finish eating, her nerves jump like they're on a hot skillet.

"Hey, let's clean up in a bit. I have something I want to show you in the basement that I've been working on." She fondles the little ring box in her pocket as she stands up. "The dishes won't be going anywhere." She smiles to cover her awkwardness. She's never been this nervous around Derek ever.

"Okay. You've got me curious." He gives her an inquisitive look. "Is this a new filming set? Something for the event?"

"It's a set for something," she says, trying to sound lighthearted.

She swings through the kitchen, grabs the champagne bottle from the fridge, and the two flutes on the counter.

"Wow, champagne, too? We need more at-home dates." He fondles her ass as she walks. "I'm so ready to smash that with my hips."

"Oh, you romantic," she teases as she dances away from his reach. But honestly, she's really ready for that, too. It will be a great stress reliever.

She leads him downstairs, feeling as if she's flying rather than walking. She rushes ahead so she can spin to watch his reaction as he enters the basement.

At the base of the stairs, he freezes in place, then leans back quickly, raising his hands in the air. "Wow! Holy shit! This is incredible!"

She sets down the bottle and glasses on the coffee table. With her heart pounding faster than she can handle, she rushes toward him, dropping to her knees when she reaches him.

"Derek," she says in a shaky voice. "I want..." she pushes her hand into her pocket as he raises his right hand abruptly, alarm crossing his face.

"Oh, whoa, now wait a minute..." He twitches, then blinks.

She presents the little ring box to him without hesitation.

"But," he protests as a little smile creeps across his face. "Can I...can you...wait right here for one minute? Just...I'll be quick..." He pauses, then hops. "It's not bad. Nothing bad. Don't freak. I just have to do something so quickly. I'll be quick. Honest. Don't move. I promise." He waves his hands as he babbles. "I'll be faster than you can think. Just hold tight. Hold tight," he chants as he scurries away. He glances back and his face is lit with so much hope and love.

She nods feeling energized, her pounding heart shaking her insides and beating so ferociously she feels she may faint. Her hands tremble as she tries to control her rapid breathing. She needs to calm down.

With him gone, panic rises in her, though, and her mind goes wild. Irrational thoughts dogpile in her head. She tries not to assume the worst but is failing. Maybe he just has to pee? What if he's not sure about marrying her anymore? Just chill. Perhaps he needs some notes he wrote down to talk about it? What if he's going run away again and doesn't come back down? She releases a big breath. But he didn't look scared or upset; more so, he looked determined. She tries to soothe herself, but she shivers. He said it wasn't bad. She can't think clearly, for shit. Her anxiety is sabotaging her, and she can't make it stop.

It's an eternity before he returns, but it's not, and she laughs at herself when he dashes back into the basement after merely a few minutes. Zooming across the room in a hurry, the last few feet he legit runs to her. He drops, kneeling before her in a flash, landing hard. They stare into each other's eyes, face-to-face.

His eyes are soft and eager. He pulls his hand out of his pocket and holds up a box parallel with hers, the same box he held when he proposed to her. "At the same time," he says breathlessly, rushed.

She nods, delight and joy filling her, making her feel like the sun inside. She pops open the lid of the box. "Will you marry me, Derek?"

He opens the box, too. "Will you marry me, Mallory?" he asks urgently.

"Yes!" she screams with a shrill voice laden with tears.

"Yes!" he shouts with exuberance, a huge smile on his face.

They both throw their arms around each other.

Mallory fills with elation as she releases a sob. Her tears stream out unhindered as relief and rhapsody take over.

Derek is crying, too.

"Yes, a million times, yes," she says through her tears.

"Same, yes, forever and eternity," he says in a shaky voice.

"Us. Always our way," she says softly.

"Yes." He leans back, his eyes watery. "And Max?"

She grins. "And Max. Yes, of course, and Max. Believe it or not, I have a story to go along with this that you will totally love, but my point is, Max actually helped me pick out your ring."

"Serious?" he asked with a gasp. "Hysterical! Well, I love it. I wouldn't have picked anything different."

"We must put them on," she says. "Or are we supposed to wait to put yours on?"

"I don't know. But who cares. Yes, let's just do it."

He removes her ring from the slot as she holds up her hand, raising her ring finger slightly. He pushes the ring down her finger.

She releases a cry of happiness, then takes out his ring and slides it on his ring finger.

His face is glowing.

Glee consumes her. They've done it. They are engaged!

"We're going to have the best wedding Max's money can buy!" Derek says with jubilation.

She laughs. "You sure have come a long way about his money. And of course, he bought the ring. How it happened, that's part of the story I have yet to tell you."

"Can't wait to hear about it. You know, I finally understand that we are together. I'm not outside the two of you anymore."

She can imagine why he felt that way in the past, and perhaps living at Max's house has helped. That and all the domination and submission acts, of course. If it weren't mutual, he wouldn't be saying this now. "You never were, Derek."

"Yeah, but I felt that way."

"No, you aren't outside us. You are integral. We are a throuple, and our marriage won't leave Max out. We can talk about all this, but Max and I have talked. I think we'll need the three of us to talk. And a lot."

"Yeah. I never thought we'd get to this point, to be honest. I used to be so jealous." His face turns sheepish. "I'm not proud of that. I behaved horribly. I hurt you, and I'm sorry."

"Hey, we're all in a better place. And I'm loving the three of us. Our dynamic might be unconventional, but it's ours. We live our way, and that's all that matters."

"Agreed." He pulls her into an embrace. "Now I get to dominate you? And we get to fuck? It's high time we fucked."

She smiles as his hungry look sends zings of arousal through her. "Oh, yes. I was trying so hard earlier. You know, I have a confession. I had Max help me get you out of my room this morning."

His face falls into shock. "No way, you did?"

"Yeah. I really wanted us to have sex after the proposal."

He leans her backward in a dipping motion. "What if I had said 'no'?" he asks in a teasing voice.

"Don't laugh. I worried about that," she says, relaxing her body into his supportive arms.

"No." He shakes his head. "You did? Never. I'd never say 'no' to marrying you."

"Well, you left last time."

"Shhh," he coos. "It's time to kiss. We can talk that out later. Right now, I want to kiss you."

He leans down with an open mouth, and she accepts his kiss with hunger. They make out. He breaks their kiss after a few minutes and carries her to the couch. Lying her down, he presses his body to hers.

She smiles as she senses his hard cock against her belly. Finally, they get to have sex.

He kisses down her neck as she plays with his hair. He peels her shirt off, then unveils her breasts from her bra cups. Suckling her nipples, she writhes beneath him.

Her desire for his cock inside her rages. She claws at his back as he feasts on her bosom.

He kisses his way down her belly, nudging at her closed pants with his nose. He undoes the zipper and slides them down her hips. Burying her covered pussy mound with kisses, he groans.

"I can't wait to be inside you," he says.

"I can't wait either," she says, her lust growing.

He pulls her panties down and inhales deeply above her pussy. "You smell incredible. Love the scent of you."

With her panties on her ankles, she moves her feet to get them off.

"Leave them, I like them on you like that."

His bedroom eyes flare. "I wanna fuck your wet pussy." He thrusts his pelvis against her abdomen. "So hard."

"Mmmm, yes, please."

"You gonna take my cock like a good cumslut?"

"Yes. Yes, I am. The best cumslut."

"You're gonna feel me mount you from behind, then my cock sliding in and out. I'll go for a titty grab, reaching around you. Then grab your hips and ram my cock in hard, repeatedly," he says during his increasingly labored breathing. "Want you to say 'I'm your fuck hungry whore. Gimme your cum.'"

She grunts as he grasps her with fervor. "Say it, 'head down, ass up.'"

She pants but manages to say, "Head down, ass up. For you."

His breath on the skin of her mound sends a shiver lighting up her clit. She slides off the couch and wriggles until her face is in front of his cock. Grabbing his thighs, she kisses along until her lips graze the base of his shaft. His groan makes her smile as she licks his cock tip, moistening his skin with her spit. She takes him in her mouth, readying for a wet, wild ride.

Bobbing on his cock, he pumps his hips, making his cock enter her mouth and exit quickly. Taking control, he fucks her mouth until she gags. Then he grabs her arms and spins her so she's facing the couch, bent over. The velvety fabric of the upholstery beneath her fingers is soft, which is a delicious contrast to his hard erection pressed between her upper thighs. He tickles his fingers along her slit, slowly dipping his fingers between her divide. Her pussy throbs as he spanks her clit rapidly with his hand. She jolts and sputters in tune with the strong sensations.

She writhes beneath him, the urgency of her movements practically begging him for more. "Please," she begs. She flutters her eyelids as his touch brings her higher in her want for him. Her yearning balloons, her impatience flares.

The aroma of their impending sex is bold in the air. She quivers in anticipation as he plays with her. She's so ready for their bodies to collide, their skin to smash together on repeat, their body heat and desire for each other turning them savage as they primally fuck.

He paws at her breasts as he humps her body. She wants to climax, and she knows he won't until she does, so she allows his fingers to launch her into her big orgasm, which makes her body tense as she arches with the strong sensations pummeling her from inside.

He keeps caressing her folds as she rises to a second peak, crying out, she twists, resisting the urge to slap his hand away even when the feel of him pressing her clit becomes too much.

Her reaction must have convinced him because he grabs his cock and lines it up at her entrance. Slowly entering her, he works himself into her body and pumps without stopping. He humps her, chasing his own orgasm like a fiend.

Every sense on overload, she's floaty with post-climax hormones coursing through her body. She's floppy and weak, ready to fall asleep if she could, but she's too hyped up at the same time.

Her breaths rage against any sort of calm. Her eyes roll in the echo of ecstasy his rubbing internally brought. Moans roll out of her mouth as the thoughts fill her brain that she's having sex with her fiancé. She welcomes his lust as he speeds up, charging full force into his own climax.

After, he lies upon her back, his breathing sounds labored and gruff. They could have kept fucking, but he helps her to spread out on the couch, then settles in beside her, maneuvering so he can look directly into her eyes. She stares back at him, baring her soul.

This man, a man she's loved for so long, one she feared she lost, but then came back, is a true gift to her. This journey started with just him and her, and it needs to keep on the right path moving forward. Kids. Family. Max. Films. Big flashy conferences. Whatever comes their way, she wants it all to be with Derek.

"I feared I lost you," she says in a soft voice.

"Never. I'd never go."

Intimacy with Derek makes her feel like she can do anything. It's a superpower. It gives her the feeling of owning that superpower. It's beautiful, lovely, freeing, empowering. Her heart soaring, she snuggles against Derek's chest.

"You fill me in so many of my hollow places that I no longer ever feel empty," he says into her hair.

"Derek, you really are everything I've always wanted and needed. And I have a lifetime of love left for you, and more."

"We get to do all this, together, you know, all of it." He caresses her face. "I'm sorry I left and had a hissy fit. I was a brat."

"I'm sorry if you felt left out."

"I don't anymore."

"Good."

"Can we freeze this moment, forever?"

She nods, a smile growing on her face. "I have already, it's written on my heart."

He smiles, too, and cuddles her head into the nook of his neck. "Us, forever. Just like this. I want to remember this feeling forever. Wherever we go, I'll always remember this moment."

The End...for now!
Stay tuned for book 3!

About the Author

Ruan Willow is an award nominated open door spicy romance author, sex blogger at https://ruanwillowauthor.com/ , sexuality and spicy romance fiction podcaster at the Oh F*ck Yeah with Ruan Willow Podcast, and an audiobook narrator/voiceover actor. She is also published on Medium, Frolic Me, and Theo Reads, plus in several anthologies. She loves spending time with family and friends, interacting with fans, cooking, sharing/chatting with and educating people about sex, reading, travel, being outdoors, swimming, learning about sex, podcasting, and more sex. Did you catch all the sex? She's giggling right now thinking about you reading all about sex. She values openness and talking about the natural act of sex. And. Yup, she loves to laugh!

Pen Names:

She writes spicy romance, open door, rom com, and menage as Ruan Willow, hotwife romance as Ruin Willow, taboo erotica as RuAnn Willhoe, and R.U. Ann for open door romantasy/horror/paranormal and dark romance fiction.

Ruan has been nominated for Best Erotic Writer by the ASN Lifestyle Magazine Awards 2025.

Thank you!

THANK YOU TO ALL MY family and friends who support me. I wouldn't be where I am without you. You are all the magic and the light in my life, the love that grows in my love. I am honestly thrilled and humbled by the supportive people in my life. Love you!

To Fans:

Thank you for purchasing and/or reviewing this book!

I peddle fantasies for the purposes of your enjoyment, entertainment, and expanding your sexuality and openness. Always remember that no fantasies are bad. You should enjoy your sexuality and your fantasy life as much and as often as you can.

Thank you for reading my book! I write for myself and for my fans. My fans are my main focus though, but of course, I want to like what I write too, and I thoroughly enjoyed writing this story.

In writing spicy romance, I'm always excited for the erotic journey! I'm personally on a path of sexual empowerment, enlightenment, and enjoyment. Thank you for reading this and I'm honored to be a part of your journey as well. I strive to spin stories where the characters get to enjoy lots of pleasure, and I hope you have also gotten pleasure from reading this book. Enjoy your own journey!

I am where I am because fans have responded to me and my content, so I owe everything to you! Thank you! Thank you! Thank you! You are a blessing in my life, and you give me more joy than you will ever know. I love interacting with all of you and I will never give that up.

My stories are open door romance, so they have a generous amount of sex in them, as I believe our relationships should have as well in real life. I hope you enjoyed this novel for what it is, literature that is in the spicy romance genre where sex is a part of the plot, storyline, and character development. It is very different from a closed door romance, and there are different levels of heat in the genre as well. Explore them all! I personally love open door romances because I want the full story of the relationship, not a partial one.

If you'd like more of my work, please see below for my list of published works on the following pages, visit my sexuality/sexual health/wellness podcast, find my audiobooks, visit my website, my Patreon, visit my profile on Medium, and my linktree with all my links at https://linktr.ee/RuanWillow

Thank you for purchasing this book, I'd love to hear your thoughts in an honest review on the site where you purchased the book from. I'd absolutely love it if you shared my book with others. It warms my heart profusely when I see someone who has taken the time to review/share my book. Love you all very much!

All my best, yours truly, with overflowing love from a full heart,

Ruan Willow, spicy romance author, sexuality/spicy romance podcaster, and book narrator

Ruan's other books and novellas:

All books:

https://books.ruanwillowauthor.com/

Collections:

Howife books:

https://books.ruanwillowauthor.com/hotwifebooks

Spring Break and Stranded with Her Best Friend's Brothers Collection:

https://books.ruanwillowauthor.com/springbreakandstrandedwithherbestfriendsbrothersseries

Servicing the Work Men, Her Filthy Hotwife Adventures Series

https://books.ruanwillowauthor.com/servicingtheworkmenseries

The Sex Challenge Series

https://books.ruanwillowauthor.com/thesexchallengeseries

The Getaway Series: age gap

https://books.ruanwillowauthor.com/ruansgetawayseries

Taboo books

https://books.ruanwillowauthor.com/taboospringbreakandstrandedwithherbestfriendsbrothersplus6men

Check out the Audiobooks:

https://books.ruanwillowauthor.com/audiobooksnarratedbyruan

Standalone by R.U. Ann:

In Scarlet's House, in ebook

https://books.ruanwillowauthor.com/inscarletshouse

In audiobook

https://books.ruanwillowauthor.com/inscarletshouseaudiobook

Arching Hunger Series (open door HEA Romantasy)
https://books.ruanwillowauthor.com/archinghungerseries

ANTHOLOGIES AND AWARD Nominations
Ruan has stories in the following anthologies:
He Will Obey (which was AWARDED THE 2020 SILVER PIGTAIL IN BEST ANTHOLOGY CATEGORY
The Femdom Coven (nominee for 2021 Golden Pigtail Smut Awards)
Inside of Ruan Willow (also available in an audiobook)
(this audiobook was a nominee for the 2021 Golden Pigtail Smut Awards)

Decadent Erotica An Anthology **3ʳᵈ Place Winner in the 2022 Golden Pigtails Smut Awards for Dark/Taboo Category**
Nominations for the 2023 Golden Pigtail Awards include:
Servicing the Trash Man, My Filthy Hotwife Adventure
Dressing Room Domme
Anthology Ruan has a story Hearts and Flowers, Whips and Chains
Nominations in 2025 for 2024 books
Narration of Emma's Policy (finalist) (Book is no longer available).
Ruan has been nominated for Best Erotic Writer by the ASN Lifestyle Magazine Awards 2025.

ANTHOLOGIES: SEASON'S Teasings: Snowbound Seductions (finalist) and the charity anthology Not So Guilty Pleasures 45 Filthy Stories for a Cause (no longer available)
Ruan was nominated for Best Erotic Writer by the ASN Lifestyle Magazine Awards for 2025.

OTHER ANTHOLOGIES:

Halloween Anthology: Trick or Tease II

Christmas/Holiday anthology: Season's Teasings: Snowbound Seductions

Summer Teases II

The Best Bi Erotica of the Year, Volume 2

OTHER LINKS/URLS:

Ruan Willow on Goodreads Ruan Willow Goodreads Author page[1]

Ruan Willow on BookBub https://www.bookbub.com/profile/ruan-willow

Sign up for Ruan's newsletter: https://subscribepage.io/ruanwillow

ARC copies are usually on BookSirens and StoryOrigin App. Check those sites for FREE ARC of books and audiobooks.

---

1.   https://www.goodreads.com/author/show/21312130.Ruan_Willow

www.ingramcontent.com/pod-product-compliance
Lightning Source LLC
Chambersburg PA
CBHW050024120726
47903CB00006B/1900